Lone Star Heiress

WINNIE GRIGGS

HARLEQUIN® LOVE INSPIRED® HISTORICAL

Recycling programs
for this product may
not exist in your area.

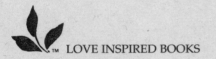

™ LOVE INSPIRED BOOKS

ISBN-13: 978-0-373-28266-1

LONE STAR HEIRESS

Printed in U.S.A.

He shall choose our inheritance for us.
—*Psalms* 47:4

To my awesome agent Michelle
and my fabulous critique partners Connie and Amy,
who all, at various points, helped me talk through
some of the tough spots I encountered while writing
this story. Thanks for your willingness to listen,
offer terrific suggestions and most of all your
belief in and enthusiasm for this story.

Chapter One

Texas
June 1896

"This doesn't look good."

Ivy gently set the hoof back down on the grassy road and patted the mule's side. "No wonder you're limping, Jubal—it 'pears like you've picked up a honey of a stone bruise."

The mule turned around to nip at her, but she avoided him easily enough. Although Jubal might be ornery at times, he usually wasn't mean. Unfortunately, these weren't usual circumstances.

Maybe she shouldn't have set such a demanding pace this past day and a half, but she'd hoped to make it to Turnabout in two days' time. A woman traveling alone for this distance, even if she was dressed as a boy, was vulnerable to gossip and worse.

But it looked as if she was doomed to spend another night on the trail.

"Not that anyone's gonna notice we're late," she told Jubal, "since no one is expecting us exactly. I'm just anxious to find out what the mysterious inheritance is that this Drum Mosley fellow is holding for me."

Ivy gave the mule's side another pat as he brayed out a complaint. "I wish there was something I could do to make you feel better." They were a day-and-a-half's ride from home and headed in the opposite direction. It had been several hours since they'd seen signs of people or habitation, so she figured they'd be better off pressing forward. "Guess we'll just have to get by as best we can."

She turned to her other traveling companion, also of the four-legged variety. "Well, Rufus, I guess I'll be walking the rest of the way alongside you."

The dog barked in response and she rubbed his head, comforted by the feel of his shaggy coat and the trusting look in his eyes.

"Let's hope we find a homestead with neighborly folks who won't mind strangers bunking in their barn." She straightened. "At least there's lots of good foraging to be had this time of year."

She took off her straw hat and wiped her forehead with her sleeve. It might be the first week in June, but the summer heat had already set in.

How far had they come since they'd started out at dawn yesterday? Other than a couple of short breaks, they'd only stopped when darkness made it unsafe to travel last night. They broke camp at daybreak this morning and she estimated it was getting on to four o'clock now. Surely they were getting close to Turnabout. Which meant it would be time to exchange her britches for a skirt soon.

She glanced down at Rufus. "Whatever this inheritance is, it sure better be worth all this trouble. 'Cause we could really use some good luck about now."

She patted Jubal's neck. "Wouldn't it be something if we could return home with enough money to rebuild the barn and buy a new milk cow? That would sure make Nana Dovie's life a lot easier."

Grabbing the reins, Ivy looked the mule in the eye. "I know you're hurting, but we need to make it a little farther before dark."

She moved forward and lightly tugged. To her relief, Jubal decided to cooperate. She glanced down the narrow, deserted road as she absently swatted a horsefly away. They hadn't seen so much as a fence post or wagon rut since before noon. Apparently this shortcut to Turnabout wasn't well used. But surely they'd spot *some* sign of civilization soon.

Not one to enjoy long silences, Ivy shared her thoughts aloud. "It's been a wearisome day and you two have been great companions. Don't think I don't appreciate it. In fact, I have a special treat for each of you that I'll hand out as soon as we stop for the night."

She glanced at Rufus, padding along beside her. "It would be nice if you and I ended up with a barn or shed to sleep in tonight, don't you think?"

Not that she minded camping out—that's what they'd done last night and, other than fighting off some pesky mosquitoes, they'd managed just fine. But those gray clouds gathering overhead would likely bring rain before morning and she didn't relish the idea of getting soaked.

But as Nana Dovie always said, worrying was like doubting God. If you truly believe He's in charge, then you have to trust He'll work everything out for the best.

Of course, it never hurt to let Him know what you'd like to have happen.

"Mind you, Lord," she said respectfully, "I know we can use a bit of rain to settle the dust. It's just that I'm not sure that sheet of canvas I brought along will keep out more than a spit and a drizzle, and I'd rather not have a mud bath. If You could help me find a dry place to sleep, it would be most welcome."

She glanced over at the mule. "And please help Jubal heal quickly. Amen."

Ivy smiled down at Rufus. "Now, whatever happens, we'll know He has it in hand."

An hour later, she frowned up at the overcast sky. The clouds had thickened like clabbered milk and the heavy air clung to her skin like a damp petticoat. And they still hadn't come across any signs of civilization. Jubal's limp was more pronounced now—she couldn't in good conscience push him further today. She had to let the injured animal rest.

"Well, boys, as Nana Dovie says, when you don't get the thing you prayed for, it don't mean God ain't listening. It just means the answer is either *no* or *not now*. So it looks like we're going to spend another night under the stars. And this is as likely a spot as any."

Mitch Parker sat comfortably in the saddle, soaking in the morning sunshine and peaceful surroundings, letting all the stress of the past few weeks dissolve away. It had rained most of last night, but the rhythmic pattering on the cozy cabin roof had added to the serenity.

And today had dawned bright and warm—perfect weather for the first full day of his vacation. The leaves on the trees had that special shine they always had after a rain and the only sounds were those of the birds and insects. He might even take out his sketch pad later.

School was out for the summer, giving him a welcome break from his teaching duties. But more than that, he was ready for a break from Hilda Swenson. The persistent widow and mother of three had made him the target of her attention for the past several weeks and seemed oblivious to his hints that he wasn't interested. She was a flibberti-gibbet of the highest order—something he had no patience for. And her determined pursuit was playing havoc with the quiet, well-ordered life he'd strived so hard to build for himself and was determined to maintain at all costs.

He never wanted to go back to what he'd once been. Nor did he want to be a husband again, not after the tragic outcome of his marriage.

His rebuffs of the widow's overtures would obviously have to be more direct in the future—a confrontation he wasn't looking forward to. Thus his decision to slip away to a friend's cabin for a week or so.

Mitch shook off those thoughts. He'd deal with that unpleasantness when he returned to Turnabout. This week was for relaxing and regaining that all-important sense of control over his life.

And this back-of-beyond cabin had been just the place to do it. He was grateful to Reggie Barr for giving him the use of it. In a way, it was a homecoming. The cabin was where he'd spent his first night in this part of the world, two years ago. Reggie had been a stranger then, but had held his fate in her hands. Now he counted her and her husband, Adam, amongst his closest friends.

He'd made it to the cabin yesterday afternoon, in time to get some fishing in. Fishing, reading and sketching, and no people around. Yes, this was going to be a fine week indeed.

Just before he'd left town yesterday, Reggie had told him he could find some mulberry trees north of the cabin. So now he was heading that way, hoping to gather a generous amount of the fruit, and curious to explore a different section of the woods. Perhaps he'd find inspiration for some of the sketching he planned to do.

A bark echoed through the trees, catching Mitch's attention. What would a dog be doing out here? It was a four-hour ride from Turnabout and as far as he knew, no one lived out this way. Then again, maybe someone had settled here recently. He grimaced at that thought. He hoped whoever it was wasn't the gregarious type—he wasn't in a sociable mood.

But he was getting ahead of himself. A dog didn't necessarily mean there were people around. The animal could have wandered all this way on his own.

Mitch slowed Seeley, then pulled the horse to a stop. Maybe he should turn around and return to the cabin. If there *were* people up ahead, there was no sense in inviting an acquaintance. Perhaps if he refrained from intruding on them, they'd return the favor.

Then he reluctantly set Seeley in motion again. If he *was* going to have neighbors, it was best he meet them at a time of his own choosing rather than have them arrive on his doorstep when he wasn't prepared. He could also drop a hint or two that he valued his privacy.

As Mitch neared the spot where the dog's bark had come from, he heard a human voice as well, though he couldn't make out the words. Well, that answered that—there *were* people out here.

He peered through the woods and spied a youth standing on a log, plucking mulberries from a tree. It appeared someone besides him had designs on the berries.

Mitch quickly scanned the surrounding area, looking for the other members of the lad's party. There was a scruffy-looking dog and a mule, but no sign of either a homestead or other people.

The dog spotted him first and began barking furiously.

"Goodness, Rufus, what's gotten into you? Is it another squirrel?" The youth turned to look and, as he caught sight of Mitch, his eyes widened and his foot slipped, losing its purchase on the log. His arms flailed as he attempted to catch his balance. The youth's hat went flying and the appearance of a long untidy braid had Mitch quickly revising his initial impression.

A moment later, *she* was flat on her back on the ground. And not moving.

Nightmare memories of another fallen woman whooshed through Mitch with the force of a flash flood. He vaulted from his horse, his heart pounding like a mad thing trying to escape his chest.

Not again. God wouldn't be so cruel as to make him relive such a tragedy a second time.

Would He?

Chapter Two

In a matter of seconds, Mitch knelt beside the all-too-still form, checking for signs of life. When he saw the rise of her chest, his frenetic heartbeat slowed slightly. But he refocused immediately. He needed to find out just how badly she was hurt.

His breath caught for a moment as he spotted reddish stains on her shirt and hands. But a heartbeat later he realized they came from berries, not blood.

Why was she out here alone, and why was she dressed as a boy?

He shoved those thoughts aside—there would be time later for those questions, once he'd made certain she was okay.

It was his fault she'd fallen. He hadn't intended to startle her, but that didn't absolve him of the fact that he had. He of all people knew that actions often had unanticipated consequences. He also knew his imposing size could make strangers uncomfortable at the best of times. For a lone female who wasn't expecting him—even one dressed as a boy—his arrival must have been a shock.

She stirred and he turned his attention to her face, only now taking in her physical appearance. Her nose and cheeks were dusted with a liberal sprinkling of freckles, giving her a youthful look. Her still-closed eyes were partially covered by a fringe of reddish-brown hair that had escaped her braid. He absently brushed the tendrils away from her face and was rewarded with a grimace and a soft moan, welcome signs that she was regaining consciousness.

"Easy," he said, still uncertain of her condition.

She started at the sound of his voice, and her eyes flew open, regarding him with wide-eyed confusion and uncertainty. The deep clover-green of her irises startled him momentarily. They were the most amazingly intense eyes he'd ever seen.

"Are you hurt?" He kept his voice calm, trying not to further alarm her.

"I don't... My head hurts, but I think I'm okay."

She made as if to sit up, but he placed a hand on her shoulder, gently restraining her. "Easy now. Take a minute before you move around too much."

She gave him a peevish frown. "I *need* to sit up—the ground's wet."

That's what she was worried about? Probably still addled from the fall. "I understand, but let's check you out first."

The suspicion in her expression deepened, and she attempted to put more distance between them. "I can check my own self, thank you."

Though her words were assertive, her tone was slurred and she seemed none too steady. He didn't want to agitate her further, however, so he nodded.

"All right, but if you insist on sitting up, at least let me assist you." He placed a hand at her elbow and helped her up, keeping close watch for signs of injuries or weakness. Once he was sure she wouldn't fall over again, he eased back on his haunches, ignoring the dampness seeping through the knees of his pants, trying to maintain a nonthreatening pose.

As soon as he moved back, she pulled a knife from somewhere and had it unsteadily pointed at his chest. "If you're thinking to rob me, mister, you should know I don't have much worth stealing, but what's mine is mine."

The dog, alerted by her tone, stiffened and bared its teeth at him.

"Whoa, there." Mitch threw his hands up, palms out, trying to assure her he wasn't a threat. The knife, while not especially large, looked sharp enough to do some damage. And although he was quite certain he could take it from her with little effort, he didn't want to do that unless he had to. "I just want to make certain you're okay, nothing more." She placed her free hand on the dog's back, but he had no illusions she was restraining him.

"I'm talking about before that. Why were you sneaking up on me that way?"

"I didn't *sneak up* on you. I *happened* on you while looking for the mulberry trees. My apologies if you were startled."

She blinked those amazing eyes as if trying to clear her vision, and the trembling in her hand grew more pronounced. Was it due to pain? Or weakness?

"Are these trees on your place?" she asked. "'Cause I didn't mean to trespass."

Trespassing should be the least of her worries right now. He didn't like the slur that had crept into her voice. Time to be firm, for her own good. "We can discuss all that later. Right now I need to know if you're badly hurt."

She still didn't lower the knife, though the effort seemed to cost her. But her left hand moved from the dog to the back of her head. "I… My head—" She pulled her hand back and stared at it as if it belonged to someone else.

It was stained with blood.

Mitch bit off an oath. "You *are* hurt. Let me have a look." He moved in closer, and she quickly raised the knife to block him, swaying slightly with the effort. Her dog let out a warning growl.

This girl had more spunk than sense. "I'm only trying to take a look at your injury—that's all. You're bleeding and it's not something you can tend to yourself."

Without a word, she nodded, her gaze never leaving his face.

Keeping his moves slow and smooth, he shifted to get a better look, ignoring the knife that unsteadily tracked his movements. A patch of blood on the back of her head stained her hair, matting it against her scalp. The wet, muddy ground she'd been lying on hadn't helped matters any, either. He tried gently parting the hair but couldn't see much beyond the blood.

He moved to face her again, and realized she'd closed her eyes. Had his ministrations hurt her?

But a moment later her eyes opened with obvious effort and her gaze held a question.

"I'm going to get my canteen so I can clean this up and get a better look. Try not to move."

She nodded wearily, then winced. "There's a shallow creek just beyond those trees." Her voice sounded strained and pain shadowed her expression.

He gave her what he hoped was a reassuring smile, crossed his fingers that she'd be all right until he returned, then sprinted back to Seeley.

Snatching up his canteen and the small cloth bag he'd intended to put the berries in, he quickly headed back, only detouring once when he saw her own canteen amongst her things.

Mitch pulled out his handkerchief as he knelt beside her again. Her hand was back on the dog's neck, but now she seemed to be using it for support rather than restraint. Not a good sign. Still, her stoicism and ability to keep her wits under the circumstances was commendable.

"I'll be as gentle as I can," he said as he wet the cloth.

She tried to raise the knife again. With a sigh, he wrested it from her in one quick move, then set it carefully out of her reach.

He regretted the spark of fear he saw in her eyes. "I'm sorry—" he kept his tone matter-of-fact "—but I can't have you hurting either yourself or me while I'm focused on fixing you up."

She watched his every move, and he saw the caution and uncertainty she was trying to hold at bay.

"I guess I should introduce myself," he said, hoping to distract her. "Mitch Parker, at your service."

"Ivy Feagan." She offered her name reluctantly, then he heard a quick intake of breath as he dabbed at the cut. She indicated the dog. "This here is Rufus." Her voice had a note of challenge in it.

Good. He preferred bravado to fear. "Glad to meet you. By the way, did you get to sample those mulberries before I interrupted you? I hear they're exceptional."

She answered affirmatively, then fell silent again. There were no indications she was hurting, other than an occasional hitch in her breathing when he touched a particularly sensitive spot. When that happened, she'd start talking, mostly rambling thoughts, as if to hide her reaction.

Despite her unfocused chatter, he found himself admiring her. She didn't complain, or dissolve into hysterics or cower—all of which would have been understandable reactions given the situation. Instead, she maintained a stoic demeanor. He'd known men who would have acted with less restraint in these circumstances.

It took all the water in his canteen, but he finally had the area clean enough to see the cut. It was a nasty-looking gash, but the bleeding had almost stopped.

He rinsed his now-soiled handkerchief, then squeezed out as much water as he could. He folded it into a thick pad, then gently covered the injury. "Do you think you can hold this in place for a few moments?"

She obediently placed a hand over the pad. He picked up the cloth bag, quickly removed the drawstring and held it up to show her. "I'm going to use this to tie the bandage in place. Okay?"

"Okay."

He secured the pad, then leaned back to study his work. With the ties dangling over her left ear, she would have looked comical if the situation weren't so serious.

"That will have to do for now." He met her gaze and frowned. He didn't like the paleness of her skin. Her freckles stood out in stark relief, her eyes looked huge and the rest of her face had a pinched look. And he could tell she was struggling to stay focused. What should he do now?

"How bad is it?" Her wariness was still evident, but he thought he also sensed the beginnings of trust.

He chose his words carefully—he didn't want to alarm her unduly. "You've lost some blood. I imagine you're going to have a whopper of a headache for the next several days, but I've seen worse." Much worse. "But right now we need to see about getting you someplace where you can rest and be tended to properly." He strived to keep the worry from his tone. "Do you have friends nearby or a place I can take you around here?" *Please let her say yes.*

"No." Her single-word answer offered no clue as to why

she was out here on her own. And that disconcerting wariness was back in full force. He couldn't really blame her for her caution—in fact he rather admired her for it. But she shouldn't have been placed in the position of fending for herself this way.

He tried again. "Is anyone traveling with you?"

"Only Rufus and Jubal."

Rufus was the dog, but who was Jubal? "Do you know where Jubal is?"

"Jubal is my mule—" Her face suddenly drained of any remaining color and her eyes fluttered closed.

Mitch managed to catch her before her head hit the ground again.

He quickly assured himself she was still breathing, and to his relief, her eyes fluttered open. As soon as she realized her position, she struggled to push him away. "What—"

He reached for her canteen and held it up to her. "You fainted. Here, drink this."

She quieted and took the canteen, raising it to her lips. Her gaze never left his.

After a few sips, she handed the canteen back, but he shook his head. "You need to drink it all," he said firmly.

She stiffened at his tone, but after a heartbeat obediently drained the canteen.

What in the world was he going to do with her?

If he had a wagon, he'd transport her directly to Turnabout and hand her over to Doc Pratt. But there was no wagon, and in her current condition, she'd never be able to sit in the saddle for the four-hour ride to town. Even if she could, she probably shouldn't.

That left him with only one option. Whether he liked it or not, he'd have to temporarily abandon his plans for solitude. "I suppose you'd better come with me to my cabin, where you can rest until you're feeling better." He only hoped she could sit in the saddle long enough to get that far.

"Thank you," she said, her suspicion obvious. "but that's not necessary. Once I rest a bit I'll be able to get on with my journey."

He knew bluster when he heard it. But he tried to navigate around her caution carefully. "Nevertheless, I'm responsible for your fall and the least I can do is share my shelter and my food with you."

She appeared to be wavering. Hoping to tip the scale in his favor, Mitch retrieved her knife.

She tensed as apprehension flared in her eyes.

He quickly held the knife out to her, hilt first. "You can hold on to this if it makes you more comfortable."

He only hoped she didn't decide to skewer him with it.

Ivy accepted the knife, wondering just how much she could trust this stranger. His size was certainly worrisome— he wasn't just taller than Goliath. He also had the broadest shoulders she'd ever seen.

Still, he'd been nothing but kind and helpful. Surely if he'd meant to harm her he'd have done so by now. And despite what she'd said, her inability to stop shaking or keep her thoughts focused was worrisome. Perhaps a hot meal and a dry place to rest would cure that. "I suppose I can rest at your cabin as well as I can here. But just for a little while."

He smiled approvingly and she decided he looked much less intimidating when he smiled. In fact, you might say he looked downright handsome, in a bigger-than-life kind of way. It was mighty tempting to let go of her worries and let this man handle them. And right now she was having trouble remembering why she shouldn't.

"Good." He nodded to his left. "I'd like to move you to that tree over there so you have something to lean against while I gather your things."

Move her? She wasn't sure she could stand and make it more than a couple of steps right now, even if he helped her.

But before she could respond, he gave her a stern look. "You appear none too steady and I wouldn't want to have to deal with you falling again."

She could see where he might feel that way, and to be honest, he had good reason. But she had a better idea. "I'll just lean against Rufus instead." She gingerly rearranged herself to demonstrate. And loyal Rufus allowed her to prop herself against him, just as she'd known he would.

She wished he would just get on with gathering her things so she could close her eyes and relax for a minute or two. But she had the nagging feeling she'd forgotten something important.

He studied her a moment, then stood. "I'll only be a few minutes and then we'll be on our way."

As soon as he turned away, she closed her eyes. Then she suddenly remembered what it was she needed to tell him and her heavy eyelids lifted reluctantly. "Mr. Parker."

He turned and took a step back toward her. "Yes? Is something wrong?"

"It's about Jubal. You should know, he turned up lame yesterday. It's why we're camped here." She hoped he'd show Jubal the same kindness he'd shown her.

His expression tightened, but he nodded and continued on his way.

Ivy watched as he made quick work of collecting her few items. For a big man, he moved with surprising grace.

She closed her eyes again. Sometime later she heard

Mr. Parker talking, though she couldn't quite make out the words. His tone was soothing and a bit distant.

Prying her eyes open, she watched him approach Jubal. The mule eyed him suspiciously, ears flicking forward. Gradually, though, the animal relaxed, and by the time Mr. Parker attempted to stroke his nose, Jubal seemed ready to eat from his hand.

Satisfied, Ivy let her lids fall shut again.

"Miss Feagan."

The voice seemed much closer this time and when she opened her eyes he stood over her, a worried look on his face. His horse stood just behind him.

"I'm okay," she assured him. "Just resting my eyes."

If anything, the concern in his expression deepened. "This is Seeley. He's a well-behaved horse with an easy gait. I know you're probably not feeling up to a ride, but the cabin isn't far and I don't know of any better way to get you there."

She tried to focus on the animal. He was big—probably had to be to carry such a rider. But how did the man expect her to mount? "I can ride, but getting into the saddle might be tricky."

His lips quirked up at that but he nodded solemnly. "I think we'll be able to work that out." He offered his hand. "Do you think you can stand for just a moment if I help?"

"Of course." At least she hoped so.

He placed his hand under her elbow and gently guided her into a shaky standing position. Unfortunately, her legs felt more like limp rope than bone and muscle. If he hadn't been supporting her she probably would have toppled over. Still, if she could get a good grip on the saddle and he formed a stirrup with his hands, she might be able to—

Before she could complete the thought, he'd scooped her up in his arms.

Caught by surprise, her arms reflexively slid around his neck. "What in blue blazes do you think you're doing?" The man, for all his well-meaning kindness, was much too high-handed for her liking.

He hefted her, pulling her unsettlingly closer against his chest. "I'm helping you into the saddle."

The ease with which he lifted and held her was impressive. She wasn't a petite woman, but he made her feel almost dainty. And the sensation of being held in such a way was unnerving. Though, strangely, she felt completely safe.

He looked down at her uncertainly. "It would be best if you rode astride rather than sidesaddle."

Ivy shrugged, or at least what passed for a shrug in her current position. She shook off her irritation at the same time. This was merely an expedient way of getting her on the horse, nothing more personal. "It's my preferred method of riding, anyway."

He stared into her eyes, and she felt the full power of his gaze. He seemed to be gauging her strength and her resolve. Would he find her wanting?

As she stared back, the flecks of gold in his deep brown eyes drew her in with surprising intensity.

She finally blinked and the connection—if it had ever been there—disappeared.

He cleared his throat. "Once I get you up there, do you think you can keep your seat?"

"Of course." She'd have to, wouldn't she?

Was he really planning to *lift* her bodily into the saddle?

As if in answer to her question, he did exactly that. Mr. Parker kept a supportive hand at her waist until she'd grasped the saddle horn and swung her leg over.

"How are you feeling?"

Was he concerned for *her* or just for the trouble her passing out would cause?

She'd felt dizzy for a moment, but that had settled into a merely foggy sensation. "I'm fine." Then she frowned. "How are you planning to travel?" Would he try to climb up behind her? How did she feel about that?

"As I said, it's not far. I'll walk."

He turned the horse and led it toward Jubal, but his gaze rarely left her. It was disconcerting to be the focus of those very direct brown eyes. He quickly tied Jubal's lead to his horse's saddle then moved to her left. She noticed Jubal only carried a saddle, and realized he'd loaded her things onto his own horse. It was more kindness for her animal than she'd expected.

"Still doing okay?" he asked.

She forced a smile. "I'm ready when you are."

"I'll be right here at your side. If you start feeling the least bit faint, let me know. Better to delay us than to risk your falling over."

She nodded and he patted the horse's side and clicked his tongue to set the animal in motion.

As they headed down the road, Ivy smiled drowsily at the thought of what an odd procession they made. She was in the lead on his horse, he walked on her left, Jubal followed on the right and Rufus alternately led and padded alongside.

The pounding in her head was amplified with each step the horse took, but she was determined not to worry her self-appointed caretaker more than necessary. She *would* remain conscious and she *would* stay in this saddle until they reached this cabin of his.

Because the alternative wasn't only dangerous and inconvenient.

It would also be altogether mortifying.

Chapter Three

Mitch kept a close eye on his injured charge as they traveled back to the cabin. He hadn't been fooled by her assurances that she was okay. He'd seen the tremble in her hands, the glaze of pain in her eyes, and the way she fought to maintain focus. The sooner he got her to the cabin, the better. But jarring her too much wouldn't do, either. He only hoped she had enough sense to let him know if she needed to stop.

The trip, which had taken only twenty minutes on his way out, took nearly an hour on the return. He paused their little caravan a few times to give her a rest from the jarring movements and make her drink some water, but otherwise he kept them moving at a slow, steady pace. At least there was no sign of fresh blood seeping from underneath her bandage. Perhaps the worst really *was* over.

Throughout that endless trip he tried to keep her talking, to make certain she was both conscious and aware. Fortunately, talking seemed to be something she enjoyed. Not that they had a coherent conversation. She mostly rambled and his contribution was limited to an occasional question whenever the pauses drew out.

Mitch learned she came from a small town called Nettles Gap and that she lived with someone she called Nana Dovie. He also learned the life history of her dog and her mule, and what great companions they'd been on this trip.

She continued to assure him she was all right whenever he inquired, but by the time he called for the third rest stop he could see she was starting to droop. So when the cabin finally came into view he wanted to shout, "Hallelujah."

"Almost there," he said bracingly.

She straightened and he could almost see her gather her strength as she squinted ahead.

He directed Seeley right up to the front porch before he called a halt. "Now you're going to have to let go of the saddle horn and slide right down into my arms. Don't worry, I'll catch you."

To his surprise, she displayed none of the suspicion she'd exhibited earlier. Perhaps it was because she was exhausted and hurting, but he hoped it was at least partly because she had begun to trust him.

A moment later, she'd half slid, half fallen into his grasp. And for the second time he thought how nice she felt in his arms, how he wanted to protect her from harm.

"If you'll set me down, I can walk from here."

He ignored her and headed up the steps. She didn't argue further, which in and of itself worried him. After a bit of tricky one-handed maneuvering, he got the door open without jostling her too badly, then carried her inside and set her on the sofa.

"I'm going to check your bandage. It won't take but a minute, then you can lie down."

Without a word, she slumped against the cushion and closed her eyes.

He watched her a moment. She looked so vulnerable, so achingly brave as she tried to hold herself together. His hand moved to brush a lock of hair from her forehead, then stopped just short of its goal. His hand slowly withdrew, as if it had a mind and conscience of its own.

This burgeoning awareness of her as more than a person in need of aid was dangerous and had to be smothered before it could go any further.

He turned and moved to the counter, ready to put some distance between them.

Ivy focused on remaining conscious, at least conscious enough to not fall over. She didn't want to get blood and dirt all over his furniture. There were probably all sorts of other things she should be worried about, but for now the only thing getting through her foggy mind was the longing for the promised bed and the chance to sleep undisturbed.

She didn't realize Rufus had followed them inside until he nudged her leg with a worried whine. She placed a hand on the dog's head without opening her eyes. "I'm okay, boy. Just need to rest for a bit."

Sometime later—she wasn't sure how long—Mr. Parker returned. "Now, let's have a look." She felt the tug as he removed the cloth pad that had stuck to the blood.

"How does it look?" she asked.

"The bleeding's stopped. I'm going to put a clean bandage on it and then let you rest while I cook some soup."

As he pressed the cloth against her head a moment later, Ivy marveled at what an amazingly gentle touch he had for such a big man.

Then he was done. She opened her eyes to see him examining his work. He made a small adjustment to the bandage, then met her gaze. "Ready for your nap?"

She'd *been* ready. But she'd rather not be carried again. It was a mite too unsettling. "Yes. If you'll lend me a hand and show me the way, I'd prefer to walk."

He frowned, but finally nodded.

Good to know he wouldn't just ignore her wishes willy-nilly.

He placed a hand at her elbow and helped her up. Then, slowly, led her to a door next to the fireplace.

Leaning on him more than she cared to admit, Ivy stepped inside a cozy bedchamber. As soon as she was seated on the edge of the bed, her rescuer knelt down and unlaced her boots.

She studied his bent head, strangely entranced by the whorl of hair at the top. What would he do if she reached down and touched it? She stopped herself just short of acting on that thought. What was wrong with her? That knock on the head must have affected her more than she thought.

When he'd removed both her shoes, he hesitated a moment, then went to work removing her socks. The sensation of his hands on her skin sent little tingles through her that caught her unawares.

She must have made an inadvertent movement because he glanced up.

"Sorry if that was uncomfortable," he said as he stood.

She wasn't sure how to respond so said nothing.

He studied her uncertainly, and she wondered if he was worried about putting her to bed. But before she could reassure him that she could take it from here, he turned, suddenlike, and marched to a chest across the room. He came back with a bundle that he shoved at her.

As she took it, she realized it was a nightgown. But whose?

He rubbed the back of his neck, looking extremely uncomfortable. "I thought you might want to change. I don't think Reggie would mind if you borrowed this." He turned and quickly moved to the door.

Once there, however, he paused. "I'll leave this open just a crack. If you need anything, call out."

He smiled as Rufus padded in. "It appears you'll have company."

As he left, she had two completely unrelated thoughts. The first was that it was kind of him to allow her dog inside the cabin.

And the second was, just who was Reggie and what was she to him?

Mitch unsaddled, then fed and watered both Seeley and Miss Feagan's mule. He patted the mule's side as the animals dipped their heads in the feed trough. Jubal's limping had gotten more pronounced the farther they'd walked. It would be best if he was allowed to rest for a couple of days before they set out again. Which meant a trip to town would not be on tomorrow's agenda, not unless they left the animal behind.

Which posed another problem. Miss Feagan's presence had become more than just an intrusion on his privacy. Now he had her reputation to worry about.

Of course, one could say that a woman who traveled alone in these backwoods probably wasn't terribly concerned with her reputation, but he didn't know the full story on that. Nor was that an excuse for him to treat the issue lightly.

There was nothing he could do to salvage the situation—it wasn't as if he could snap his fingers and make a chaperone appear. He'd just have to do what he could to make her comfortable and hope for the best.

On the way back to the cabin, Mitch noticed the stack of firewood was low, so he grabbed the ax from the shed and spent the next twenty minutes replenishing the pile.

Wiping his face with the tail of his shirt, he decided a quick dip in the lake to cool off and clean up wouldn't be amiss.

He quietly entered the house, wanting to check on the patient before he got out of hailing distance. He pushed her bedchamber door open just enough to look inside. The dog, lying beside the bed, lifted its head to stare at him. He stared back, keeping his demeanor impassive, and after a moment the dog lowered its head again. However, the animal's watchful gaze never left Mitch's face.

Miss Feagan, on the other hand, didn't stir. She lay on her side under the covers with that thick mahogany braid of hers mostly unbound. He watched her a moment, assuring himself she was sleeping and hadn't passed out again.

In sleep her expression lost most of the hardness that suspicion and pain had given it. With her hair flowing over her shoulder and that generous sprinkle of freckles, she had the look of a schoolgirl. The guilt he'd felt for his part in her fall washed over him again. Along with something protective and tender.

He wanted to find whoever was responsible for her and give them a piece of his mind for allowing her to end up in this situation. She deserved better.

Then Mitch remembered something he'd heard once about head injuries, something about not letting the injured party sleep too deeply. He hated to rouse her, but he'd hate it even more if he didn't and she got worse.

He squeezed her hand while he said her name. He had to do it three times before her eyes opened.

She glanced up at him, obviously disoriented. "What is it?"

"Nothing important. Go back to sleep."

With a nod, she closed her eyes and snuggled down deeper into the pillow. He pulled out his pocket watch and noted the time. He'd repeat the process every thirty minutes for the next several hours, just to be safe.

Mitch started to ease back out when he spotted the pile

of dirty clothing she'd left on the floor. She'd need something clean to wear whenever she recovered enough to leave the bed. He crossed the room under Rufus's watchful gaze, gathered up the discarded clothing, then left, pulling the door behind him until only the barest crack remained.

Pausing just long enough to give the soup simmering on the stove another stir, he headed back out.

Ivy frowned as a soft *woof* intruded on the peace of her sleep. Rufus did it again and she reluctantly gave up on trying to sink back into oblivion.

"What is it, Rufus?" Even to her, her tone sounded petulant. Then she saw Mr. Parker standing in the doorway and her cheeks heated.

"Sorry if I disturbed you," he said. "I was just checking to see if you were ready for some soup. If you'd rather continue sleeping, though, the food will keep until you're ready."

She eased herself up against the pillows, wincing at the throbbing of her head. "Actually, food sounds good." Her cheeks heated again as her stomach loudly echoed those sentiments. She certainly wasn't making a very good impression. "If you give me a minute to collect myself, I'll join you at the table." She wondered if there was a robe in that trunk he'd pulled the nightgown from.

But he shook his head. "You stay put and I'll fetch you a bowl."

Before she could argue, he changed the subject. "How's your head?"

"Better." Not exactly a lie. The throbbing had eased.

From the corner of her eye, she spotted her knife resting in easy reach on the bedside table. It was likely his way of trying to reassure her that she had nothing to fear from him, and her heart softened a little more. He really was a very kind, honorable man. She was no longer worried about his intentions, even though she was still at his mercy.

He stepped closer. "Mind if I check?"

It took her a moment to realize he was referring to her injury, and she turned to give him access to the back of her head. As he bent nearer to study the bandage, she felt suddenly shy and vulnerable. Both feelings were foreign to her and that made her edgy and unsettled. It didn't help that as he checked the bandage, his hands brushed against the nape of her neck and she shivered in reaction.

It was just an aftereffect of her fall, she told herself.

He stilled. "Sorry. Did I hurt you?"

"No." She tried to keep her tone light. "I guess I'm more woozy than I'd thought."

"Understandable." He straightened and stepped back. "I'll get that soup. Food and rest are what you need."

He was right—that was all she needed. Then she'd be back to her old self.

She tried to shake off those earlier feelings as she settled more comfortably and watched him exit. Better to focus on the savory smell wafting in from the kitchen. If the aroma was any indication, he was as good a cook as he was a caretaker.

Rufus plastered his front paws onto the mattress. "Hello, boy. I guess I haven't been very good company the past—" She paused. How long *had* she slept? Ivy glanced toward the window and frowned at the lengthening shadows. It had obviously been more than an hour or so.

Then her brow furrowed as hazy images of him repeatedly checking in on her floated at the edge of her memory. Had that really happened? Or had she dreamed it?

When he returned a few minutes later carrying a steaming bowl balanced on a tray, she edged up straighter. "How long was I asleep?"

"About six hours."

"Oh, my goodness. You must think me an awful slugabed."

"Rest is the best medicine at times like this."

As he helped her settle the tray onto her lap, she inhaled appreciatively. "Smells good."

He gave a small smile. "Only because you're hungry. I don't usually cook for anyone but myself and I make no claims that it's more than passable."

"I'm sure you're being too hard on yourself." She picked up the spoon, then frowned when he pulled up a chair. "Aren't you going to eat something, too?"

"I ate earlier. I'll get more later." He settled back in the chair. "I thought I'd keep you company, if that's okay?"

What was he up to?

Then she took herself to task. She had to stop being so suspicious of menfolk—not everyone was a mean-spirited polecat like Lester Stokes. Mr. Parker was nice and seemed to expect nothing in return. He probably just wanted to make sure she didn't faint into her bowl while she ate.

She tasted a spoonful, then smiled. "As I suspected, this is a good sight better than merely passable."

He spread his hands as if to dispute her words but didn't say anything.

Feeling the need to fill the silence, she asked after her mule. "How's Jubal doing after that long walk here?"

"He's had some feed and water, and now he and Seeley are grazing." He met her gaze squarely. "As for the hoof, I think you were right about the stone bruise. I let him soak it in warm water to try to draw out the infection, but he's going to need a couple days' rest, I'm afraid."

Poor Jubal—she hoped she hadn't done him permanent harm. But this also meant more delays. Nana Dovie would be worried if she didn't hear something from her soon. But that wasn't Mr. Parker's fault. "It was real nice of you to be looking out for him. And me, too, of course."

"And how are you feeling now that you've had something to eat?"

The way he looked at her one would think he actually cared about *her,* not just the trouble she was causing. "Much better." She deposited her spoon in the now empty bowl. "That nap and this meal have fixed me right up." No need to burden him with her aching head and shaky feeling.

But Mr. Parker didn't look convinced. "You shouldn't attempt anything that requires effort today. You need to give yourself time to heal."

Be that as it may, Ivy certainly didn't intend to spend what was left of the day in bed.

"Mind if I ask how you came to be out here alone?" he asked.

She took a sip from her glass, trying to decide how much to tell him. She wasn't much on sharing her personal business with strangers, even kind-hearted ones. "I've got business to take care of over in Turnabout. And this shortcut seemed the fastest way to get there."

"You said you were from somewhere called Nettles Gap? How far away is that?"

"Don't know how many miles, exactly, but I set out at sunup the day before yesterday."

He stiffened. "Two days alone on the road."

It was nice of him to be concerned, but she was perfectly capable of taking care of herself. "I wasn't really alone," she said, trying to reassure him. "I had Rufus and Jubal with me. And I took precautions."

But his frown deepened. "By precautions I assume you mean that getup you were wearing and that knife you pulled out of your pocket."

He made it sound as if her efforts had been ineffective at best.

"And a dog and mule are hardly adequate escorts for a young lady. Wasn't your family at all concerned about your safety?"

Ivy blinked. Hadn't anyone called her a lady in a long time.

But she quickly pushed that thought away. He could talk about her precautions all he wanted, but *no one* was going to lay blame at Nana Dovie's door.

"Nana Dovie cares about me something fierce—don't you be thinking she doesn't. But she wasn't in any condition to come with me." No, sir, she wasn't about to let anyone speak ill of Nana Dovie, not even someone who'd been as nice as this gent.

But he didn't seem to take offense. "You mentioned this Nana Dovie before. Who is she?"

"Her name's Dovie Jacobs, and she's sort of my mother."

His brow went up. "Sort of?"

How to explain? "When you get right down to it, Nana Dovie isn't exactly blood kin. But she's family just the same. She took me in and raised me when my folks passed on. I was just a babe at the time."

"Sounds like a special lady."

Ivy nodded, pleased he'd understood. "And now that she's getting on in years and needs someone to take care of her, I aim to do my best to return the favor."

"So what was so important that you had to leave her side and set out alone?"

Ivy stiffened. "You sure do ask a passel of nosey questions."

Mr. Parker grimaced. "My apologies for prying. I'm afraid I've been cursed with a curious mind. I suppose that's why I became a schoolteacher."

She leaned back, diverted by this bit of information. "You're a schoolteacher? I guess that means you have a lot of book learning." That didn't surprise her much—he seemed like the educated type.

His lips quirked up at that. "I do like a good book."

She narrowed her eyes. "Are you making fun of me?"

"Not at all. I wouldn't dare."

Not certain how to respond to that, she took another sip from her glass.

This time he broke the silence. "You didn't answer my question."

"What question?"

"Why are you traveling to Turnabout?"

He was like a hound on a scent—he just didn't give up.

"I learned a few days ago that I might have an inheritance waiting there. And I aim to find out, 'cause if I do, I plan to sell whatever it is so Nana Dovie and I can pay off some debts and make some purchases we sorely need."

"I see."

It was time for her to ask a few questions of her own. "Are you familiar with Turnabout?"

He nodded. "I've lived there two years now."

"You mean this cabin isn't your home?" A heartbeat later, she realized she should've figured that out when he said he was a schoolteacher. He'd need to live in a town where there were actual schools and students, not out in the woods.

"This cabin belongs to friends of mine," he explained. "They let me borrow it for a few days."

"Oh." Her mind made a totally irrelevant connection. "Then this Reggie whose clothes I'm wearing..."

"Is the owner of this place."

So, Reggie wasn't his wife, then.

Not that that was important.

"And speaking of that," he continued, "I still think you should take it easy today. But if you do decide you want to sit out on the porch, you'll find more of Reggie's clothing in that chest. Oh, and your saddlebags are on top of the trunk if you need any of your own things."

"Thank you. But how far away is Turnabout?"

"It's about a four-hour ride from here."

She glanced toward the window. How much daylight was left?

As if reading her mind, he gave her a stern look. "Don't even think about trying to travel today. Even if you were up to it—which I very much doubt—your mule is not. Besides, it'll be dark in less than three hours."

She blew a stray tendril of hair off her forehead in frustration. He was right, of course. But that didn't make it easier to accept.

"I want you to know," he said, looking decidedly uncomfortable, "that I am an honorable, God-fearing man. You're perfectly safe in my company and I plan to spend the night outside so you can sleep without worry about your reputation."

As if that would stop any true gossipmonger's tongue from wagging if word got out. "I appreciate you trying to do what's proper and all, but there's no need for that, considering the circumstances." It said a good deal about him that he was worried about propriety and her feelings, but if he only knew how unnecessary that really was...

Not that she planned to enlighten him.

"Nevertheless, I feel it's important that we attend to all the proper social conventions while we're out here."

She'd be hanged if she'd let him make her even more beholden to him. "If you're going to be that muleheaded about it, then I should be the one sleeping outside. After all, your friends loaned this place to you, not me. I'm the intruder here."

He stiffened as if she'd insulted him. "If you think I'll allow that, then you must have a very low opinion of me."

Have mercy, the man could certainly look intimidating when he got up on his high horse. Not that such tactics would work on her. "I just think it's silly to worry about such things at a time like this. If it makes you feel better, Rufus can sleep in here with me and be my chaperone. Why, I'll even bar the door."

He stood. "I think I'll get a bite to eat. Would you like more soup?"

Did he take her for a simpleton? "Mr. Parker, now you're the one who's sidestepping the question. Do I have your word that you'll sleep under this roof tonight?"

His lips compressed and he was silent for a long moment. Then he nodded.

Ivy leaned back, reassured.

She might not know him well, but she knew in her gut that he was absolutely a man of his word.

Mitch sat at the table, absently eating his soup. If temperament was any indication, Miss Feagan was definitely regaining her strength. She was quickly turning into one of the most independent-minded, strong-willed, intriguing women he'd ever met.

But there were pros *and* cons to that. While she might make interesting company, she would also need watching to make certain she didn't take on more than she could handle.

He'd been pleased to see color back in her cheeks. And her hands had almost been steady as she'd ladled up the soup. So physically it appeared she really was on the mend.

That just left the *other* issue.

He stood and stepped out onto the porch, frustrated by the situation. He wouldn't sleep in the house with her, of course. But that was just for his own conscience. If word got out that they'd been here alone overnight, she'd be just as ruined as if he'd spent the night in her room.

He had trouble believing she was as unconcerned by the situation as she would have him think. Perhaps she was just being pragmatic. Or perhaps she wanted to relieve him of any guilt he might be feeling.

Or perhaps it was just that she recognized as much as he did that, other than giving them clear consciences, his sleeping outside wouldn't do much good if word of their situation got out.

Whatever her reasons, however, he intended to adhere to the proprieties as much as possible. A clear conscience was something to strive for. The promise he'd made was to sleep under the roof, and he would keep his word—the roof covered the porch, as well.

Besides, it wasn't just *her* reputation at stake. As a schoolteacher, it was important that he keep his own conduct above reproach.

What a tangle.

There'd been a time when he would have prayed for direction, but that time had long passed. He and God had stopped communicating with each other some time ago. Ever since that tragic night over two years ago.

The night he'd killed his wife and unborn child.

Chapter Four

Thirty minutes after Mr. Parker left her room, Ivy had had enough of lying about in bed. She looked down at Rufus as she threw off the covers and swung her legs over the side of the mattress. "I think exercise and fresh air are just the things to make me feel better."

But first she had to find her clothes. She glanced around. Where were they? The garments had been muddy and damp. They'd also absorbed wet-dog smell from Rufus. Mr. Parker had probably decided to get the messy things out of the cabin and she couldn't say she blamed him.

Ignoring Mr. Parker's suggestion that she help herself to his friend's clothing, Ivy turned instead to her own bag. As she crossed the room, she was pleased to find she wasn't nearly as wobbly as she'd been earlier. It took her a bit longer to change than usual, but she did it and carefully placed the borrowed nightdress over the back of the chair.

She wished she had a mirror so she could see how she looked. Then she grimaced—maybe it was better that she didn't. She likely looked a fright with her hair all a mess and her fingers stained from the berries. She pulled the comb from her saddlebag and tried to remove the worst of the tangles without disturbing the bandage. Then she quickly plaited a loose braid and let it fall down her back. With the bandage around her head, there wasn't much else to be done with it. Besides, Mr. Parker had already seen it in much worse condition so it wasn't as if this would shock him further.

Taking a deep breath and giving Rufus a pat, Ivy stepped out of the bedchamber. Her rescuer wasn't anywhere in sight. She paused a moment to study her surroundings— she hadn't been in any shape to pay attention when she'd first arrived.

To her right was a large fireplace. It was clean and tidy with wood stacked nearby. Facing the fireplace was the sofa she'd rested on when she'd first arrived. Thankfully she saw no signs of blood or dirt. There was a cozy little kitchen and a dining table across the room. The curtains at the windows and the apron hanging on a peg by the door spoke of a woman's touch. Off to one side, a ladder led up to a small loft tucked in under the eaves.

On the opposite side of the common room was a curtained-off area. Another bedchamber, perhaps?

Rufus padded out the open front door and she heard him give a friendly woof. A masculine voice returned the greeting. Well, that solved the mystery of Mr. Parker's whereabouts.

When she stepped outside, she was greeted by the sight of her missing clothing draped over the porch rail. A closer look showed that the pieces weren't just airing out but were clean.

Had he actually done her laundry? She wasn't normally missish, but the thought of him doing such a personal thing for her sent the warmth climbing up her neck and into her cheeks.

"Miss Feagan. What are you doing out of bed?"

She started at the sound of his voice. The sight of her

clothes and thoughts of what it meant had momentarily made her forget she wasn't alone.

Mr. Parker sat off to her right in a ladder-backed chair. He had a large pad of paper in his lap, a pencil in his hand and a frown on his face.

She quickly collected herself—his washing her clothes likely meant nothing more than that he liked everything around him to be all neat and tidy.

Besides, the question about what he was doing with that oversize pad of paper was much more interesting.

And a much safer focus for her thoughts.

As soon as Mr. Parker saw her glance at his paper, he closed the pad, set down his pencil and stood. "Are you sure you should be up so soon?"

Was it just worry for her well-being that put the edge in his tone, or was she intruding? Choosing to believe the former, Ivy brushed his concern aside with a wave of her hand. "I'm feeling much better, thank you. And Nana Dovie always says, sunshine and fresh air go a long way toward healing an ailing body."

Ignoring his frown, she changed the subject. "Thank you for taking care of my clothes—seems I just keep getting deeper into your debt."

His expression shifted as he rubbed the back of his neck. "I just tossed them in the lake when I went down to wash up earlier. It didn't take much effort."

She could tell he'd done more than soak her things— they'd had a good scrubbing. But she let it pass and instead sat in the rocker next to his chair. Then she pointed to his pad of paper. "Please don't let me stop you from finishing whatever it was you were working on."

He sat back down. "It's just some idle sketching— nothing that can't wait."

This man was full of surprises. Intrigued, she leaned forward. "Mind if I look?"

He hesitated, then shrugged. "Help yourself."

She took the tablet and flipped it open. Then her eyes widened. She was looking at a perfect likeness of a hummingbird hovering over a morning glory. It was done all in pencil, but he'd somehow managed to capture the movement of the bird and the early morning dewiness of the flower with simple lines and a bit of shading.

She turned the page and found yet another remarkable work. It was his horse, contentedly grazing near an old wooden fence. A dandelion was bent by a breeze that had teased some of the fluff from the stalk. Again, the level of detail he'd managed to capture with just a pencil was remarkable.

When she turned the page yet again, she found an unfinished drawing. It was the view from the porch. The railings and support post were in the foreground, and beyond that was an open area and then a stand of brush and trees. A quick glance verified that he'd faithfully captured the image of the tree line up ahead.

She turned and found him watching her closely. Was he worried about her opinion? "These drawings are *very* good."

Such God-given talent was surely a treasure to be nurtured and shared. He should be displaying them proudly, not trying to hide them away.

This Mr. Parker was definitely a puzzle—one she was coming to wish she had time to figure out.

Mitch had watched her closely as she studied his work. He rarely showed his sketches to anyone—it was only a hobby, after all, and much too personal to share casually.

Not that he cared much what others thought.

But her genuine smile of delight was oddly gratifying. "Thank you. It's just something I do to pass the time." He took the sketchbook and set it on the table, then changed the subject. "Are you hungry? There's more soup on the stove."

She shook her head, then went right back to the subject of his sketches. "Do you ever draw people?"

Was she hinting that she wanted him to sketch her? "Not often."

"So you do sometimes," she pressed. "I'd love to have you sketch Nana Dovie."

That surprised him. "You might do better to get a photograph. Reggie, the lady who owns this cabin, is a photographer and her work is quite good."

She wrinkled her nose consideringly. "I think I'd rather a sketch. Photographs seem so stiff." Then she sighed. "Not that it matters. Nana Dovie would never travel this far for something she'd think was nonsensical."

She looked around then, obviously done with the subject of his artwork. "Where are Jubal and your horse?"

"Around back."

"And where does that trail lead?" she asked, waving to her left.

"There's a small lake about three hundred yards down that way. It's where the water I've been using comes from, and there's good fishing there, too."

Her eyes lit up. "Is there a spare fishing pole around here?"

"Several. They're in the lean-to out back."

"I'm pretty good with a pole and a hook," she said with a hopeful glance his way.

"Perhaps tomorrow you can try your luck."

Her sigh had a note of disappointment, but she grinned. "Luck has nothing to do with it."

He returned her smile. "I look forward to seeing if the reality matches the boast."

"Challenge accepted." Then she stood. "Please, continue with your drawing. I'm going to plop down in that chair over in the sunshine and just enjoy the fresh air for a bit."

Mitch opened his sketchbook as she settled into her chair. She ruffled the fur on her dog's neck. When the mutt ran off, she leaned back and watched him, laughing and talking to the animal as if he could understand her.

Mitch tried to lose himself in his drawing again, to transfer the essence of the view before him onto the page. But the sound of Ivy's laughter, the sight of her blissful enjoyment of her surroundings, was making it surprisingly difficult to do much of anything but look at her.

Ivy watched Rufus sniff the ground, obviously picking up the scent of some critter or other. It was nice out here—warm but with a breeze to stir her hair. She heard the rat-a-tat-tat of a woodpecker in the distance.

The sun slipped out from behind a cloud, and she closed her eyes against the sudden glare. Rufus barked from what seemed like far away, and she wondered if he'd treed a squirrel. She heard buzzing and wondered idly if it was a bee or a deerfly. But it wasn't really worth the effort to open her eyes to find out.

A moment later, someone cleared his throat right above her, breaking the stillness of the afternoon. Her eyes flew open to focus on Mr. Parker, standing beside her, his sketchbook in hand. Had he finished his drawing already?

Then she noticed the shadows had lengthened and she was no longer in full sunshine. The heat rose in her cheeks as she saw his amused glance. Despite the fact that she'd thought herself well rested, she'd fallen asleep again.

"You must think me a real lazybones."

He smiled. "You have good reason to rest." He reached down to help her rise. "Why don't we head back inside? If you're not hungry or tired, I can pull out a checkerboard, if you feel up to a game."

She took his hand, accepting his assistance. "You'll soon learn I rarely back down from a challenge."

With a smile on his face, Mitch let her precede him back into the cabin. The woman was intriguing. She was certainly unpredictable. And seemingly unflappable.

And totally unlike any woman he'd met before.

Shaking off that thought—an exercise he seemed to be doing a lot of lately—he dug out the checkerboard and set it on the table.

As she sat across from him, he raised an eyebrow in challenge. "I assume you know how to play."

She grinned. "It's been a while, but I think I remember how it goes."

Miss Feagan proved to be an aggressive player, approaching the game with more verve than strategy. He won the first two games, though they were by no means runaway victories. Those defeats didn't seem to dampen her enthusiasm, however. She merely grinned and vowed to get him next time.

He stood. "Before you try again, why don't we eat?"

She grinned. "I came close to beating you just now. Are you by any chance wanting to fortify yourself before facing me again?"

He couldn't remember the last time anyone had taken that teasing tone with him. But he found he rather liked it. "I was thinking I needed to give you an opportunity to sharpen *your* wits so you'd have a fighting chance."

"Ha!" She put her hands on her hips and glowered melodramatically. "That sounds like a challenge. I demand we play a third game so I can defend my honor as a checker player."

"After we eat." He moved toward the stove. "There ought to be just enough soup left for each of us to have a nice bowlful." She stood, but he waved her back down. "Keep your seat. This won't take but a minute."

She ignored him. Naturally. "Don't be silly." She crossed to the counter. "The least I can do is set the table. I assume the dishes are kept in here." She opened the cupboard, then reached inside.

A moment later Mitch saw her sway unsteadily, and he quickly crossed the space between them. "Whoa, there." He took her elbow and put an arm around her shoulders. "Are you okay?"

She gave him a shaky smile. "Just got dizzy for a moment."

"That does it." He led her firmly back to the table. "I want you to sit here and not get up again until it's time to turn in."

"Don't be silly. It was just—"

"No arguments." He pointed to the chair. "Sit."

She stared at him mutinously for another heartbeat. Then she relaxed and gave him a pert grin. "I suppose," she said, sitting with exaggerated care, "that if you insist on waiting on me, I should just let you."

His lips quirked at that, and he gave a ceremonious bow. "At your service, m'lady."

Ivy propped her elbows on the table and watched as Mr. Parker went back to the stove. He certainly was a puzzle of a man. Big as a grizzly but graceful as a wolf. All prickly and proper when it came to matters of propriety but able to take her teasing with good humor and even give it back to her at times. Able to carry heavy loads—

like a fully grown woman—and with those same hands he could draw the most amazing pictures. And for all his stern exterior, she was beginning to believe he was soft as a mossy creek bank on the inside.

Maybe not such a puzzle after all—he was just a good man.

Rufus padded over and she reached down to pat his head. "Hello, boy. Getting restless, are you?" She glanced up at her host. "Has he eaten anything today?"

Mr. Parker turned and frowned down at Rufus. "I gave him a bit of pemmican and some broth earlier."

She should have known he'd take care of her dog. He ladled the soup into two bowls. "I suppose the mutt can have anything left in the pot when we've eaten our fill tonight."

He carried one of the bowls to the table and set it in front of her with a stern look. "I expect you to eat all of it. You need to keep your strength up."

Without waiting for her response, he turned to fetch his own bowl.

Normally she'd get her back up at being ordered around, but she found herself smiling instead. He was being outlandishly high-handed, of course. But she also knew she'd scared him with her momentary light-headedness and this was likely how he dealt with it.

A moment later, he rejoined her at the table. As he settled into his seat, she met his gaze expectantly. "Would you like to say grace?"

Mr. Parker stilled and something she couldn't read flitted across his expression. Was he not a praying man?

But then he bowed his head. "Dear Lord, we thank You for providing this food we are about to partake of, and for the blessings You have bestowed on us this day." He paused a heartbeat, then added, "We also ask that You restore good health to Miss Feagan."

"And to Jubal, as well," Ivy interjected quickly. "Amen."

Mr. Parker echoed her amen, then picked up his spoon. Before taking a bite, he glanced her way. "Earlier you mentioned you *might* have an inheritance waiting for you in Turnabout. If you don't mind my asking, what did you mean by *might?*"

"Reverend Tomlin got a letter a few days ago that said if Robert Feagan's daughter was still alive then there was an inheritance waiting for her in Turnabout. And I'm Robert Feagan's daughter so I just figured I'd head on over to check it out."

"Just like that?"

She shrugged. "I've never been one to let others make decisions for me." She grinned. "And I'm also not very patient. Nana Dovie says it's one of my biggest faults."

"And the letter didn't give you any other details?"

"No, and I'm more than a tad curious." Then she realized he might be able to fill in some of the blanks for her. "Do you know a man named Drum Mosley?"

"Only well enough to exchange greetings. He owns a large ranch outside of town. Is he a relative?"

Something in his tone made her think he knew more than he was saying. "No. But it seems he knew my father. According to the letter, he's been holding something in trust on my father's behalf and if I can prove I'm my father's child, he'll turn it over to me, whatever *it* is."

"My condolences on the loss of your father."

She shrugged. "Thanks. But he passed on when I was just a babe, so I didn't know him."

"Drum's expecting you, then?"

"Don't know about that."

"You didn't send a response to his letter?"

"I figured there wasn't much use since I'd get there at about the same time as a letter." She grimaced. "Or at least

I would have if I hadn't run into these delays." She'd had enough of talking about herself. She'd much rather learn more about him. "Tell me something about yourself."

"Anything specific you'd like to know?"

"Do you have any family?"

"I have two sisters."

"Older or younger than you?"

"Both are younger."

She imagined he'd make a fine older brother, always there to look out for his little sisters. "I've always wished I was part of a larger family," she said wistfully. "Don't get me wrong, I couldn't ask for a better person than Nana Dovie to raise me, but it always seemed kind of lonesome out in the country with no other young'uns to play with."

She dipped her spoon back in her bowl. "So, how often do you get to see them?"

"Not often. They're both happily married. Erica, the elder of the two, married a doctor and they moved to San Francisco. They now have four children—three girls and a boy. Katie, my baby sister, married an Italian concert pianist, of all things, and spends much of her time in Europe. They have three little boys."

"Oh, my goodness, your family is scattered all over creation. No wonder you don't see them often."

"We keep in touch with letters."

"What about your parents?"

"They've both passed on."

So he was an orphan, too. "I'm sorry." She hesitated a moment, then plunged in with a more personal question. "And you never married?"

From the way his expression immediately closed off, she knew she'd overstepped. "That was rude—forget I asked. Sometimes I speak before I think."

"I married once. She, also, has passed away."

Now she *really* felt bad. Obviously it still stirred up painful memories. "I'm sorry," she said again, feeling the words were entirely inadequate.

"I appreciate your sympathy." He stood. "Looks like you finished your soup. Would you like another serving?"

He obviously wanted to put some distance between them, and she didn't blame him. "No, thank you—I'm full." She stood, as well. "I should probably check on Jubal before it gets dark.".

But he shook his head. "I'll take care of that. Why don't you feed Rufus?"

"I appreciate your concern, but I'm perfectly capable of taking care of my own animal."

"Then take care of your dog."

She bit her tongue, trying to remember that, despite his bossiness, he meant well. She gave a short nod.

For tonight, she'd hold her peace. But come tomorrow it would be a different story.

Mitch added a couple of buckets of water to the trough.

He'd felt like a fraud earlier when he'd said grace, especially when he'd looked up afterward to see the soft approval in Ivy Feagan's eyes.

Though he went to church services regularly and attended meals in friends' homes, where prayers were offered, it had been a long time since he'd truly prayed himself, much less done so publicly. But he did believe in the Almighty and he'd felt strangely reluctant to refuse her request.

The words had come naturally to him, as if riding a horse again after a long convalescence.

Had God, knowing his heart, been offended by his prayer?

Which, for some reason, brought his thoughts around to that moment when Ivy had asked him if he was married.

It had taken all of his control not to react as the painful memories returned. Sweet-tempered, turn-the-other-cheek Gretchen, the woman he'd vowed to cherish and protect, hadn't deserved the violent, senseless death that had been her lot. And he may not have actually pulled the trigger, but her death was as much his fault as if he had.

He could never forgive himself for that.

Mitch pushed away those fruitless thoughts and focused on Jubal. He firmly nudged the animal, forcing him to take a few reluctant steps, and studied his gait. It was quickly apparent that the mule would indeed need more time before he could make the trip to Turnabout.

"Sorry you had to make that long walk this morning, but it couldn't be helped." He gave the animal a handful of oats and patted his side. "But I'll make you as comfortable as I can while you recover."

He dug out another scoop of grain and turned to Seeley. "Here you go." He stroked the animal's nose. "You didn't think I'd forgotten about you, did you?"

As he tended to the animals, his thoughts drifted back to Miss Feagan's mention of that possible inheritance. The conversation had raised as many questions as it had answered. If her father had been dead for all these years, then why was she just now hearing about her inheritance?

And it was even stranger that Drum Mosley was involved. The man had a reputation as a penny-pincher. Mitch couldn't picture him voluntarily giving away any of his holdings. Then again, he vaguely remembered hearing that Drum had taken to his sickbed recently. Perhaps the rancher was getting his affairs in order.

Whatever the case, it was none of his business. As soon

as he could get her to Turnabout, his involvement in her affairs would be over.

He picked up the water bucket and headed back to the cabin, ignoring the little voice inside him that whispered his involvement in Miss Feagan's affairs was actually just beginning.

When Mitch returned to the cabin, the dishes had been cleaned and put away, and the checkerboard set up for another game.

"I see you've been busy," he said with what he considered commendable restraint. He should have known she wouldn't take it easy.

She waved toward the game board. "Didn't want anything standing in the way of my getting my revenge."

"Are you sure you wouldn't rather turn in? I wouldn't want you to suffer yet a third defeat."

"That does it. Sit yourself down and prepare to eat those words."

And to his surprise, she actually won.

Mitch found himself smiling as she crowed about her victory. Then he started collecting the checkers. "I believe I'd better quit while I'm ahead. And dusk settled in while we weren't looking, so it's time to call it a night. It's been a long day and we both could use some rest."

She grimaced. "All I've done today is rest."

But since she followed that statement with a broad yawn, he had no compunction in insisting. "Is there anything you need before you retire?" he asked as he stood.

Miss Feagan shook her head. "I'll be fine, thank you. Good night." She crossed the room then paused and eyed him suspiciously. "You *do* remember you promised not to sleep outside, don't you?"

He'd hoped she wouldn't bring that up again. But maybe it was best that she knew his plans so she could speak honestly if questions came up later. "What I *promised* was to sleep under this roof. I'm going to drag the mattress from the other bed out to the porch. It's a nice night and I'll be quite comfortable." He raised a hand to stop the protest already forming on her lips. "My mind is made up."

She crossed her arms, glaring at him, frustration etched on her face. "It just doesn't seem right."

"Still, the decision is mine so you'll just have to accept it."

She glared a moment longer, then lifted her hands in surrender. "Have it your way."

As she turned to her room, he called out, "Take Rufus with you."

Just before she closed her door, Mitch thought he heard her mutter something that contained the phrase "more stubborn than Jubal."

He grinned as he wrestled the unwieldy mattress out the front door. She certainly wasn't bashful about speaking her mind. But at least she was smart enough to know when arguments were useless.

His smile faded as he stretched out on the mattress and stared out at the stars. If he was being entirely honest with himself, despite his desire for solitude, he hadn't really minded her presence here today. Which was troubling.

Because he had to hold himself apart. He couldn't risk hurting someone else the way he'd hurt Gretchen.

Chapter Five

As Ivy settled into bed, she marveled at how the day had turned out to be so different from what she'd imagined when she woke this morning. She'd been worried about Jubal's hoof and whether or not she'd be able to stretch her provisions if they were delayed much longer. And now, here she was, a roof over her head and a warm, dry bed to sleep in, plenty of provisions to carry her through and a proper place to let Jubal rest and heal.

And befriending Mr. Parker was an unexpected blessing for sure. Even though he was something of a stiff-necked gent at times, his concern for both her physical well-being and her reputation was touching. She no longer found his size intimidating—rather it was comforting to know that so much strength was tempered by restraint and kindness.

And as much as she considered herself independent, knowing there would be someone in Turnabout she could turn to if the need arose was also very comforting.

Lord, despite these unexpected delays, You've sure been kind to me. Of all the folks who could have happened across me out here, You sent the most honorable man I've ever met. Thank You for that grace.

Amen.

* * *

By the time Ivy rose the next morning she could hear Mr. Parker moving around in the kitchen. The smell of coffee brewing had her rushing through her morning ablutions to join him.

When she opened the door, he looked up with a smile. "You're just in time for breakfast."

"Smells mighty good."

He shrugged. "It's nothing fancy—just hardtack biscuits and strawberry preserves. But I softened the biscuits in the skillet with a little bacon grease."

"Apologies not necessary—it sounds like just the thing."

He gave her a searching look. "How are you feeling today?"

"Much more myself, thanks." She refused to let him mollycoddle her today. "The smell of coffee was sure nice to wake up to."

"It's ready if you want to help yourself. The cups are on that shelf next to the window."

She crossed the room and reached for the cups. "Want me to pour you some, too?"

He nodded as he set the dish of warm biscuits on the table. "Thank you."

Ivy carefully carried the nearly full cups to the table and took her seat. He seemed cheerful and rested today—maybe sleeping on the porch hadn't bothered him as much as she'd feared. "I hope the mosquitoes didn't pester you too much last night."

"I managed to sleep through it."

His dry tone made her wonder if he was downplaying the amount of aggravation he'd experienced.

After they said the blessing, she slathered some jelly on her biscuit. "I should be up to that four-hour ride to Turnabout today."

He gave no outward reaction, but she could tell he had reservations. Not surprising—did the man ever do anything spontaneously? But she would've thought he'd be glad to get rid of her by now.

Mr. Parker took a sip of coffee before responding. "I checked on Jubal when I got the wood for the stove this morning. He needs at least one more day's rest before he undertakes that long trip."

She tried to rein in her disappointment. "Of course I don't want to push him if he's not ready. I'll take a look at him after breakfast and decide."

His left brow rose. "Does this matter in Turnabout require your immediate attention?"

She waved dismissively. "That's not it. This inheritance thing has waited more than twenty years so another day or two won't make much difference." She rubbed her cheek. "But Nana Dovie's going to worry if she doesn't hear from me soon. I promised to send her a telegram when I got to Turnabout so she'd know I'd arrived safely."

He nodded. "I see." Then he studied her a moment longer. "This Nana Dovie means a great deal to you. I can hear it in your voice when you speak of her."

Ivy nodded. "She's the only family I have," she said simply.

"And how will she react to not having heard from you yet?"

"Nana Dovie's not one to panic easily," she said. "We discussed this trip before I left, and much as I'd hoped to make the trip in two days, we both knew it might take longer. But if she doesn't hear from me by tomorrow, she'll fear the worst." Ivy hated the idea of putting the only mother she'd ever known through such needless worry.

"Don't worry—we'll send word as soon as we're able."

Ivy found it interesting that he'd said "we" and not "you."

"There's something else. Nana Dovie doesn't leave the farm, ever, so she'll have to wait until the reverend pays a visit to send an inquiry."

She saw the flicker of speculation in his eyes at her statement, but he didn't press. She was coming to appreciate his tact.

He stood and carried his dishes to the counter. "Then it's best we plan to leave first thing in the morning."

It wasn't ideal, but perhaps Nana Dovie wouldn't start imagining the worst before then. She followed him to the counter with her own dishes. "So you think Jubal will be ready for the trip by then?"

"We'll get to town tomorrow, one way or the other."

"What do you mean by that?"

"Why don't we wait and see what tomorrow brings?"

Was he being deliberately evasive?

Before she could ask for an explanation, he changed the subject. "Now, Miss Feagan, do you prefer to wash or dry?"

She grabbed a dishrag. "Wash." She dunked a plate in the basin, which already contained fresh water. "And don't you think, all things considered, there's no need for you to continue to refer to me as Miss Feagan? The name's Ivy."

Predictably, he raised a brow. "*All things considered,* I think it best we stick to the formalities."

She refused to back down. "Hogwash. You've bandaged me, bodily lifted me onto your horse, removed my shoes and stockings, practically tucked me in—you even did my laundry, for goodness' sake. Standing on ceremony at this point is just silly."

Mitch stiffened and she hid a grin. He probably didn't get called silly very often.

He accepted the clean plate and rubbed it with extra vigor. "*Miss Feagan,* we'll have enough speculation to deal with when we ride into town together from this all-but-forsaken backwoods. Any overfamiliarity we show with each other will just intensify that scrutiny."

She sighed melodramatically. "I've *never* met such a fusspot before." She'd deliberately used that word, knowing it would get his back up. And she was right.

She quickly spoke up again before he could protest further. "If you feel that strongly, why don't we compromise? While we're alone, we use first names. When we get to town, we get all formal and particular again. After all, I don't expect to be in Turnabout more than a couple of days."

He frowned but finally nodded stiffly. "Very well."

She rewarded him with a broad smile as she handed him another plate. "Good to see you can unbend on occasion."

That earned her a startled look and then the hint of a sheepish grin.

Five minutes later, Ivy patted Jubal's side sympathetically as Mitch set the animal's hoof down and brushed his hands against his pants. Unfortunately, she agreed with his assessment—Jubal was in no shape to make that trip today. She only hoped one more day would improve his condition enough to let them get underway again.

As they strolled back to the front of the cabin, she looked at the trail thoughtfully. "You did say there was a lake out that way, didn't you?"

He nodded. "Thinking about going fishing?"

She hesitated a moment. He was so straightlaced—would he think her indelicate if she told him what was on her mind?

Then again, he'd likely already figured out she wasn't

a prim and proper miss. And the urge to get clean *was* almost overwhelming.

She tilted her chin up. "Actually, if you don't mind, I'd appreciate a chance to take a bath."

He didn't so much as blink. "Of course. Gather what you need and I'll show you the way."

Relieved that he hadn't argued with her, she nodded and all but sprinted up the porch steps.

In addition to a change of clothes, she grabbed the borrowed nightdress and the sheets from the bed. Might as well do laundry while she was bathing.

When she stepped outside, she discovered Mitch had towels and a bar of soap. He also had his sketchpad.

That last gave her pause. "Just what is it you aim to do with that?"

"While you're occupied at the lake, I thought I'd search out a spot to do some sketching."

Of course. He was probably tired of playing nursemaid to her and was ready for some privacy of his own.

He insisted she hold his arm for steadying support as they walked down the trail. That and the slow pace he set had her rolling her eyes. Even Rufus didn't stay beside them for long—within a few minutes he'd scampered ahead to explore on his own.

Ivy wasn't used to being treated as if she were fragile and she'd never cottoned much to being mollycoddled. But she had to admit, at least to herself, that it wasn't altogether unpleasant to have someone so concerned for her well-being.

In fact, it made her feel special.

When the trail finally opened to reveal the lake, her eyes widened, trying to take everything in at once. Everywhere she looked there was something to delight the eye. The sun glinted across the water like crystals from a chandelier. Colorful dragonflies darted here and there A pair of turtles sunned on a half-submerged log as a hawk skimmed the air high overhead.

She turned and touched his arm. "It's perfect. And the water looks so inviting—I can't wait to wade in."

He glanced at her hand on his sleeve and she quickly removed it, embarrassed by her impulsive gesture.

But his expression didn't change. "Then I'll leave you to it. And don't worry. It's not deep on this end, and it's entirely private." He took a step back. "I'll be up the trail just a little ways, close enough to hear if you call. Take whatever time you need."

Ivy watched him until he rounded a turn. Then she began unbraiding her hair. If she had to be stuck somewhere while Jubal healed, this was not a bad place to be.

And the company was quite nice, as well.

In fact, if she weren't in such a hurry to get back and check on Nana Dovie, she wouldn't mind the delay at all.

Mitch found a comfortable spot and settled on the ground with his back against a tree. He heard her break out in song and smiled at her slightly off-key but enthusiastic rendition of "Shall We Gather at the River?" as he opened his sketchbook.

Even injured, she was the most attack-life-head-on woman he'd ever met. Now that she was feeling better, she was definitely a force to be reckoned with. It was exhausting just being around her.

And strangely exhilarating, as well.

Did she really think him a fusspot? He wasn't exactly certain what that was, but it definitely didn't sound flattering. He had to admit, if only to himself, that it had been her name-calling that had made him give in on the subject of using first names. Was he so easily manipulated?

But the smile she'd given him when he capitulated had seemed strangely compelling. It had been quite some time since anyone had looked at him with such unabashed approval.

Shaking off the thought, Mitch took up his pencil and waited for inspiration. Normally he had no trouble finding a subject, but for some reason today was different. He finally settled on the image of the turtles sunning down by the lake.

Forty-five minutes later, Mitch looked up to see Ivy approaching. Her still-damp hair was loosely braided and she carried a load of wet laundry. The smile on her face reflected satisfaction and her eyes sparkled.

Her pleasure was infectious.

Closing his sketchbook, he stood and moved to meet her.

"Sorry I took so long," she said, "but the water felt absolutely wonderful and I didn't want to get out." She nodded toward his sketchbook. "Did you get any drawing done?"

"I did." He set his pad and pencil down. "Here, let's swap. I'll take those wet things from you and you take my sketch pad."

To his surprise, she didn't argue, but merely said thank you as she surrendered her load of soggy laundry.

Then he discovered why. As soon as she retrieved his pad, she opened it and studied the image inside. "It's beautiful. You have such a wonderful God-given talent."

Ivy certainly had a way about her.

"I see why you like coming here," she said, interrupting his thoughts. "It's such a marvelous place."

"It's only my second visit, but I'm enjoying this visit more than the first." He was definitely enjoying the company more than he had that first time.

She gave him a questioning look. Then her gaze sharpened. "Aren't those blackberries?"

Mitch followed the line of her gaze. "What do you know, a few end-of-season stragglers."

She was already moving toward the brambly vines, and before he could so much as blink, she had popped one in her mouth. She closed her eyes and tilted her chin up. "Mmm."

He watched, captivated by her expression of pure bliss. He couldn't have moved if his boots were on fire.

She opened her eyes again.

"You should try some of these. They're really good." Then she looked contrite. "Oh, your hands are full. Allow me."

She plucked a couple of berries and held them up to him. Without a word, he opened his mouth. Their eyes locked and she froze with her hand inches from his lips. Her eyes widened and her breath hitched. They were so close, he could count the freckles on her nose if he tried. He knew he should step back, but for the life of him he couldn't do it. But closer, oh, yes, he could move closer with very little effort.

Then Rufus returned and Ivy took a step back.

Mitch silently berated himself. The temptation to kiss her had caught him unawares, surprising him with its swift intensity. But that was no excuse. He should have had tighter control of himself. What would have happened if Rufus hadn't interrupted them?

He'd assured her he was an honorable man, that she had nothing to fear from him. Did she still believe it?

Did *he?*

His earlier thoughts about enjoying her company had come back to haunt him. For the first time since Gretchen's death he'd let his guard down enough to take pleasure in a woman's company. And look what had happened.

What was it about Ivy that she could get under his skin so easily?

Then he focused on her again.

Her cheeks were a becoming shade of pink, her expression reflected confusion. He felt a cad for having done that to her.

She turned to greet her dog, giving them both an opportunity to gather their composure.

He knew offering an apology would only make matters worse. His best course of action was to get things back on an easy, comfortable footing.

He cleared his throat. "What do you say we try out those cane poles? I've a hankering for some fried fish for lunch."

"That sounds like fun." She stood. "I seem to recall I'm supposed to show you how it's done."

He was relieved to see she'd already recovered some of her spirit. "Is that a challenge?"

"Yes, sir, I do believe it is."

Ivy arranged the wet laundry on the porch railings. As soon as they'd made it back to the cabin, Mitch had disappeared around back to fetch the poles.

She wasn't sure what had happened back there, but she *was* fairly certain it had been her fault. And she'd hate to think she'd done anything to make him think less of her. What on earth had she been thinking, offering to *feed* him those berries?

Mitch reappeared carrying a pair of cane poles and leading his horse.

She nodded toward Seeley. "Are you going somewhere?"

"Since we're headed to the lake, I thought I'd refill the water barrel."

She frowned. "You use your horse for that?"

"Yep."

Puzzled, she watched as he maneuvered Seeley so the animal was backed up to the barrel. She moved closer and discovered the barrel sat on a low wooden platform outfitted with wheels. "How clever."

"Reggie's husband built it. It has a harness so you can hitch a horse for easy transport."

She nodded appreciatively. "That would definitely save lots of time and effort hauling buckets of water."

"That's the idea." Mitch started fitting his horse with the special harness. "I figure, once I fill it, Seeley can graze until we're done fishing."

He had the horse hitched in short order and then they retraced their steps to the lake.

"If I help you fill the barrel," she offered, "it'll get done in half the time."

"No need—I've got the job in hand and it won't take long."

She knew he was mollycoddling her again, but before she could protest he picked up the small spade he'd brought along.

"I'll dig some worms for you so you can start fishing while I fill the barrel."

"No need," she said, mimicking him, "I've got *that* job well in hand."

That nudged his brow up a notch. "You plan to collect your own worms?"

"Of course." It wasn't as if she'd had anyone around to do it for her back home.

"And bait your own hooks?"

He seemed even more surprised at that. She supposed it

wasn't the most ladylike of tasks. But she refused to apologize for it. "It's like threading a needle."

That teased a grin from him. "I suppose that's one way of looking at it."

She watched surreptitiously as he scooped water with the pail and dumped it into the barrel. His very broad, solid back was to her. She didn't figure there was much as could stand against a man with a back like that. Especially one with as good a heart as Mitch seemed to have.

That combination of strength and heart was mighty attractive in a man. A woman would be lucky to have a man like Mitch looking out for her.

For a heartbeat she recalled that moment on the trail, how the light in his eyes had deepened as he'd stared at her and everything else had seemed to fall away. Then she gave her head a shake and quickly turned to bait her hook.

As she dropped her line in the water, she noticed a slight tremble in her hands.

As they cleaned their catch at the water's edge, Ivy argued that her five fish to his three clearly indicated she was the better fisherman. He insisted it was more about the quality of the catch and his three easily outweighed her five.

Ivy enjoyed their spirited discussion—it was the kind comfortable friends would have. And she hadn't had a friend like that in a long time, thanks to the outcast status Lester Stokes had foisted on her.

When they arrived back at the cabin, Ivy left Mitch to tend to Seeley while she went inside with the fish. Poking around in the kitchen, she found cornmeal, salt and a small crock with bacon grease. She also found a jar of pickled tomatoes—just the thing to go with pan-fried fish.

By the time she had all the fixings for their meal gathered up, Mitch had returned. "Thanks again for taking care of the animals," she said.

He merely nodded. For a schoolteacher he certainly wasn't talkative. Was he this way in his classroom, too?

Then he waved toward the stove. "I can do the cooking," he said. "You've had an active morning for someone still recuperating." His serious expression lightened as he gave a lopsided smile. "I'm not much of a cook, but I *do* know how to fry fish."

She shook her head. "It's *your* turn to sample *my* cooking."

He didn't argue further, but she felt him watching while she worked. As she added cornmeal and seasoning to the fish, she asked, "You said you're a schoolteacher—is drawing one of the things you teach your students?"

"No."

It was like squeezing tears from a rock to get him to elaborate on anything. "Why? I reckon there's some who'd enjoy those lessons more than reading and 'rithmetic."

"But reading and arithmetic, along with geography, history and literature, are the more important things for them to learn."

"You know all those subjects?" she asked.

"I know *something* about all of them. What I don't know I find in the books I teach from."

She glanced over her shoulder. "So you draw, fish, rescue injured travelers and have a lot of book learning. That's quite a list of talents."

He gave that crooked smile again. "You make it sound more impressive than it is. I have faults enough to offset those talents, believe me."

She turned the fish in the skillet. Was he just being modest or did he think so little of himself? "Have you always lived in Turnabout?"

"No, I moved there about two years ago."

"Where did you live before that?"

"Pennsylvania, near Philadelphia." His tone implied the topic was off-limits.

Which, naturally, piqued her curiosity. She decided to see if coming at it sideways would make him more forthcoming.

"Philadelphia—that's over on the East Coast, isn't it? Seems like that's a far piece from here."

Some of the tension she'd heard in his voice eased. "About fourteen hundred miles."

She looked at him over her shoulder. "Oh, my stars, you traveled all that way? Whatever for?" She couldn't even imagine such a distance, or why someone would cross it to come here.

But his expression had closed off again. "I was ready for a change, and moving all the way to Texas seemed like a good start."

It appeared she'd gotten too close to whatever it was he didn't want to talk about. Time to drop the subject—she owed him that courtesy at least. Did it have something to do with his deceased wife? Had grief put that bleak shadow in his expression? Or was it something more? She was human enough to be curious.

Very curious.

Mitch didn't want to think about his life back in Philadelphia, much less discuss it. He'd rather forget that period of his life.

As if he ever could.

"How are those fish coming along?" he asked.

"Just about done."

He crossed the room to get the dishes and set a couple of plates in easy reach for her. Then he filled a pair of glasses from the jug of water he'd brought inside. In short order they were seated and ready to dig into their meal. "This is quite good," he said after taking his first bite.

Her cheeks pinkened in pleasure. "Glad you like it. Nana Dovie used to do most of the cooking at our place. Lately, though, she's been insisting I do more of it."

He saw the slight furrow of her brow. "And that worries you?"

"It's as if she's trying to prepare me for life without her."

"Perhaps she's merely preparing you for when you marry and have a kitchen of your own to manage."

Her expression closed off. What nerve had he struck? Didn't she dream of marriage the way other females did?

She made a noncommittal sound and focused on eating. Then she pointed her fork at him. "Have you always liked to draw?"

"I suppose."

"Did you take lessons?"

"No, just trial and error."

"Were you a schoolteacher back in Philadelphia?"

She certainly wasn't shy with her questions. "For a time. Then I bought a farm and worked that for a while." Which brought him back to memories he didn't want to relive.

He speared another bite of fish and changed the subject. "When you're not traveling long distances to claim an unspecified inheritance, what do you enjoy doing?"

"Working in the garden," she said without hesitation. "And I'm good at it, if I do say so myself. Nana Dovie says I have the greenest thumb she ever did see."

Mitch let her continue to talk about gardening for the rest of the meal, only occasionally commenting or asking a question when she paused. Later he insisted she nap while he stepped out onto the porch with his sketch pad.

But he didn't pick up his pencil. Instead he stared at the tree line, focusing on nothing in particular.

Thankfully that near-kiss on the trail didn't seem to have affected her trust in him. Which was a good thing, of course.

So why was he staring off into space, wishing things could be different?

Chapter Six

"What's the verdict? Can Jubal travel today?"

Ivy wasn't certain which answer she wanted Mitch to give. Yesterday had been just downright enjoyable. After her nap, Mitch had taken her to a beautiful meadow and she'd brought armloads of wildflowers back to the cabin, filling jars and pitchers with them and setting them all around. She could tell Mitch was amused by it all, but not in an unkind way.

She'd give a lot to have just one more day in this idyllic spot. But she had obligations that she couldn't fulfill here.

"Ideally, he could use another day of rest," Mitch answered, "but I know you're worried about Nana Dovie. So I think, if we take it slow and easy, he can probably make it to Turnabout without experiencing much of a setback—as long as you're not riding him."

Ivy was puzzled. "Are you saying I should walk?"

"There is another option." His tone was carefully neutral, his gaze assessing. "We can ride double on Seeley."

Ivy blinked, not certain she'd heard right. Was the always-concerned-with-propriety Mitch Parker actually suggesting they ride double?

"We'll have to go slow and take frequent breaks to make

certain we don't overtax either animal," he continued. "But we should still make it to town well before dark if we leave in the next few hours."

Apparently he *was* serious. She felt a sudden shyness at the thought of that long ride together.

He must have sensed her hesitation. "It's your choice. We can wait until tomorrow if you prefer."

This was no time for missishness. Ivy shook her head. "Not at all. But do you think Seeley can carry us both that far? I don't want to pamper Jubal at your horse's expense."

"Seeley will be fine, especially at the pace we'll be setting."

"Then that's what we should do. I'll sure feel better once I've sent that telegram to Nana Dovie." And surely he wouldn't have suggested this if there were anything really improper about it.

He nodded, his expression still unreadable.

They set to work and made preparations to leave. And all the while, she kept telling herself not to be such a nervous twit about the upcoming trip.

When they finally closed the door on the cabin, Ivy had the strangest feeling she was leaving a special haven, a place where nothing more troublesome than hungry mosquitoes had been able to touch them.

But now it was time to head back into the real world and face whatever challenges awaited her. If only she had a little more time alone with her white knight—

She shook that thought off before she could complete it—she should focus on practical considerations, not daydreams and foolishness.

Mitch led the animals to the front of the cabin, and Ivy approached Jubal and petted his nose. "Sorry to press you back into service so soon, but we'll go as easy as we can."

When she stepped aside, Mitch attached Jubal's lead to

Seeley's saddle. Then he faced her. "I think this will work best if I ride in front."

She nodded, that shy feeling returning. Hopefully Mitch didn't seem to notice anything unusual in her demeanor. He turned and mounted in one quick, fluid motion; then he nudged Seeley, prompting the horse to move next to the porch steps. Ivy took his hand and was in the saddle almost before she could give it much thought. She'd changed into the britches again, deciding that would be the easiest way to do this. She'd change back into more ladylike clothing before they reached town.

"Wrap your arms around my waist," Mitch said. "I assure you, it won't restrain or hurt me."

Ivy hesitated. That meant she'd be all but embracing him for whatever time it took to get to Turnabout. Despite the fact that Lester had succeeded in convincing the folks back in Nettles Gap that she was a fallen woman, it was a familiarity she hadn't ever experienced before.

But this was a purely practical accommodation, driven by necessity. Besides, if Mr. Fusspot saw no problem with the arrangement, it had to be perfectly respectable.

She took a deep breath and did as he'd instructed.

Her arms didn't come close to reaching all the way around his broad chest. Not that she tried. Instead, she held herself stiffly upright, trying to leave a bit of space between them.

"Relax," he said gently. "I won't let you fall. And it's going to be a long ride."

She was relieved that he thought she was only worried about falling, though his words and his tone did ease some of her tension. She shifted, tightening her hold and allowing herself to lean against his broad back.

"That's better." He gathered the reins. "Ready?"

"Ready." She supposed *better* was one way to describe it. Very safe and altogether too cozy was another.

With a click of his tongue and a slight movement of his knees, her white knight set his steed in motion.

Ivy was obviously on edge. Was she uncomfortable with this enforced closeness? For all her apparent independence, Mitch sensed she was still naive and innocent in many ways. Which was as it should be.

The best way to put her at ease was to get her mind focused elsewhere. And it wouldn't be a bad thing to find something for him to focus on besides the feel of her pressed against his back, either.

"Tell me about your Nana Dovie. What's she like—as a person, I mean?"

"Oh, my, that's a tall order. Let's see, if you were just to look at her while she's resting, you wouldn't think there was much to her. She's a little woman, not quite five feet tall and skinny as a possum's tail. But, like a banty rooster, she can be very forceful when she needs to be, and she can turn a grown man into a stammering schoolboy with just a look."

He felt Ivy relax against him a bit more as she talked.

"But that ain't to say she's mean or vengeful or anything like that," she explained. "It's just that she's not afraid to give you the benefit of her opinion. She's God-fearing and generous, and stands up for what she feels is right, even if it means she has to stand alone. And she might not have much book learning, but she's the wisest person I know."

"She sounds like quite a woman." And very like Ivy herself.

Ivy nodded in agreement. "I owe her everything I have and am. That's the main reason I have to see this thing through, and as quickly as possible."

"We're working on that. How did you come to live with her?"

"She was a friend of my ma's and also a midwife. She was there when I was born and when my ma died. When my pa died a few days later, she took me in."

He hadn't realized she'd been orphaned so young. No wonder Ivy was so loyal to the woman. "So the two of you run a farm on your own?"

"It's not a big place. We have a nice-size garden and some chickens…and a goat."

He sensed there was something she'd left unsaid. "No other livestock?"

"We used to have a milk cow, and a horse, too. But…" He felt her shudder as she paused. "But four months ago the barn burned down and we couldn't get the animals out in time."

Sympathy washed through him. "I'm sorry. That must have been hard to watch."

"I've never felt so helpless and heartsick in my life. Both Buttercup and Homer were more than just farm animals— they were like pets. It's the one and only time I've seen Nana Dovie cry."

She shuddered again and he had to fight the urge to stop the horse and take her in his arms to console her. But he didn't have that right. Instead he tried to turn her thoughts to other matters. "Did you rebuild your barn?"

"Not yet. That's one reason I'm so anxious to see what this inheritance business is all about. We need a new barn and new animals. As it is, we had to borrow—"

She stopped talking abruptly, as if afraid she'd said too much. "Sorry, didn't mean to rattle on about my troubles."

"I don't mind." In fact, he wished she felt comfortable sharing more. Exactly how deep in debt had they gotten?

"After you send your Nana Dovie that telegram, what's your next move going to be?"

"I figure I'll go see Mr. Mosley and show him my proof that Robert Feagan was my father. You said he has a ranch outside of town. Is it on our way?"

"I'm afraid not—it's about a forty-five-minute ride to the other side of town. I'll get a wagon from the livery and escort you there."

She didn't say anything. Had he overstepped by inviting himself along?

Instead of pressing her, he moved on. "Before we do any of that, though, I intend to have Dr. Pratt take a look at that injury of yours."

She was quick to respond. "There's no need. My head feels much better."

No matter how much she protested, it wasn't a point he intended to give in on. "That's for the doctor to decide."

"You sure can be mighty bossy." There was a grumpy note to her voice that succeeded only in making him smile.

"I prefer to think of it as determined," he said dryly.

She made a rather indelicate noise at that.

He chose to ignore it. "Do you have a place to stay while you're in Turnabout?"

"I assume there's an inn there."

"There's a hotel called The Rose Palace."

"Sounds fancy."

He shrugged and found he liked the way she reflexively tightened her hold. "I wouldn't describe it as fancy, but it's clean and comfortable."

"Then that's all I need. Besides, I won't be staying long."

Strange how talk of her leaving needled him. "Just ride in, claim your inheritance and head home again."

"Of course." She sounded happy about it. "The sooner I get back to Nana Dovie, the better."

And why would she stay?

"Miss Jacobs is lucky to have someone like you to care for her."

"I'm the lucky one." Then she sighed. "Though I have to learn not to be such a worrier. As Nana Dovie reminds me, God has everything under His control. And He can make all things work for good, even if we don't see it at the time."

Mitch shifted. There was a time when he'd shared that belief. But where had the good been in Gretchen's senseless death? Where had God's mercy been when those bullets were flying?

"Is something wrong?"

Apparently his silence on the matter had caught her attention. He pasted a smile on his face in the hopes it would lighten his tone. "We've been on the road for about an hour. Time to stop and give the animals a rest."

It wouldn't hurt to put a bit of distance between them, as well.

Ivy realized he hadn't answered her question. She noticed he often tried to sidestep when her questions got too personal.

She didn't want to press too hard, though. Besides, she was more than happy to climb down and stretch her legs.

As soon as she had her feet on the ground, she moved to Jubal. "How are you doing, old friend? I promise when we get to town I'll find you a nice place to rest with lots of comfy straw. And I'm going to get you the juiciest apples I can find."

"Speaking of feed…"

She turned to see Mitch untying the food sack from the saddle.

"I think I'll have a bite to eat," he said. "How about you?"

They ate some berries and hardtack and shared water from his canteen to wash it down, as they stood in companionable silence.

When they were done, Mitch reattached the food sack, then quickly mounted up. As soon as he was settled, he reached down to her. With an ease that still surprised her, he lifted her into the saddle.

Once they were on their way, Ivy took stock of how far they'd traveled and where the sun was in the sky. "We're not going to make it to town in time for me to see Mr. Mosley today, are we?"

"Probably not."

"At least I'll be able to send that telegram. The rest can wait until morning."

He cleared his throat. "You will undoubtedly encounter Reggie and Adam, the couple who own the cabin, while you're in town. When you do, I know your first tendency will be to thank them." He turned enough to give her a stern look. "But it would be best if you refrained."

"But—"

He faced forward again. "If we're going to hide the fact that we were alone out there for two days, then we must keep silent about *every* aspect of our time there."

Really, he could be like an old biddy hen with her chicks. Only she wasn't a helpless little hatchling. "I don't plan to lie to anyone."

"Neither do I. It's just best we don't volunteer any information unnecessarily. Surely you don't want to burden my friends with keeping our secret as well, do you?"

That gave her pause. "I hadn't thought of it that way."

Perhaps she'd been selfish in her thinking. "Very well, we'll do this your way."

But the thought that this decision would come back to haunt them wouldn't let her go. These were his friends so she would bow to his wishes. But it had been her experience that secrets had a way of coming to light.

And when they did, feelings would be hurt and trusts would be broken.

Chapter Seven

Ivy discovered yet another reason to be grateful Mitch was with her. Thanks to his familiarity with the area, she was able to don her skirt before they reached the first farmhouse. And when they did reach that first farmhouse, Mitch, who seemed acquainted with the family living there, convinced them to loan him a wagon.

So when they finally rolled into town, they did so with at least a smidgeon of the propriety Mitch so diligently strove for. Of course, with Seeley and Jubal tied behind and Rufus riding on the floor between them, a smidgeon was the best they could hope for.

As further proof of that, several townsfolk along the sidewalks were eyeing their little procession curiously. Not that she blamed them. The makeup of their group was unconventional, and she was a stranger who'd arrived out of the blue with the town's schoolteacher.

She tried to ignore the stares and instead focus on the town itself. Turnabout was larger than Nettles Gap. The street they were on had businesses lining both sides. She spotted a barbershop, a boot store, an apothecary and others whose signs she missed. Mitch finally stopped the wagon in front of a redbrick building with fancy double doors that were propped open. The gold-lettered sign above the entrance read The Rose Palace Hotel.

"Here we are," he announced unnecessarily.

"Shouldn't we go to the livery stable first and see Jubal settled in?"

"Better to get your things unloaded first so we don't have to carry them through town."

He dismounted, then helped her down. After hitching the horse to the rail, he retrieved her things and then glanced down at Rufus. "I don't believe animals are allowed inside. Will he be okay out here?"

Ivy nodded and stooped so that she was practically nose to nose with Rufus. "I need you to stay out here and guard Jubal." She ruffled his fur with both hands. "We won't be gone long."

The animal responded with a couple of yips and Ivy gave him a final pat before she stood and met Mitch's gaze. "He'll be fine," she said confidently.

His raised brow indicated he was skeptical, but he nodded and escorted her inside.

Ivy looked around as they entered the lobby. There were faded red velvet chairs and large potted plants arranged near the stairway. The front desk was made of a rich-looking wood that had a high polish to it and there was an ornate brass bell on the desk.

Mitch might not think of this place as grand, but it was nicer than anyplace *she'd* ever been. Would her meager funds cover her stay?

He ushered her to the desk and greeted the bespectacled man standing there. "Hello, Edgar, I have a customer for you—Miss Ivy Feagan. Miss Feagan, this is Edgar Crandall."

It appeared they were back to formal address, which she

should have expected, given their earlier agreement to adhere to the proprieties once they were among his friends.

The clerk gave her a friendly smile. "Welcome to The Rose Palace Hotel, miss. Always glad to have fresh faces around here."

Ivy doubted her face was very fresh right now, but she returned his smile. "Thank you. This seems like a mighty fine establishment."

The man's smile broadened at her compliment. "We take a lot of pride in this place." He opened a ledger. "Now, let's see if we can get you fixed up. How many nights will you be staying?"

Ivy hesitated. "I'm not sure."

But the man didn't so much as blink. "We'll just leave that open-ended for now." He pointed to a blank line in the ledger. "If you'll just sign here."

She did as he asked, and by the time she'd finished the man was holding out a key. "I've put you in room three. Turn right at the top of the stairs and it'll be the second door."

Ivy reached for her bag, but Mitch was ahead of her.

"Allow me." He waved her to the stairs and she had no choice but to go along unless she wanted to make a scene. She was very aware of his presence behind her as she climbed. When they reached the room she'd been assigned, he finally handed over her bag. "Take whatever time you need. I'll wait downstairs. The livery is on the way to the train station, where the telegraph office is, so we can take care of both of those things when you're ready."

With a nod and a promise not to take long, Ivy opened the door. The room was slightly larger than her bedchamber back home. The furnishings consisted of a bed, a dressing table and mirror, two chairs, a bedside table and a stand that held a basin and ewer. More than adequate for her needs.

She was pleased to see fresh water in the ewer and a clean towel nearby, so she took a moment to wipe some of the travel dust from her face and hands.

She had to admit, having someone as solicitous as Mitch to smooth the path for her entry into town was quite nice. It was clear he intended to make sure she was comfortably settled rather than just wash his hands of her right away.

She hoped this resumption of formal terms of address didn't dampen any other part of their friendship. She headed downstairs with a spring in her step.

As promised, Mitch was patiently waiting for her when she returned to the lobby. And when they stepped outside, the ever-faithful Rufus was waiting, as well. "I just thought of something," she said as he handed her back up into the wagon. "Where's Rufus going to spend his nights?"

Mitch stared at the dog a moment, then climbed up beside her. "I suppose he can stay at my house."

"You'd do that?" His offer surprised her more than anything he'd done so far. She didn't think he even liked Rufus.

He shrugged. "He doesn't seem to be much trouble."

Ivy was touched by his gesture, more than she knew how to say.

When they arrived at the livery, Mitch introduced her to Fred Humphries, the owner.

"Glad to meet you, miss." Mr. Humphries turned back to Mitch. "You're back in town early, ain't you?"

Mitch shrugged. "My plans changed." Then he changed the subject. "Miss Feagan's mule here has come up lame. We were hoping you'd take a look at it."

Mr. Humphries examined Jubal's hoof, then declared it

to be healing nicely and promised to apply a special poultice he had for such injuries.

Then they walked to the train depot. Ivy quickly dictated the telegram she wanted to send to Nana Dovie and was pleased when Mitch didn't argue over her insistence that she pay for this herself.

But as soon as they stepped outside, his high-handedness returned. "Our next stop is Dr. Pratt's office."

"That's not necessary. It's hardly even tender anymore."

"Nevertheless, I insist."

She rolled her eyes, but his expression remained set. She finally decided it would be easier just to get it over with.

Along the way they passed a building with a sign that caught Ivy's eye and she stopped in her tracks—The Blue Bottle Sweet Shop and Toy Store. She turned to Mitch in delight. "Is it really a store that sells nothing but sweets and toys?"

He nodded, a hint of amusement on his face. "There's a tea shop inside, as well."

She couldn't help herself. "Can we go inside?"

"Yes." He gave her arm a little tug to get her moving again. "*After* we see Dr. Pratt."

She resisted the urge to stick her tongue out at him, but it wasn't easy.

When they reached the doctor's home, where he apparently had his office, an older woman with a friendly smile answered his knock. "Why, hello, Mitch." She opened the screen door wider. "I thought you were going to be gone for several more days."

Did everyone in town know his plans?

Mitch removed his hat. "Good afternoon, Mrs. Pratt. I hope I'm not disturbing you, but I have a young lady here who needs to see your husband."

"Of course, come right on in. Grover's still back in the clinic."

As they stepped inside, Ivy turned back to Rufus. "Wait here, boy. We won't be long."

Rufus obediently sat on his haunches and watched her with tongue hanging out.

Mitch made the introductions. "Mrs. Pratt, this is Miss Ivy Feagan. She's in town on business." He turned to Ivy. "Miss Feagan, this is Mrs. Pratt, the doctor's wife."

Ivy extended her hand. "Pleased to meet you, ma'am."

Mrs. Pratt took Ivy's outstretched hand and gave it a pat. "It's nice to meet you, too, dear. I hope there's nothing serious ailing you."

"Oh, no, ma'am. Mr. Parker is just being a bit of a worrywart."

Mitch cleared his throat. "Actually, Miss Feagan fell and ended up with a nasty cut on the back of her head. She claims to be feeling better, but I thought it best your husband look at it."

"Quite right. Always better to be safe than sorry. Come along back to Grover's office."

Ivy resisted the urge to roll her eyes Mitch's way as they followed the woman down the hall. This was a total waste of time, but they were here because Mitch was concerned for her welfare, and as misguided as that concern might be, she couldn't fault him for it.

In fact, it felt quite nice to have someone so squarely in her corner for a change.

Mitch sat in the outer office as Dr. Pratt examined Ivy. The examination seemed to be taking quite some time, but according to his pocket watch it had only been fifteen minutes. He supposed if she could read his thoughts she'd call him a fusspot again, but it was only natural to worry when someone had been injured.

As soon as Dr. Pratt opened the door, Mitch stood. "How is she?"

The physician closed the door behind him. "She's got quite a knot on the back of her head, but I don't think there'll be any lasting effects. With a head injury, the first twenty-four hours are usually the trickiest and it seems we're beyond that."

Mitch felt an immense sense of relief—he refused to think that it might be out of proportion for the situation.

He ignored the questioning look the doctor gave him. "Are there any special instructions for her care?"

Before Dr. Pratt could respond, the door opened and Ivy stepped out.

"What did I tell you?" Her tone held a triumphant note. "Doc here says I'm right as rain."

Dr. Pratt gave a stern *humph*. "That's not exactly what I said, young lady. I said there should be no lasting effects. You should take it easy for the next few days, just to be safe." He wagged a finger. "And if you feel the least bit dizzy, I want you to come back to see me right away."

"Yes, sir."

Now that that was settled, Mitch brought up another topic. "By the way, I heard Drum Mosley had taken ill. How is he doing? Miss Feagan is here specifically to see him."

The doctor's expression turned somber. "I'm sorry to be the one to deliver the bad news, but Drum passed away yesterday." He gave Ivy a sympathetic look. "Was he a relative or friend of yours?"

She shook her head. "No. I just had some business to discuss with him."

Ivy was doing a good job hiding her disappointment, but Mitch could see what a blow this news was.

He cleared his throat, reclaiming Dr. Pratt's attention and giving her time to collect herself. "I suppose Carter is handling the estate?"

The doctor spread his hands. "I'd assume so. As Drum's only relative, it makes sense he'd inherit it all."

Mitch glanced at Ivy. When she held her peace, he straightened. "Thank you for your assistance, but we should be going now."

"You make certain you do as I said and take it easy."

Ivy nodded. "Thank you, Dr. Pratt. I will."

"And I'll hold her to it," Mitch added.

Mitch insisted that Dr. Pratt put the bill on his tab, countering Ivy's protest with a stern reminder that the visit had been undertaken at his insistence. A moment later they were back out on the front porch. As soon as the door closed behind them, Ivy bent to pet Rufus's head.

"Who's Carter?" she asked without looking up.

"Drum's nephew. He's helped Drum manage the ranch for a number of years now," Mitch added.

He kept a close eye on her, trying to figure out what she was thinking, but she didn't meet his gaze. Instead, she straightened and started down the walk.

She brushed at her skirt. "Would Drum have confided in him about my father?"

"I honestly don't know. But we can certainly speak to him and find out."

She cast him a sideways look. "We? You still want to go along?"

"Of course." Did she think he would abandon her at this stage? He felt a certain responsibility for her—after all, he *had* been responsible for her fall.

She was quiet a moment, but her chin seemed the slightest bit higher and her step a little lighter. Was she pleased to know he was sticking around? "Perhaps I should talk to this Mr. Barr person first," she said.

Mitch nearly missed a step. "Adam's involved in this?"

She gave him a puzzled look. "Yes, I believe his first name *is* Adam. Do you know him? He sent the letter on Mr. Mosley's behalf."

Mitch nodded. "He's one of the men who traveled here from Philadelphia with me. And he's married to Reggie, the lady who owns the cabin we stayed at."

"Oh." She looked at him uncertainly. "I hadn't realized he was *that* Adam. Then I guess he's trustworthy."

"Absolutely." It made sense Drum would have enlisted Adam's assistance. Adam had worked as an attorney before he came to Texas, and folks still turned to him when they needed legal advice.

"Come on, I'll take you to meet him. It's probably best you and he discuss this before we pay Carter a visit."

"Do you think we should just drop in on him without an appointment?"

"We're not going to his office—he'll be at home for the evening. And he won't mind. Besides, I need to let Reggie know I'm no longer at the cabin, anyway."

He glanced at the dog padding along beside them. "But we should drop Rufus off at my place first."

She nodded, but her mind was apparently on his earlier statement. "You said Mr. Barr was *one* of the men who traveled from Philadelphia with you. How many were there?"

"There were two others—four of us in total."

"You must have been really good friends to just up and leave your homes, and move here together."

"Actually, we didn't know each other before we planned

the trip." And they hadn't gotten along very well at first, either. That had been a very uncomfortable trip.

Ivy paused a heartbeat, staring at him in confusion. Then she started walking again. "Four gentlemen from Philadelphia all decide to travel way out here to Turnabout at the same time? Sounds like one whopper of a coincidence."

"There was no coincidence. You see, we had a common acquaintance—Reggie's grandfather, as a matter of fact—who pulled us together for a unique business opportunity." The opportunity being to participate in a marriage lottery for Reggie's very unwilling hand.

And the less said about that, the better.

She nodded. "So y'all went into business together."

He could see why she'd be confused, but he really wasn't at liberty to reveal the whole story. And to be honest, he wasn't sure he'd want to even if he were.

"No. We've all gone our separate ways. Adam married Reggie shortly after we moved here and now he manages the bank and gives legal advice on occasion. Everett runs the local newspaper and married Daisy, who runs a restaurant. And Chance and his wife, Eve, run that toy and candy shop you saw earlier." He spread his hands. "And I'm one of the town's two schoolteachers." Did that sound as anticlimactic next to the accomplishments of the other three as he thought it did?

"Do you consider these men your friends *now?*"

He didn't have to think about that one. "Of course." The four of them had had their differences during the trip here and during those tense days when they had been waiting for Reggie to make her decision.

To be honest, during that trip his mind had been more on his reason for leaving Philadelphia than on what company he was in. Gretchen's death, and his guilt, had been fresh then. Getting close to anyone had been beyond his abilities.

But in time the four men and Reggie had forged a mutual respect and friendship.

But he hadn't allowed anyone to get really close since he'd moved here. He wasn't certain he even knew how any longer.

Ivy wondered if Mitch knew how telling his words had been. Each of the men who'd traveled here with him had found love and established a family. Each one except him.

That didn't make sense. Mitch was a tall, handsome man with a strong sense of honor and a good heart. Any girl would be lucky to have him for a husband.

Which was not an appropriate topic for her to dwell on.

As soon as Mitch pointed out his house, she studied it with interest. It was a white two-story structure, very simple and plain in design. It was just the right size, she decided—small enough to be cozy, but large enough so he wouldn't feel cramped.

It was a bit stark, though. Unlike many of the homes they'd passed, there were no swings or rockers or even benches on the front porch. The yard appeared well maintained, but there were only a few bushes flanking the front gate—no flowering plants or flashes of color. No woman's touch.

The fence guarding his yard was wooden, about waist high, and it seemed sturdy enough to hold Rufus, as long as the dog didn't want out very badly.

Mitch stepped forward to open the gate. "Let me get a bowl of water for the mutt and then we'll head to Adam and Reggie's place." He paused, then added, "Perhaps it would be best if you waited here with Rufus. I'll just be a minute."

She nodded—this was likely another of his attempts to protect her reputation. But despite his stiff-necked tendencies, he'd been thoughtful enough to take time to get Rufus a bowl of water.

Then she saw his front door and she couldn't help the grin that spread across her face. Unlike the stark formality of the rest of his place, the door was painted a deep apple-red. Perhaps Mitch wasn't quite as reserved as he tried to pretend.

True to his word, Mitch returned a few minutes later. He set a large pan on the porch, then closed the front door behind him.

Ivy bent down and rubbed the dog's ears. "Okay, Rufus, there's plenty of water and lots of room to run around. You be good and don't make Mr. Parker sorry he volunteered to keep you."

The dog followed them as far as the gate, then sat on his haunches as she closed him in. For a moment, Ivy worried about abandoning him in a strange place. Then he caught sight of a squirrel and took off, chasing the animal across the yard and around to the back of the house.

She smiled. He'd be fine.

"I like your door," she said as they started down the walk.

His only reply was a noncommittal *"Hmm,"* but she thought she detected a slight self-conscious wince.

Deciding not to tease him further, she contented herself with asking questions about the town.

Finally, he waved a hand. "That's the Barr home just up ahead."

The Barr home was a two-story white structure, larger than Mitch's, with a nice-size lawn and some well-cared-for rose bushes brightening up the front porch.

"Remember, don't mention the cabin," Mitch reminded her. "And no first names."

Ivy nodded, trying to ignore the spurt of exasperation at his stern warning. Did he think she would be so indiscreet?

But a bit of irritation was a small price to pay for all he'd done for her. Having Mitch introduce her to Mr. Barr would make her meeting with the man less awkward than it might have been otherwise.

And she clearly needed all the help she could get, now that Drum Mosley was dead. She still couldn't wrap her mind around that and what it meant for her. Had her chance to claim a windfall inheritance died with him? Had she made this long, trouble-plagued trip to Turnabout for nothing?

She certainly hoped Mr. Barr had some answers for her. But knowing he was a friend of Mitch's already inspired her with confidence that things would work out.

And if they didn't, well, having Mitch in her corner was still a win any way you looked at it.

Chapter Eight

Mitch placed a hand at the small of her back as they turned up the front walk.

She drew comfort from his touch, suddenly feeling unaccountably nervous. Not only was her access to that mysterious inheritance on the line, but these people were Mitch's friends and she didn't want to do or say anything that would embarrass him.

A lady with vivid blue-green eyes and coffee-brown hair answered his knock.

"Mitch." The woman opened the screen door, concern in her expression. "I thought you planned to stay at the cabin for another four or five days. I hope nothing's happened." Then she noticed Ivy. "Oh, hello."

As Ivy stepped forward, Mitch smiled reassuringly. "Don't worry, nothing untoward happened. My plans just changed."

Ivy smiled at the woman. "That was my fault, I'm afraid."

"Reggie, this is Miss Ivy Feagan." Mitch turned to Ivy. "Miss Feagan, this is Regina Barr."

Reggie smiled a greeting. "Pleased to meet you. And

I'm dying to hear how you changed Mitch's plans. But first, come inside so we can speak more comfortably."

"Call me Ivy, please. And I'm very glad to meet you, too."

When Ivy entered she found herself in a warmly furnished entryway. The hat rack and hall table had both seen better days, but the wood had a lovely glow to it. The oval mirror above the narrow table had an ornately carved frame, and was flanked by lovely photographs.

Before Ivy could take in any more, Reggie gave her arm a friendly pat. "As I said, I'm very interested in hearing how you managed to pry Mitch away from his vacation."

Mindful of Mitch's concerns, Ivy chose her words carefully. "I was on my way here from Nettles Gap and ran into a bit of trouble. My mule came up lame and then I fell and bumped my head. Mr. Parker stumbled on me, so to speak, bandaged me up and offered to escort me to town." She gave Mitch a teasing look. "I think he was afraid I'd hurt myself further if he'd didn't keep an eye on me."

"How chivalrous of him." Reggie eyed Mitch thoughtfully, then turned back to her. "You say you bumped your head—I hope you weren't badly hurt."

Ivy waved dismissively. "I bumped my head, but I'm okay now. Even Dr. Pratt says so."

"Well, that's a relief."

Mitch cleared his throat. "Actually, the other reason we're here is that Miss Feagan has some business to discuss with Adam."

"I see. Well, Adam is right in here." She stepped aside as they reached the open doorway to a parlor, where a man was watching a toddler play on the floor.

He stood as soon as he saw them.

"Adam, Mitch brought a new friend of his round to see

us," Reggie said. "This is Ivy Feagan. Ivy, this is my husband, Adam."

Mr. Barr's eyebrow went up momentarily at the introduction, and Ivy wondered if he'd recognized her last name. But he merely nodded politely. "Miss Feagan."

"Nice to meet you, Mr. Barr."

The toddler started fussing and Reggie scooped her up. "And this little doll is our daughter, Patricia." She gave the child an affectionate squeeze, then turned to her guests. "Patricia and I will leave you to your business with Adam. But I warn you I will be back later for that chat."

Reggie exited, closing the door behind her, and Ivy took a seat on the sofa while Mitch sat on a nearby chair.

Mr. Barr glanced from her to Mitch. "May I inquire how you two are acquainted?"

Mitch gave him the same story they'd relayed to Reggie earlier.

Then Reggie's husband turned to Ivy. "I assume you're here in response to the letter I sent out on Drum Mosley's behalf."

Ivy nodded. "I understand Mr. Mosley passed away yesterday."

Mr. Barr nodded. "He'd been quite ill for some time." Then he eyed her curiously. "What is your relationship to Robert Feagan?"

"He was my father."

"I see."

Mitch leaned forward. "What are Miss Feagan's options now? Does she need to take this up with Carter?"

Rather than answer the question, Mr. Barr asked Ivy a question of his own. "How much do you know about your father's relationship with Drum Mosley?"

"I didn't even know there *was* a relationship. I was just a few days old when my pa died. The lady who raised me, Dovie Jacobs, couldn't remember much, either. When your letter came, she thought on it a bit. All she could remember was that my pa was setting up a new home for us when he got word about my ma taking ill. But it all happened so long ago, she doesn't remember much else." Ivy leaned forward with her hands clasped together. "Do *you* know the story?"

"Only what Drum shared with me."

"And that was?"

Mr. Barr leaned back and rubbed his jaw. "Drum requested you bring proof that you are who you say you are. Do you have that with you?"

"It's back at the hotel with my things."

"May I ask what it consists of?"

"I brought a letter from Nana Dovie, the midwife who delivered me. And I have my ma's Bible that has her name in it, along with a family tree that goes back three generations." She started to rise. "I can fetch them if you need to see them."

Mitch placed a restraining hand on her arm. "I don't think that's necessary." He turned to Adam. "I'll vouch for her. If she says she has them, then she does."

Ivy was touched by Mitch's trust.

Adam gave a short nod. "Then that's good enough for me. At least as far as telling you this part of the story."

What did that mean?

"Nine days ago, Drum sent word that he needed to see me. It seems that, once he knew he was nearing the end of his life, he had a crisis of conscience and wanted to make sure his affairs were in order. He wanted my advice on how to right a wrong that may or may not have been committed twenty-one years ago."

"Something to do with my pa?"

"Yes."

Ivy felt a fluttering beneath her breastbone. She would finally learn what this was all about.

"From what Drum told me," Mr. Barr continued, "back in their younger days, he and your father worked together on a number of cattle drives. They became friends and decided they were tired of working for others, so they agreed to buy a parcel of land together and develop their own ranching operation."

"They were partners?"

Mr. Barr nodded. "They pooled their money and bought a parcel of land just outside of Turnabout. They spent the first year just getting the land ready. Then they borrowed heavily to purchase a bull and a few dozen head of cattle to establish their herd."

Her father had been a cattle rancher. "Where was my ma all this time?"

"According to Drum, your mother stayed in Nettles Gap. She had a delicate constitution and your father didn't want to bring her here until he'd built a proper house for her. He and Drum had just about put everything else in motion when he learned she was expecting. So he and your mother decided to wait a little longer so she could be with folks she knew and felt comfortable with until the child was born."

Ivy found this story fascinating—she hadn't heard any of it before now. The puzzle was finally starting to make sense.

Mr. Barr looked at her with a kindness she hadn't expected from a near stranger. "Do you know the circumstances around your parents' passing?"

"Nana Dovie told me I came too early and that my ma died in childbirth. Not long after, my pa died of grief."

When she was younger she'd thought dying of grief was romantic. Later, she'd wondered why her pa hadn't decided to stick around for her sake—didn't he love her, too? And come to think of it, how did one die of grief, anyway?

She suddenly became aware of Mitch's strong presence beside her, quietly supportive as she absorbed this new information about her parents. She gave him a quick smile, then turned back to Mr. Barr. She wasn't sure she wanted to hear the answer to her next question, but it had to be asked. "What was Mr. Mosley's version of my pa's story?"

He shifted slightly, but nodded. "Something similar. After your father buried your mother, he returned here and threw himself into his work. Drum said that all he could get out of him was that your mother had passed and that the baby wasn't expected to live."

She winced at that. "Nana Dovie *did* say it was touch and go for a while as to whether I would live." But why hadn't her father stuck around to find out?

"At any rate, your father died a few days later when he fell from his horse."

It wasn't grief, then. Or maybe it was grief that made him careless. She supposed she'd never know. "So what does all this mean?"

"As for the particulars of Drum's will, that should wait until I have both you and Carter together. I had planned to speak to him after the funeral tomorrow. Perhaps you should come as well so we can attend to the matter properly."

"We'll be there," Mitch said before Ivy could answer.

He was being high-handed again, but in this particular case, she couldn't say she minded. She nodded. "I'd like to pay my respects." After all, even though she'd never met him, Drum Mosley had given her a glimpse into who her parents had been.

Mitch spoke up again. "What else can you tell Miss Feagan about her prospects?"

Mr. Barr turned to speak to her directly, which she appreciated. "I can tell you your father and Drum had a formal partnership agreement, which stated that if either of them died without a direct heir, then their share of the property would go to the other partner. As far as Drum knew, your father had no direct heir remaining, so he assumed ownership of the entire ranch. And no one came forward to challenge his claim."

Did that mean she *did* own some land? "What made Mr. Mosley decide to check his facts now?"

"I think he always wondered in the back of his mind if Robert's child had really passed away. But he ignored those niggling doubts and continued to build on, and profit from, the ranch." He rubbed his chin. "Then, as I said, facing his own mortality forced him to reevaluate."

Mitch leaned forward. "Does Carter know about this?"

"When last we spoke, Drum instructed me that no one, including Carter, was to know about this unless an heir stepped forward. So unless he changed his mind, I'd say no."

Before she or Mitch could ask anything further, Mr. Barr leaned back. "Now, I'd prefer to defer the rest of this discussion until we meet with Carter tomorrow."

Ivy nodded. "Of course. And I appreciate you taking the time to tell me this much."

As if she'd been waiting for her cue, Reggie reentered the parlor with a now smiling and cooing toddler. She hefted the child on her hip. "I've waited long enough. Surely your business is complete by now."

Mr. Barr stepped forward and gave his wife a peck on the cheek. "So impatient. But yes, we're done."

"Well, then, Mrs. Peavy tells me supper is ready." She turned to Ivy and Mitch. "And I insist you join us."

"That's mighty kind, ma'am, but I wouldn't want to intrude," Ivy said.

"First of all, I'll have none of this 'ma'am' fustiness—it's Reggie. And second, there's more than enough for two guests, and it will give me a chance to visit with you properly. Besides, I want you to meet our son, Jack, as well as Mrs. Peavy and her husband, Ira, who live here, as well."

Mitch spoke up before she could refuse again. "Thank you, we accept."

Reggie smiled. "That's better." She handed the toddler over to her husband and linked her arm through Ivy's. "Now, I want to hear all about how you and Mitch met."

Ivy sent a quick glance Mitch's way, unsure how to reply to that. He immediately came to her rescue.

"When Miss Feagan fell, I got to play white knight to her damsel in distress."

"A white knight, was it?" Reggie grinned. "I always thought there was hero material inside you—you just needed the right circumstances to bring it out." She cut a quick glance Ivy's way. "Or the right person."

Ivy's cheeks warmed at that and she quickly turned the conversation in a different direction. "Mr. Parker tells me you're a photographer. That sounds like an interesting skill to have."

Reggie accepted her change of subject. "I enjoy it. Stop by my studio while you're here and I'll show you some of my work." Then she tilted her head. "Speaking of which, how long are you planning to be in town?"

"I'm not sure. It depends on how long it takes to settle this business with Mr. Mosley."

"Well, we'll do our best to make certain you want to stay for a nice long visit."

"Thank you, but I left Nana Dovie—that's the woman

who raised me—on her own and I don't like to be gone for too long."

Reggie patted her arm. "In that case, I suppose we'll have to wish for a speedy and happy conclusion to your business here."

As Ivy thanked her again, she cast a quick look at Mitch, the man who'd stood by her ever since he'd first stumbled upon her, and had helped her in more ways than she could count.

Would he miss her when she left?

Because she had a feeling she would definitely miss him.

As Mitch walked Ivy back to the hotel, he saw the lamplighter starting his rounds on Second Street. It was hard to believe they'd left the cabin only this morning.

"The Barrs seem like real nice people," Ivy said.

"They are."

She paused for a moment, then added, "Like you."

She thought he was nice? He wasn't sure how to respond to that. So he changed the subject. "How are you feeling about all of these new details you're learning about your parents?" She'd been uncharacteristically silent on the subject.

"It was unexpected, of course. But after thinking on it a bit I find it fills in a lot of gaps for me. I just wish I would've made it here before Mr. Mosley passed on. It would have been really nice to speak to someone who knew my pa so well."

So she was more focused on her father than on the legacy he'd left her. The way her mind worked never ceased to surprise him.

"I appreciate all you've done to help me," she continued, "but I don't want you to feel like you have to keep going out of your way on my behalf. There's no need for you to go out to Mr. Mosley's ranch tomorrow if you want to head back to the cabin and finish your vacation."

Was she tired of his company? He found himself strangely reluctant to step away. "You don't think I'm going to come this far and not be there when the end plays out, do you?"

"Well, if you're sure it's something you *want* to do..."

"It is."

A yawn escaped her as they arrived at the hotel. She gave him a sheepish look. "I'm sorry. I—"

"No need to apologize. You've had an eventful day. A good night's sleep will do you a world of good." He escorted her just inside the lobby. "I'll see you in the morning."

"Thanks again for taking care of Rufus."

"All I did was pen him up in my yard."

She rolled her eyes at him, then turned serious. With a vulnerable smile that tugged at all his protective instincts, she placed a hand on his sleeve. "In case I haven't said it enough, I'm truly grateful for everything you've done for me these past few days. And I don't just mean tending to my injury." She waved her free hand. "I didn't realize just how unprepared I was. You've made this whole situation unbelievably easier for me."

Then, as if embarrassed by her own seriousness, she dropped her hand and gave him a tongue-in-cheek smile. "I guess there are some benefits to your being such a fusspot, after all."

And with that she turned and moved quickly to the stairs.

Mitch walked the three blocks to his house down quiet, dusk-shadowed streets, a smile tugging at his lips. He still wasn't sure what to make of this teasing affection she treated him with. No one had dared do that since he and his sisters were in the schoolroom.

Then he sobered. They'd managed to avoid any sort of gossip, salacious or otherwise. But the real test would come tomorrow, once word of his return and the new visitor to town got around.

He turned into his yard, bending down to absently scratch an enthusiastic Rufus behind the ears.

Would they really be able to pull this off and remain unscathed by gossip?

And if not, what would he do about it?

Ivy settled into bed, exhausted.

Last night she'd been at the cabin, with Mitch out on the porch. He was so thoughtful, so uncomplaining.

Of course, he probably would have done the same for any female in her situation. Still, it had made her feel special. Which could be dangerous, given that she'd be returning to Nettles Gap soon.

She rolled over, wondering what tomorrow would bring. Hard to believe her father had been a landowner all those years ago, but if Mr. Mosley had been willing to acknowledge it then it must be true. Were her money woes truly over?

She stared at the ceiling. Better not to count on that just yet, though. If Mr. Barr was right, Mr. Mosley's nephew didn't know about her or her claim yet. The poor man had just lost his uncle—how would he react to her claim?

Whatever happened, she was glad she'd be facing it with Mitch at her side.

Chapter Nine

The next morning Drum's funeral was held on the ranch at the Mosley family cemetery. Once it was over and the attendees had offered their condolences to Carter, folks began drifting back to their carriages and wagons, leaving the gravediggers to complete their job.

Adam and Reggie were among the last to speak to Carter, and afterward Adam gave Mitch a subtle signal that they should proceed to Carter's house. Then Adam handed Reggie up into their carriage to send her back to town on her own before climbing into the carriage Mitch had rented from the livery.

Mitch eased the carriage into the procession slowly exiting the cemetery, but rather than turning onto the road to town, he followed Adam's directions and took the fork that led to the ranch house.

Ivy looked around. "How big is this place?"

"Around fifteen hundred acres, I believe," Adam said.

"Mercy me! I can't believe my pa owned part of this."

Mitch wondered if it had sunk in yet that soon, she would, too.

When they pulled up in front of the house, Carter was

waiting on them. "You said we needed to talk about the estate," he said distractedly. "Can we make this quick?"

Adam took the lead. "We'll do our best. But first, let me offer my condolences once again on the loss of your uncle."

Carter nodded acceptance. "Thank you."

"I believe you already know Mitchell Parker."

Carter gave a short nod. "The schoolteacher, right?"

Mitch returned his nod, not sure he liked the man's impatient tone. "That's correct." He drew Ivy forward. "And this is Miss Ivy Feagan."

Carter touched the brim of his hat in acknowledgment. "Miss Feagan," he said, looking slightly puzzled.

It was clear to Mitch that Carter didn't recognize Ivy's last name, which meant Carter didn't know about Drum's plans. How would he react when he heard the story?

Carter had already turned back to Adam. "I assume you need to talk to me about Drum's estate." He gave Adam a puzzled look. "Though I'm not sure why. I've seen Drum's will and it looks pretty straightforward to me."

Adam indicated the folder of papers he held. "There's been a change. Drum called me out here a little over a week ago and asked me to revise his will."

That definitely sharpened Carter's attention. "Revise it how?"

"For one, he named me executor." Adam nodded toward the house. "It might be best if we go inside to discuss this."

Carter nodded, then paused. "Not to be rude, but why are these two with you?"

Mitch stiffened and touched Ivy's arm protectively.

But Adam's expression never changed. "Miss Feagan is here at my invitation because this affects her, too. And Mitch is here as her friend and adviser."

Her friend and adviser—Mitch liked that.

Carter's frown deepened and he gave Ivy a speculative look. But a moment later he turned without comment and led them into the house. They walked through a short hallway and entered a room that appeared to be an office.

Drum's nephew took a seat behind the desk and waved them to the other chairs. Mitch seated Ivy, and he and Adam sat on either side of her.

"So, let's get to it," Carter said. "What are the terms of this new will?"

Adam folded his hands over the file in his lap. "First, I need to give you some history. Have you heard of Robert Feagan?" When Carter shook his head, Adam gave a quick rundown of the partnership agreement, Drum's actions after Mr. Feagan's death and his recent crisis of conscience.

Mitch watched Carter, noting his deepening displeasure. Apparently Carter was getting an idea of where the conversation was headed.

When Adam finished his story, he pulled a paper from the file. "Drum amended his will to indicate that if Robert Feagan's child had survived, and could prove her paternity, she was entitled to a portion of the estate."

Carter's posture was fence-post stiff. "If all this were true, Uncle Drum would have told me."

"Your uncle didn't want to say anything to you until he learned whether the heir was still alive." Adam's tone and expression remained businesslike. "I assure you, there is no subterfuge here—he did amend his will. He also instructed me to tell you that you would find his copy of the will folded in the pages of his Bible."

Carter made no move to verify the presence of that copy. "Uncle Drum is barely in the ground and already someone is trying to stake a claim on this place."

"I'm truly sorry for your loss," Ivy said softly. "And I agree the timing ain't the best. But, and I mean no disrespect by this, the timing is your uncle's, since he only recently contacted me."

How did she manage to sound so understanding, Mitch wondered, when faced with blatant hostility?

Carter stared at her a moment without responding, then turned back to Adam. "What if I wanted to contest the will?" he asked.

Mitch stiffened at this hint that Drum's nephew would attempt to keep Ivy's portion of the estate from her.

Adam, however, merely pulled out another document. "That's your right, of course. But Drum gave me his copy of the partnership agreement between himself and Robert Feagan. So, whether he added Miss Feagan to his will or not, she has a legitimate claim on the estate."

Carter's jaw tightened and his brow drew down, narrowing his eyes. "I've heard Uncle Drum talk about the early years of the ranch. That agreement, if it's legitimate, was drawn up when this place was barely more than rock-strewn dirt and scrub, and the herd that ran here could be contained in a small pen."

"Be that as it may, Miss Feagan still has a rightful claim."

"Rightful." Carter looked as if he wanted to spit the words. "There's been a lot of blood, sweat and tears poured into this place over the past twenty-one years, and Robert Feagan—" he cast a quick, hostile look Ivy's way "—not to mention his heirs, had no part in any of it. To my way of thinking there's nothing *rightful* about her claim."

Before he or Adam could respond, Ivy leaned forward. "Mr. Mosley, I understand why you would feel that way," she said, her tone surprisingly polite, "and I sure don't expect you to split this place down the middle. I'm willing to talk about a more reasonable arrangement."

Her words didn't seem to appease the man. He glared

at her a moment, then turned back to Adam without responding. Mitch felt Ivy stiffen and he didn't blame her.

"How do we even know she is who she says she is?" Carter demanded. "After all, from what you've told me, this Robert Feagan didn't expect his daughter to live."

Mitch couldn't hold his peace any longer. "Because she's not a liar," he said. "And because your uncle would never have sent that letter if he hadn't believed there was a chance she was still alive."

Ivy gave his arm a quick touch, then turned back to Carter. "I brought a letter from the midwife who delivered me, and I also brought my mother's family Bible."

The man made a sharp, dismissive gesture. "Folks can be bribed to write whatever they're told to, and that Bible could have been acquired another way." He leaned back in his chair. "Seems to me we really don't have much more than her word to go on."

"I didn't bribe anyone," Ivy said indignantly. "And that Bible came straight from my ma—Nana Dovie said so and she's as honest as a baby's cry."

Again Carter ignored her. "You're the lawyer, Mr. Barr. What options do I have to fight this?" He narrowed his eyes. "Or maybe I shouldn't ask you since you're obviously on her side."

Adam remained unruffled. "I have no problem answering objectively. As I said, your uncle named me executor of the estate, and my only interest is to see that his wishes are carried out. If you want to fight Miss Feagan's claim, then you'll need to take her to court and let a judge decide the case."

Carter nodded decisively. "Then that's what I'll do. We can both take our chances with the judge."

Adam put the papers back in the folder. "That's your right, of course. I'll write to the circuit judge and let him know we have a case for him the next time he comes through."

He met Carter's gaze evenly. "Of course, right now, the will states Robert Feagan's heir gets half the *original* estate, which was five hundred acres. Your uncle tripled that since his partner's death. If you take this to court, you run the risk of having the judge divide the whole thing right down the middle."

The man blinked uncertainly, but then lifted his jaw. "I'll take my chances."

Ivy rubbed her chin. "How long will all this take?"

Adam turned to her. "I believe Judge Andrews is due back through here in about three weeks."

"Three weeks!" Ivy plopped back in dismay. "I didn't plan on sticking around that long."

Carter shrugged. "Suit yourself. You can always go back where you came from and drop this whole matter."

Mitch had had enough of the man's rudeness. "She's staying. And we'll see what the judge has to say when he looks over the proof she brought with her, and learns how your uncle cheated her out of her inheritance for twenty-one years."

Carter narrowed his gaze. "Tell me again what your role is in all of this, schoolteacher. Are you maybe looking to snag a rich wife?"

Mitch surged to his feet, ready to defend both his and Ivy's honor. But Adam stood as well and placed a hand on his shoulder, holding Mitch's gaze for a long moment, bringing him back to his senses.

When his friend finally turned to Carter, Mitch cast a quick glance Ivy's way and saw her puzzled expression.

Before he could do more than offer her a tight smile, Adam was speaking again.

"I understand this has come as a shock to you," his

friend said with his unblinking gaze now focused on Carter, "especially on top of your uncle's passing, but there's no need to toss around insults."

Mitch said a silent amen to that. "I think it's time for us to take our leave." He had to get out of here.

"I agree." Adam looked at Carter levelly. "Think over all I've told you and look over your uncle's will for yourself. Then decide if you really want to pursue this course of action. In the meantime, I'll contact Judge Andrews."

"I don't need to think about it."

Mitch held himself very still. The fact that he'd nearly lost his temper a moment ago had shaken him to the core. He'd thought he'd come a long way in getting that beast inside him under control—apparently it still had the capability to slip its chains when provoked.

He couldn't let that happen again.

Not ever again.

A few minutes later, Ivy leaned back against the seat of the carriage, trying to gather her thoughts while Mitch drove and Mr. Barr sat behind them. She'd been shocked by the accusation Mr. Mosley had flung at Mitch, and equally surprised by the vehemence of Mitch's reaction. The last thing she'd wanted was to bring trouble to this man who'd shown her such kindness.

Perhaps she should do as Carter wanted and just drop the whole thing. Not much good ever came from getting something for nothing, anyway.

Then again, there was still the matter of how Nana Dovie would pay her debts. And it sure would be nice to have a milk cow again.

She took a deep breath. Here she went again, trying to figure things out on her own. That wasn't the way to tackle this at all. She bowed her head and closed her eyes.

Dear Lord Jesus, I sure am all discombobulated by this. It seems wrong to come all this way and then not see the matter through, especially when this whole out-of-the-blue windfall seemed to be the answer to our prayers. But I sure don't want to put material things above friendship, or above Nana Dovie's welfare.

And another thing to consider is that I don't have the money to stay in that fancy hotel for three weeks—I barely have enough to stay three nights.

So please, help me figure out what I should do.

She kept her eyes closed a few moments longer, letting her thoughts settle.

It was several minutes before she realized a heavy silence had fallen. This wouldn't do. She turned to Mitch. "Thank you again for accompanying me today and for speaking up on my behalf. I'm sorry if it caused you any discomfort."

Mitch nodded without taking his gaze from the road. "No need to apologize. I'm just sorry you were subjected to that."

His voice was tight, controlled. Was he still upset over the man's accusation? Of course it was ridiculous to think he might be interested in *marrying* her, whether for money or not. Surely Mitch didn't think anyone would take that accusation seriously?

Though the idea of marriage to the man beside her wasn't something she'd look amiss on. Assuming he was interested, which he obviously wasn't.

Quickly squashing that line of thought, she decided to steer the conversation onto a safer track. "Mr. Mosley's reaction isn't hard to understand. He just lost his uncle and now a stranger comes along and stakes a claim on a place he's been led to believe is rightfully his. And I think it hurt his feelings that his uncle confided in Mr. Barr and not him."

"Feelings! You're being too kind."

She gave Mitch a reproving look. "There's no such thing as being *too* kind. And all I meant was that I don't suppose anybody could rightly blame him for not taking the news well."

Mitch made a noise that was neither agreement nor disagreement. "Adam, how good are Carter's chances of winning his challenge in court?"

Mr. Barr rubbed his chin. "Unless he can throw serious doubt on Miss Feagan's status as Robert Feagan's daughter, her claim should stand. The fact that I have in writing that Drum himself admitted to not having followed up at the time of his partner's demise will work in her favor."

Ivy spoke up, irritated that they were talking about her as if she weren't sitting right here. "He does have a point about all the work he and his uncle poured into that place. What little I've seen of it, it looks like a mighty nice spread with a fine house. I wouldn't want to take anything that wasn't rightfully mine."

Mitch snorted. "Nonsense. Keep in mind, Drum thought you had a right to a share of the place."

Ivy stiffened. He didn't need to sound so superior. "I only meant—"

Mr. Barr cleared his throat. "Why don't we wait until the judge hears the case and validates your claim to worry about all of that?"

Mr. Barr was right. She twisted around to face him. "Can you explain how this is supposed to work? I mean, if the judge says my claim is legitimate, then do Mr. Mosley and I just sit down together and figure out how we want to divide up the estate?"

"That's one way to do it." His tone was carefully neutral. "Or if that doesn't seem feasible, the judge can appoint someone to mediate the process."

Ivy nodded and faced forward. This was all getting so complicated. And she still felt a bit like a circling buzzard. She wished Nana Dovie were here so they could talk it over.

Which brought up the issue that had been niggling at her since talk of this three-week delay came up. Could she leave Nana Dovie on her own that long?

"What's wrong?"

How did Mitch know she was worried? Was she so easy to read?

"I was just thinking three weeks is a much longer time than I'd planned to be away." She turned to face Mr. Barr. "Is there any way to speed this up?"

He gave a regretful shake of his head. "I'm afraid the judge's schedule is pretty well-set. And as important as this is to you and Carter, it would take something much more significant to have him alter his normal circuit route."

"I see." Not the answer she'd wanted but about what she'd expected.

Mitch gave her a quizzical look. "Getting homesick?"

"I've never been away this long before." Not quite an answer, but hopefully it would satisfy him.

Truth to tell, she was actually enjoying her time here more than she'd expected. She'd seen new sights and had new experiences in the short time she'd been away. And folks around here didn't treat her like a leper the way they did back home.

Of course, another part of the reason she was enjoying herself was sitting right next to her.

Best not to dwell on that, though.

Chapter Ten

By the time Mitch dropped Mr. Barr at his home, it was nearly noon and Ivy was no closer to figuring out her next move than she'd been when she'd left the ranch. She wasn't one for giving up just because things got difficult, but she also wasn't sure this was a battle she really should be fighting.

Once they'd delivered the carriage back to the livery, Mitch gave her a searching look. "Come along, we can have lunch at Daisy's while we discuss what happens next."

So he wasn't ready to wash his hands of her just yet. Suddenly feeling her mood lighten, she raised a brow. "Daisy's?"

"Daisy Fulton runs a restaurant here in town. The hotel's food is okay, but Daisy's cooking is much better."

She grinned. "Then lead on."

As they strolled along the sidewalk, Ivy paused to admire a frock in the window of a dress shop. It was simply made, out of a pretty blue-and-yellow fabric. But the touches of lace at the collar, yoke and cuffs gave it a special-occasion look.

"Thinking about getting a new dress?"

Ivy cut him a quick smile. "Nana Dovie has a birthday

coming up and I would love to get that dress for her. But she'd give me such a scold if I did."

"Why?"

"Because there are more practical things to spend our money on."

"My sisters always believed birthdays were a time to forgo the practical and indulge in the frivolous."

Ivy grinned. "I think I'd get along very well with your sisters."

"I think you would, too."

The half smile with which he delivered those words did something funny to her insides.

Before she could form a response, someone stepped out of the dress shop. The woman looked to be in her fifties, and had dark hair and a solid build. Her gaze darted with keen interest between her and Mitch, and she approached them with an eager smile.

"Why, hello," the woman said to Mitch. "And good day to your friend, as well."

Was it her imagination or did Mitch stiffen slightly?

Mitch nearly groaned. Eunice Ortolon was a well-meaning woman, but she was also the most notorious gossip in town. If there was a secret to be ferreted out, Eunice was the one to do it. He only hoped Ivy wouldn't say anything to put her on the scent.

He touched the brim of his hat. "Mrs. Ortolon, allow me to introduce you to Miss Ivy Feagan." He turned to Ivy. "Mrs. Ortolon runs the town's boardinghouse."

Ivy gave a neighborly nod. "Pleased to meet you, ma'am."

"So you're the young lady who rode into town with Mr. Parker yesterday." She didn't wait for a response before rushing on. "I saw you at the funeral this morning but didn't have the opportunity to say hello. Was Mr. Carter a relative of yours?"

Mitch held his breath. How would Ivy respond?

"No, ma'am. He was an old friend of my father's."

Of course—the perfect answer.

Mrs. Ortolon nodded sympathetically. "How very kind of you to travel here to attend his funeral. Did you have to come far?"

"I came from Nettles Gap."

That raised the woman's brow a bit. Was she wondering why Ivy hadn't arrived by train? Mitch took Ivy's elbow. "If you will excuse us, we were headed to Daisy's."

"Of course. Enjoy your meal."

As they walked away, Mitch imagined the woman's eyes boring into their backs.

"She seems very friendly," Ivy said, though her tone was tentative. "She must make a very good boardinghouse proprietor."

"She does run a very tidy and comfortable place." Mitch believed in giving credit where credit was due. "I stayed there for a few weeks when I first moved to Turnabout. All four of us did." That's when he'd learned the woman had a talent for extracting a juicy bit of blather from the most unwitting of sources. She wasn't malicious, just drawn to gossip like a bee to nectar.

Still, it would be best if he kept Ivy away from Eunice Ortolon—and any other gossips—as much as possible.

Ivy studied the colorful sign above the door proclaiming the establishment to be Daisy's Restaurant. It had a charming little daisy dotting the *i,* and somehow it made her feel welcome. This was going to be another eagerly anticipated first for her—she'd never eaten in a restaurant before.

When they stepped inside, Ivy was further delighted. The place was decorated with a sunny, playful brightness reflected in everything from the yellow walls to the flowery curtains. And if the aromas were any indication, the food would be every bit as good as Mitch had promised.

As for Daisy herself, she was as down-to-earth and friendly as the flower she was named after.

While they were waiting for their meal, Daisy's husband, Everett, popped in to talk to Daisy for a minute, and she brought him over for introductions. It turned out that her husband, who spoke with a slight accent, was another of the men Mitch had traveled from Philadelphia with.

After the couple moved away, Ivy asked Mitch about the accent.

"Everett was born in England," Mitch explained. "He didn't move here until his adolescence."

"Oh, my. I thought Philadelphia was a far piece from here, but he crossed an ocean." It certainly put her two-day trip—that had turned into four—into perspective. "What's that over there?" She indicated the wall that was lined with bookshelves, and fronted by a small desk and cabinet.

"That's Abigail's circulating library."

"Is it normal to have a library inside a restaurant?"

"Not usually, but Everett's sister, Abigail, moved here and decided she wanted to open a library, so Daisy gave her a section of the restaurant to use. It's become a popular spot."

Ivy had enjoyed reading while she was in school, but she hadn't had the opportunity to do much since. Maybe she'd give it another try while she was here.

Then she paused. She was acting as if her staying here had already been decided. And that was far from true.

"You're worried about your Nana Dovie, aren't you?"

Ivy met his gaze, surprised by his ability to read her.

"Much as I'd like to see this through, I just don't like the idea of leaving her alone for so long."

"Is it because you believe she needs someone to look after her?"

Ivy grinned. "She'd get a switch after me if she ever heard me say so. But, for all that she's determined to do for herself, she's getting on in years and I worry about her not having someone to help with the chores and just generally keep an eye on her."

"You said the preacher was checking in on her while you were gone. Would he be willing to continue doing so for the next few weeks?"

His questions and tone were logical, but she thought she detected a hint of concern just below the surface. Or maybe that was just wishful thinking. "More than likely, but that's not the same as someone being there all the time."

"I agree it's not ideal, but it is workable. Other than your concern about her well-being, is there another reason you're reluctant to delay your departure?"

She hesitated, not wanting to appear vulnerable or pitiful. But there was no getting around the facts, and after all he'd done for her, he deserved the truth. She absently stabbed a green bean with her fork, dragging it across her plate.

"I don't have the wherewithal to pay for a stay of three weeks."

Mitch mentally chided himself as he saw the color rise in her cheeks. He should have realized her dilemma. "I'm certain Reggie would let you stay in her guest bedroom," he offered quickly. But his words didn't have the desired effect.

Ivy stiffened. "You shouldn't go speaking for her. She hardly knows me. And besides, it's bad enough I slept in her bed down at the cabin and wore her clothes without being able to thank her. I won't take advantage of her generosity knowing that I already have an unpaid debt she isn't even aware of."

Mitch quickly looked around. He knew she was distracted by other concerns, but a slip of the tongue like that could cost her dearly. Thankfully no one appeared to be paying attention.

"Even if all that wasn't an issue," she said, waving a hand dismissively, "I still don't like the notion of leaving Nana Dovie alone for so long. No, I figure the best thing for me to do is to head back to Nettles Gap in the morning."

He took hope from the fact that she didn't sound happy about it. "You're going to just give up your claim?"

"I can always return here when it's closer to the time for the judge to show up."

Mitch didn't approve of that plan at all, but he didn't stop to analyze why. "Think this through. What if the judge comes early? His schedule isn't always precise. If that should happen, you risk missing him altogether and allowing Carter to present his case without you there."

She rubbed her chin. "I hadn't thought of that. I wouldn't want to stand the judge up."

Seeing she was weakening, he pressed his advantage. "Exactly. Even though your case is strong, there's no telling how he might rule if you're not here to counter Carter's arguments."

"I suppose, if I decided to stay and plead my case, the preacher could keep a close eye on Nana Dovie for me." Then she sighed. "But none of that matters if I don't figure out how to pay my way."

They were back to that. "If you're absolutely set against staying with Reggie, there are other people here in town who'd provide you with a room. I can ask around."

She speared him with a glare. "I won't go begging, or let you do it for me. I've always been one to pay my way or I do without."

"You do know that pride is a sin, don't you?"

She lifted her chin. "Only false pride."

He hid a smile and let her comment pass. "Fortunately, I think there's another option."

"And that is?"

"You could rent a room in someone's home for much less than what the hotel costs."

Her suspicion didn't appear to abate any. "I told you, I won't live on charity—not yours or anybody else's."

"That's not what I'm suggesting. Eileen Pierce, a young widow, put the word out a month or so back that she'd be willing to take in a boarder so she could have some extra pin money."

Ivy looked at him as if trying to decipher an ulterior motive. "A month ago. And nobody's taken her up on the offer? Is there something wrong with it, or just not much call for rooms around here?"

Mitch chose his words carefully. He wanted to let her know what she'd be walking into without being judgmental of the young widow. "She's not the most popular individual in these parts. Not for any reason that would put you at risk, I assure you. But there are things in her past some folks still hold against her."

Just after Mitch had arrived in Turnabout two years ago, Eileen's husband, who'd embezzled money from the local bank, had committed suicide when it had become obvious his guilt would be discovered. Many in town blamed his downfall on his young wife's extravagant tastes and spending habits.

But Mitch wasn't one to give credence to gossip. Nor was he one to spread it. Though to be fair, the woman's withdrawal from everyone after the tragedy hadn't helped her cause.

To his surprise—and relief—Ivy didn't press for details. Instead she seemed to brush right past the issue. "When it comes down to it," she said matter-of-factly, "most of us have things in our past we wish we could change."

He added a silent amen to that. But there'd been a hint of poignancy in her voice that piqued his curiosity. "Including yourself?" he asked before he could stop himself.

She gave him a that's-off-limits look. Then, instead of answering, she took the conversation back to its original focus. "Anyway, I prefer to form my own opinion about folks."

"Very commendable," he said quickly, embarrassed by his prying. But he was even more curious about what she might be hiding than he had been before. Not that it was any of his business. "If you're agreeable, then," he said, following her lead, "I'll take you round to Mrs. Pierce's place and introduce you. The two of you can take it from there and work out the details."

Her brows went up. "You mean now?"

"Of course. I assumed you wanted to get this settled right away."

He also didn't want her second-guessing her decision to stay.

When she still hesitated, he gave her a challenging look. "I thought you said Mrs. Pierce's reputation didn't bother you."

"It's not that." She rubbed her neck absently. "The thing is, even if she only charges half of what the hotel does, it'll still cost me money I don't have."

Ivy said this with more frustration than embarrassment. She was the practical sort, he'd give her that. And she'd already made it clear she'd never accept a gift of money from him, or even a loan.

But perhaps there was another way he could both help her and keep an eye on her during her stay. "Are you opposed to taking a job while you're here?"

Her eyes lit up and her shoulders straightened. "Not at all. In fact, I'd be mighty grateful to have a chance to earn my way." She leaned forward eagerly. "Are you saying you know of something like that?"

"I certainly do."

It didn't take Ivy but a moment to figure things out. When she did her smile faded and she sat back with a thump. "You're talking about working for you, aren't you?" Irritation colored her tone.

But Mitch was ready for her resistance. He put on his haughtiest expression. "I assure you, if you take this job, you won't get any special treatment just because you know me. I'll expect you to earn every cent I pay you. There's a *real* house to clean and *real* meals to cook, and I have high standards for both." Which was absolutely true.

He'd never before considered hiring anyone, though. His home was his private retreat, a place where he could insulate himself from the world. Very few individuals— very few friends—had ever stepped across his threshold. And that was just the way he liked it.

Or at least the way he needed it to be if he was to maintain his distance. But this situation called for extreme measures. *And* it was just for a few weeks. Afterward, he could slip back into his solitary routine and things would return to normal.

Although he wasn't so sure how he felt about "normal" anymore since Ivy Feagan had burst into his life and reminded him how intriguing the unconventional could be.

* * *

Ivy knew he was waiting for her answer, but she wasn't sure what to make of his offer, which still smacked of a handout. She didn't have a lot of choices, though, not if she wanted to remain in town until the judge arrived. And despite her worries over leaving Nana Dovie alone, she found she really did want to stay.

Besides, as long as she put in an honest day's work, kept it strictly businesslike and didn't accept more pay than was reasonable, she supposed it didn't really matter what his motives were.

Of course, she could—and should—question her own motives in ignoring her better judgment and taking him up on his offer.

"I don't expect any kind of special treatment," she warned.

He held up his hands. "Understood. We can work out the details after you settle the matter of lodging. Shall we head over to Mrs. Pierce's now?"

He'd certainly changed the subject fast enough. Was he hiding something? Deciding to trust him, she nodded, and in a matter of minutes they were on the sidewalk.

Once they'd settled into a comfortable stroll, Ivy said, "Tell me about this Mrs. Pierce. Not about her past," she added quickly. "Just in general what sort of person she is, so I'll know what to expect."

"I thought you liked to form your own opinions?"

Surely that wasn't a hint of amusement in his tone? "I'm not looking for judgments on her character. I only meant things like is she chatty or quiet, more down-to-earth or highfalutin, does she have a sense of humor—that sort of thing."

"Of course. Let's see, before her husband's death she was quite social, loved to throw and attend parties, wore stylish clothing and surrounded herself with beautiful things. Since her husband's death she's become more reserved and keeps to herself more often than not."

Sort of like him. Had his wife's death affected him in the same way it appeared to have affected Mrs. Pierce?

"As for her stylishness," he continued, "even though her husband has been gone nearly two years now, she still wears black."

"She must have loved him very much." That was the sort of love she hoped to find one day—the forever kind. It was the reason she'd spurned Lester's advances, the start of all her troubles. Still, if she could find that kind of love, the hardships of these past five years would have been worth it.

"I didn't know either of them well" was his only comment. There was something in his tone, though, that made her think perhaps he didn't view it as romantically as she did. Had something in his own marriage affected his views?

"That's it, up ahead," he said, pointing. "The three-story brick one with all the flowers in the yard."

Ivy studied the house with interest. It was an impressively large structure with white columns supporting the front porch. Did Mrs. Pierce live in this huge house alone?

But what really caught her eye was the lovely flower garden. She identified rosebushes, irises, snapdragons, lilies and camellia bushes. And there were others she'd never seen before. Despite what Mitch had said about the widow, Ivy found herself immediately predisposed to like this Mrs. Pierce. A woman who took such pride in her garden had to have a good heart.

Mitch escorted her to the front door without sparing so much as a glance for the flamboyant array of colors, and twisted the ornate brass doorbell.

The chimes echoed musically inside the house, and a moment later, the door opened. Her first impression of Mrs. Pierce was that she was an elegant, slender woman who seemed very poised. She oozed sophistication, from her impeccably arranged dark blond hair to the hem of her black silk skirt.

"Good afternoon, ma'am," Mitch said. "I hope we're not disturbing you."

She gave him a smile that was more polite than warm. "Mr. Parker. To what do I owe the pleasure of this unexpected call?"

"Please allow me to introduce you to Miss Ivy Feagan."

Ivy stepped forward, and the widow studied her with an unreadable expression, then dipped her head regally. "Miss Feagan."

"I'm pleased to make your acquaintance, ma'am. And to answer your question, I've come to inquire about renting a room from you."

There was a flicker of surprise and something Ivy couldn't quite identify in the widow's expression. "I see." She stepped back. "Please come inside where we can discuss this more comfortably."

Ivy was a little disconcerted by Mrs. Pierce. She'd never before encountered anyone who was so closed off. But she took hope from the fact that the widow hadn't dismissed them.

Once they were inside, Mrs. Pierce ushered them into a parlor that was sparsely but impeccably furnished. As she waved them to a seat, she focused on Ivy. "You're the young woman who rode into town with Mr. Parker yesterday afternoon, aren't you?"

Ivy resisted the urge to shift, instead returning the woman's gaze without blinking. "I am."

"Tell me what you're looking for."

"Of course. It turns out my business here in Turnabout is going to take longer than I'd planned. Unfortunately, I don't have the funds to stay at the hotel for that long."

From the corner of her eye, Ivy noticed something akin to a wince flash across Mitch's face. Had it been indelicate to mention money?

She refocused on Mrs. Pierce. "When Mr. Parker remembered you'd wanted to rent out a room at one time, I figured I'd pay you a visit."

"I see. Since you mentioned finances, I would need to know that you can meet your obligations. And that would mean payment by the week, in advance."

Ivy's heart sank. Would the meager funds she still had cover the first week's payment? Before she could ask what the rate would be, Mitch spoke up again.

"You do understand that Miss Feagan will be expecting to pay significantly less than she would at the hotel or boardinghouse."

"What exactly do you mean by 'significantly less'?"

He named a figure that was about a third of what she was paying at The Rose Palace.

Mrs. Pierce frowned. "That is somewhat less than what I had in mind."

Ivy spoke up before Mitch could speak for her again. "I would be willing to perform some chores around the place to make up the difference."

Mitch frowned. "You'll hardly have time to be a housekeeper here if you're performing the same function for me."

His speaking for her was getting to be annoying.

Mrs. Pierce eyed them both speculatively. "So you'll be working for Mr. Parker while you're in town?"

"I will." Ivy left it at that. "And I'm certain I could manage a few added responsibilities in exchange for my lodging. Assuming you're agreeable."

Mrs. Pierce folded her hands in her lap. "As I said, I was hoping to get a little more for the room. After all, it hardly seems worth the trouble of having a stranger in my home for such a pittance. But perhaps we can work something out along the lines you suggested. If you were to, say, do my laundry once a week, that might be acceptable."

Mitch frowned, but Ivy nodded. "Agreed. I can take care of your wash at the same time I do mine."

Mrs. Pierce inclined her head graciously. "Very well. And may I ask how long you're planning to stay?"

"I'm hoping to wrap up my business in about three weeks, but it might be a little longer." She smiled hopefully. "Does this mean you'll lease me the room at that rate?"

"Before I agree, I have some very specific rules for any boarder staying with me that you need to know about."

"And those are?"

"I guard my privacy very jealously, so you would need to respect the boundaries I set. You would have access to your room, this parlor and the kitchen—not any other area of my home. The rest of the rooms are strictly off-limits unless I specifically invite you inside."

If the woman's tone was any indication, there would be no such invitation forthcoming.

She cast a meaningful glance Mitch's way. "Visitors must be entertained on the front porch, not inside the house, and only during daylight hours."

"That won't be a problem," Ivy responded. "Since I'm a stranger here, I don't expect to have callers. And besides, I'm going to be working as Mr. Parker's cook and housekeeper so I won't be around most of the day."

Mrs. Pierce nodded approval. "You would also be expected to care for your own room and linens, and provide for and cook your own meals. I will be your landlady, not your maid." She lifted her chin. "Those are my terms and they are not negotiable."

Her list was restrictive, but fair. "Those terms are perfectly acceptable."

"Then we have a deal."

Ivy shot a quick, triumphant glance Mitch's way.

"How soon would you like to move in?" Mrs. Pierce asked.

"This afternoon, if possible."

The widow nodded. "That's acceptable. Give me four hours to get things in order and then the room is yours." She stood, sending a clear signal that they were dismissed. "And please have your first week's rent with you when you return."

Ivy nodded and shook hands with the widow, sealing the deal, then made her exit, closely followed by Mitch.

As they stepped onto the sidewalk, he frowned at her. "I think we could have negotiated for a deal that wouldn't have included you becoming her washerwoman."

It was sweet of him to want to champion her, but the widow had dealt fairly with her. "It's a fair arrangement," she responded calmly. "As long as I'm happy with it, I don't see where you have any cause to complain." Then she had another thought. "If you're thinking it'll interfere with my work for you, I give you my word it won't."

He gave a dismissive wave. "That thought never even entered my mind."

She relaxed, encouraged by his show of faith. "Looks like I have four hours to fill until I move," she said, firmly changing the subject. "Which is good, since there are a few things I need to take care of."

"Such as?"

At least his grumpy frown had faded. "I need to send a

telegram to Reverend Tomlin about continuing to keep an eye on Nana Dovie while I'm gone. Because if he's unable to do that, none of the rest of this matters."

He nodded. "We'll head to the depot first."

"And after that, I should look in on Jubal again." She grimaced. "I also need to arrange for extended stabling." Another expense she hadn't planned for.

"Don't worry," he said. "Fred's fees are quite reasonable." He tugged on his cuff, cutting her a knowing look. "And I suppose after that you'll want to check in on Rufus."

"He *has* been alone all day and he's not used to being penned up."

He raised a hand. "No need to explain. You probably should get a look at my place while you're there anyway. That way you can see what you're in for."

Ivy had to admit, to herself at least, that she was looking forward to seeing what the inside of his house looked like. Would his walls be covered with his sketches? Would there be pictures of his sisters and his late wife?

Would there be anything at all to give her insights to other parts of his personality?

He'd probably be irritated by her interest in learning more about him, but it was his own fault for being so intriguing. A girl couldn't be blamed for wanting to get to know her own personal knight in shining armor a bit better, could she?

Besides, what could it hurt? She'd be leaving here soon enough and when she did they'd likely never see each other again.

For some reason, that thought dimmed the sunshine of her day just a smidge.

Chapter Eleven

As they approached The Blue Bottle—the building that housed that intriguing sweet shop Ivy had noticed yesterday—a woman and three young boys stepped out onto the sidewalk. Each child had a parchment-wrapped treat in his hand.

As soon as she spotted them, the woman gave Mitch an arch smile and waited for them to draw near. "Mr. Parker, it's so good to see you. I heard you had returned to town early. I trust there's nothing amiss."

The woman was surprisingly tall and big-boned with blond hair and fair skin. She also seemed to have a particular interest in Mitch, which brought a frown to Ivy's face. Did she not already have a husband? Then Ivy mentally chided herself. This was none of her business. Just because Mitch was being kind to her didn't mean she had any sort of claim on him.

Mitch touched the brim of his hat. "Good day to you, Mrs. Swenson. Allow me to introduce my friend Miss Ivy Feagan. Miss Feagan, this is Mrs. Hilda Swenson."

Was it her imagination or was his tone even more reserved than normal?

But the woman was studying her with an oddly assessing look, so Ivy pushed aside her thoughts and flashed a smile. "Pleased to meet you, ma'am. Those are handsome children you have."

The woman relaxed slightly. "Thank you. And I'm pleased to meet you, as well. Are you in town for long?"

Was there an edge to her voice?

"About three weeks or so," Ivy answered.

"Well, I certainly hope you enjoy your stay."

"Thank you. I'm sure I will." Ivy couldn't help but notice how well matched this woman and Mitch would be. With their striking heights and complimentary light and dark good looks, they would command attention wherever they went. She felt absolutely mousy beside this woman.

Mitch placed a hand at her elbow, and it seemed to Ivy there was something sweetly protective and slightly possessive in the gesture.

And it didn't go unnoticed by Mrs. Swenson, whose eyes narrowed slightly.

"If you will excuse us," Mitch said politely, "Miss Feagan and I have business to attend to at the train depot."

"Of course."

As they moved away, Ivy couldn't help but do a bit of probing. "She seems nice. What does her husband do?"

He looked at her as if trying to determine the motive behind the question. "Mr. Swenson passed away about a year and a half ago."

"Oh. It must be difficult for her, especially with three sons to raise." Ivy couldn't blame the woman for hoping that Mitch would step in and fill those shoes.

He gave a noncommittal response and this time she let the subject drop. But that didn't mean she forgot it.

The telegram was dispatched quickly, with just a pang of guilt. And to her surprise, Mitch had been right about the stabling fees. Not only was the cost less than she would have thought, but it turned out Mr. Humphries was willing to wait until she was ready to leave town for her to settle the bill. Ivy wasn't naive enough to believe this was something he offered to every visitor—undoubtedly it was because Mitch was there to vouch for her. But his earlier comment about her pride was still uppermost in her mind. Besides, she wasn't in a position right now to look this particular gift horse in the mouth.

Ten minutes later, they turned onto the block where Mitch's house was located. As soon as Rufus spotted her, he ran to the front gate, wagging his tail furiously and barking a joyful greeting.

Ivy quickened her pace and reached the gate well before Mitch. As soon as the gate was open, the dog jumped up, planting his paws on her skirt, trying to lick her face.

Ivy laughed and ruffled his neck fur. She could always count on Rufus to lavish affection on her. "Hi, boy. I missed you, too. I hope you're behaving yourself for Mr. Parker."

Mitch rolled his eyes. "If you and that mutt are finished greeting one another, I'll show you the inside of the house."

As he opened the red door, she smiled again at the color. Someday, she'd have to get the story of that red door.

She stepped across the threshold and paused to take in the house. Her first impression was that he was indeed a very tidy, orderly man. There didn't seem to be a thing out of place. Nor was there anything of a personal nature visible from the entry.

He waved her into the parlor, and to her disappointment, the rows of books in his bookcase were the only personal touch to be seen. The curtains at the windows were a nondescript brown without ruffle or trim. The mantel over the fireplace was as empty as the walls were blank. There were no pictures, trinkets or memorabilia in sight.

Why didn't he at least display his sketches?

She itched to add some clutter and color to the place, to move a few books off the shelf and onto a table, set out a vase or two of wildflowers, replace his curtains with a less bland set.

If the rest of his house was like this, the only housekeeping she'd be doing would be a daily sweep of the floors.

She glanced at him. "How long have you lived here?"

"Nearly two years."

How could he *not* have put his own stamp on the place in all that time? She knew, deep down, this man had a flamboyant expressive streak—he couldn't draw those wonderful sketches if he didn't. So why did he work so hard to keep it bottled up inside?

"Do you have many visitors?"

"No."

She was surprised by his response. He seemed to have so many friends here. Everywhere they went he was greeted with respect.

But his expression told her not to press. "What exactly will my duties be?"

"Sweeping, dusting, mopping—that sort of thing."

"That should take me all of an hour." She couldn't accept a full day's pay for so little work.

"Don't forget the cooking. Come on, I'll show you the rest of the house."

She stepped inside the room across the hall and found two walls lined with bookcases, a solid-looking desk and a pair of comfortable chairs situated in front of a fireplace.

"Oh, I'd expected this to be a dining room."

He shrugged. "I didn't need a dining room. I *did* need a study." He waved her back into the hallway. "Shall we move on to the kitchen?"

She followed him down the hall and found herself in

another very stark, almost sterile room. The kitchen, of all rooms, should be warm and inviting. Back home, it was where she and Nana Dovie spent the most time together; it was where they'd had countless talks as she'd grown up and it was where Nana Dovie had comforted her when that awfulness with Lester had happened five years ago.

Mitch, however, seemed perfectly happy with it the way it was. "The pots and dishes are stored over there," he said, indicating a cupboard across the room. Then he moved to a door set in the wall to their left. When he opened it, she saw a well-organized pantry with shelves of perfectly arranged foodstuffs.

"I think you'll find it's well stocked for someone with my simple tastes. But I'll set you up on my line of credit at the mercantile and butcher shop so you can shop for whatever you need."

She tried to match his businesslike tone. "Tell me what kind of food you like."

"Other than not caring for liver or beets, I'm easy to please."

Clearly she'd have to draw her inspiration from elsewhere. She moved to the back door. "How big is your kitchen garden?"

"I don't have one."

Ivy turned to stare at him in disbelief. "No fresh herbs or vegetables?"

He shrugged. "I get what I need from the mercantile or local farmers."

"But *every* home should have a garden. If for nothing else than the satisfaction of eating something you've grown yourself."

He seemed to find that amusing. "I haven't seen the need."

Perhaps he just needed someone to show him the way.

"I know it's late to be planting, but do you mind if I put a garden in for you?" The thought of actually doing something meaningful for him lifted her spirits tremendously. Not only would she be doing work she loved, it would also help her feel as if she were actually earning her pay.

But he raised a brow. "It hardly seems worth the effort since you won't be here to reap the benefits."

He had a very flawed view of what a garden could be. "Planting things and watching them grow is *always* worth the effort."

That drew a smile from him. "Then by all means, plant." He stepped past her to open the back door. "My entire yard is at your disposal."

She stepped out onto the back porch, working out the logistics in her mind. "Let's see, it's not too late to plant a few herbs and maybe some tomatoes, peppers and beans. They'll need lots of watering and loving attention at this late stage, but if we got some hearty cuttings we could probably coax some produce from them." She eyed him. "But I would expect you to keep it going after I'm gone."

He raised his hands palms up. "I make no promises."

"If it's a matter of not knowing how to care for a garden, I could teach you."

In fact, sharing something she loved so much with him would be rather nice.

But when a shadow of some strong emotion crossed his face, Ivy realized she'd gone too far.

Mitch did his best not to let her see how his gut twisted at her simple offer. She couldn't know that he'd been a farmer at the time his world had exploded around him. He forced a smile. "Scratching in the dirt is something I'm not particularly interested in."

From the expression on her face, he could tell some

harshness had spilled into his tone despite his efforts. He tried to cover with a more conciliatory tone. "But I'm not averse to you getting your hands as dirty as you like."

There'd been a time when he'd taken pride in tilling the soil and reaping the crops he'd grown himself for the family table. He could still see Gretchen smiling in triumph when she'd harvested her first ear of corn from the land they'd built their home on.

"Oh, you have a swing!"

The utter delight in Ivy's voice shook him out of his sober thoughts. She was staring at the oak tree that shaded one end of his backyard. Whoever had owned this place before him had attached both ends of a long chain to one of the sturdy branches and used a notched board for the seat.

Other than noting it was there, he'd paid very little attention to it in the time he'd been here.

She turned back to him with a teasing grin. "It appears there's a bit of playfulness in you after all."

"I hate to disappoint you, but that swing was already there when I moved in." He regretted the words as soon as he saw the disappointment flash across her face.

But she rallied quickly. "It's yours now, though. And it looks strong enough to support even you."

He was relieved to hear her teasing tone. Apparently she wasn't holding his lack of enthusiasm against him. "I wouldn't know."

She fisted a hand on her hip. "You mean to tell me that in the two years you've lived here you've never once even *sat* in that swing?"

"Guilty."

"Well, I call that downright wasteful."

He smiled at her nonsensical notion and waved a hand toward the swing. "Feel free to make use of it while you're here."

She gave him a challenging grin. "Well, you can be all stuffy and grumpy, but I like a bit of play in my life. And there's no time like the present." With a saucy smile she started across the lawn, a defiant spring in her step.

He leaned against a porch support, crossing his arms and enjoying the view.

Ivy sat on the board and set the swing in motion, soaring high and laughing aloud at the pure joy of it. She pumped her legs and threw her head back with as much enthusiasm and abandon as would any of his students during recess. Rufus followed the movements of the swing, barking encouragement and running to and fro.

As Mitch watched her, it occurred to him that perhaps her presence in his heretofore serene household was going to change his life more than he'd considered.

He watched her with her unruly braid flying out behind her and her unapologetic laughter ringing around him, and couldn't find it in himself to be sorry.

He told himself if he had any modicum of sense remaining he'd head inside. But for some reason he never followed through on the thought. It was fifteen minutes later before Ivy abandoned the swing, and even then, she did so reluctantly.

When she finally rejoined him on the porch after a quick game of fetch with Rufus, she was grinning. "That was fun. You ought to try it sometime."

He decided not to grace that comment with a response. "Have you selected a patch of ground for your garden yet?"

She surveyed his backyard. "I think that spot right there by that clump of clover flowers will work for a small herb garden. The vegetables can go next to your east fence."

He studied the two spots she'd indicated and nodded. "You have a good eye."

"I told you, I have a knack for gardening. Nana Dovie

says that God gives each of us at least one thing we're good at. He gave you the ability to draw those wonderful pictures. And to open your students' minds to learning new things. I guess gardening is what He gave me."

She continued to surprise him with her homespun insights.

"Any idea where I could get some cuttings?" she asked. "It's late to be trying to plant from seeds."

He thought about that for a moment. "Reggie has a nice garden out behind her house. And her place is near Mrs. Pierce's. Perhaps after we get your things moved in, we can stop by and speak to her."

He looked at his pocket watch. "Speaking of which, we have another two hours before Mrs. Pierce will be ready for you. Is there anything in particular you'd like to do?"

She didn't hesitate. "I can start working the ground for the garden. I've actually missed mine these past few days."

"Then by all means, till away."

"Do you have any gardening tools?"

"There were some left by the previous owner. They'd be in the toolshed. Come on, let's see what we can find."

He led her to a small outbuilding in his backyard. When he opened the door, he paused a moment to let his eyes adjust to the dim interior. He ducked his head to step inside the small room, and she followed him without hesitation.

He heard her chuckle. "Even your toolshed is organized."

She said that as if it were a bad thing. He had actually spent a great deal of time organizing this place when he'd first moved in and was quite proud of the result. There were tools of all sorts arranged on shelves or hanging from pegs. The center of the room held a couple of sawhorses, three small kegs—one with chains, one with nails and one with wooden stakes—and a lawn mower.

"What's that?" she asked, pointing.

"That's a lawn mower."

"A lawn mower?" Her nose wrinkled in question.

"I push it across the yard and it cuts the grass."

Her expression cleared. "Well, now, ain't that something. It sounds a mite easier than using a scythe."

"It is." He crossed to the wall to his left. "Here's a spade, a garden fork and a trowel." He handed them to her. "I'll grab the hoe and shovel. Is there anything else you see here that you think you'll need?"

"I'll need a bucket for watering, but otherwise I think that's it."

He waved her toward the exit. "There's a bucket on the back porch you can use. Now, let's break some ground."

"Does that mean you're going to help me?" she asked with a smile.

"I figured I'd help get the ground ready. Then you're on your own."

They started with the patch of ground she'd earmarked for the herb garden and worked side by side, digging up the sod and turning the soil until they had what looked like a proper planting bed.

Ivy sat back and admired their handiwork. Then she gave him an approving look. "I do believe you *have* done this before."

He wiped his forehead with the back of his hand. "I never said I hadn't. Just that I wasn't particularly fond of it." He grabbed the shovel and hoe and moved toward the toolshed, wishing he could push the memories away as easily.

Then he paused, struck by a startling thought. It was only now, when they were done, that the memories of his other life, the one he'd shared with Gretchen, had intruded.

Up until then he'd actually been enjoying working side by side with Ivy.

He wasn't sure whether that was a good thing or not. It was definitely unsettling. And he wasn't ready to face what that might mean just yet. "I think we've done enough for today," he told Ivy. "Time to clean up and get your things moved from the hotel."

Chapter Twelve

Ivy slowly rose and trailed behind him with the hand tools, wondering at his change of mood. What was it about gardening that put that stiffness in his demeanor? No, not stiffness exactly. More like a deep sadness.

There was obviously something in his past eating at him, shadowing his happiness in the here and now. Such a kind, generous man didn't deserve to be robbed of joy that way. She ached to ask him about it, so she could help him get past whatever it was. But she didn't have that right. Not yet, anyway.

Something inside her stirred. She might only be here for three more weeks, but she planned to do everything she could in that time to discover his secret pain and help him through it.

Whether he wanted her to or not.

She owed him that much and so much more.

After they stowed the tools back in the shed, they made their way to the porch, where they poured water into a chipped basin and washed their hands and faces.

When they were done, Mitch handed her a cloth to dry her face and took a second one for himself. "I'll help you move your things."

"Thank you, but don't feel obliged. I can manage on my own."

"Obligation has nothing to do with this," he said matter-of-factly. "I'm merely one friend helping another."

So he thought of them as friends now. That lightened her mood. She hadn't had many friends since Lester had made everyone believe the worst of her. "Then I accept your offer."

"Good. Before we head out, though, perhaps we should find something to eat. Mrs. Pierce did say you were responsible for your own meals."

Ivy knew if they went back to Daisy's he'd insist on paying again and she wasn't really comfortable with getting deeper in his debt. "Why don't I fix us up something from your pantry?"

"I hadn't intended for you to start working for me today."

"It'll be a practice run of sorts. I can get used to your stove and figure out what supplies I'll need." She gave a little smirk. "Besides, it'll just be one friend cooking for another."

His lips twitched. "Very well. I'll stoke the stove while you gather the ingredients."

Ivy stepped over to the pantry and studied the contents. Without access to perishables she'd have to get creative. And she'd definitely need to do some shopping before she fixed breakfast in the morning.

There were several jars of various vegetable preserves—had he purchased these or had friends such as Reggie and Daisy given them to him? She studied the jars and identified several kinds of beans, carrots, squash and pickled tomatoes and cucumbers. There were a few she couldn't identify without further scrutiny and she decided to ignore them for now.

On another shelf, she found sweet ingredients such as honey, jams, preserves and syrups. So he possessed a sweet tooth—good. It gave her hope that he was still open to a bit of frivolity in his life.

Then she spotted the cornmeal. Did he have molasses? Yes, there it was. She turned to him. "Do you like corn bread?"

He nodded without looking up from the stove.

"Nana Dovie has a recipe she uses for when the hens aren't laying. It looks like you have everything I need if you want me to fix up a batch."

Mitch straightened. "As long as you're eating with me, I'm game to give it a try."

She grinned. "You just want to make sure I won't feed you something I wouldn't eat myself."

"Something like that."

His tone was dry, but she saw that half smile tease his lips again.

"Fair enough." Ivy began pulling ingredients from the pantry. He crossed the room and took the sack of cornmeal and the jar of molasses from her and carried them to the table. When she had everything else she needed for the corn bread, she started looking for a mixing bowl.

He moved to help, but she stopped him with a raised hand. "You take a seat and leave me to figure things out. Like I said, consider this a dry run." She looked around. "I don't suppose you own an apron?"

He shook his head. "Sorry."

"Never mind. I can do without."

Ivy went to work. Mitch stayed in the kitchen with her, watching while she worked. He said it was so he'd be on hand if she had questions, but she got the strangest feeling he had other motives, as well.

Not that she'd let herself think on what those motives

might be. That would involve a bit of wishful thinking. And a woman who was leaving town in three weeks couldn't afford to do such a thing.

Mitch watched as Ivy busied herself in his kitchen. Her movements were confident and sure, and in very little time she had the pan of corn bread in the oven.

"Now, let's see what we can fix to go with that." She moved back to the pantry, still talking to herself as she considered and discarded several options.

It was fascinating to listen to her one-sided conversation, so full of whimsy and humor. Did she have any idea how revealing of her unique outlook on life it was?

She cast a glance over her shoulder. "You must like bland food—I don't see much in the way of herbs or seasonings."

"As I said, I'm a man of simple tastes."

"Simple doesn't have to be tasteless." She turned back to his pantry and finally pulled out two jars. "Field peas and pickled tomatoes—I might be able to do something with these."

It was an unusual combination but he didn't question her. To his surprise, she poured the beans into a pot, then poured about half the jar of pickled tomatoes into the same pot, adding a bit of molasses to go with it.

Well, he'd said he was game to try anything she would eat herself. He supposed she was taking him at his word.

And to his surprise, the unusual mix of sweet and tangy turned out to be quite satisfying when taken as a whole.

Much like the woman herself.

Once the meal was over, Mitch insisted on helping her clean up.

"That's my job," she insisted.

But he was having none of that. "Not until Monday.

Now, why don't you scrape these plates into that bowl on the back porch for your dog while I fill the basin with water."

Without giving her a chance to argue further, he turned and headed for the counter.

He allowed himself a small smile at the sound of her grumbling about stubborn, bossy know-it-alls, but there were no further arguments. She washed and he dried, and in no time they had the kitchen set back to rights.

As he rolled down his sleeves, he had another thought and went to the pantry. Quickly scanning the contents, he pulled out a jar of fig preserves and a tin of crackers, and held them out to Ivy. "Take these, please."

She took them with a puzzled frown. "What do you want me to do with them?"

"Since you haven't had time to do any shopping yet, you'll need something for breakfast in the morning."

She held them out to him. "That's very kind, but—"

He raised his hands palms out. "You'll be doing me a favor—Mrs. Peavy gave me the preserves, but I'm not overly fond of figs."

And without waiting for her response, he turned and moved to the door.

Why did she have to be so all-fired stubborn about accepting his help? Her constant questioning of his offers was making him have to think about the reasons he was doing this.

And *that* was making him decidedly uncomfortable.

Ivy walked beside Mitch as they headed for the hotel and tried to decide whether to be angry with his I-know-best attitude or not. One part of her wanted to just relax and enjoy the flattering attention. But the other part of her, the one that knew she would be leaving Turnabout soon, warned her not to grow accustomed to such gallantry.

She left Mitch in the hotel lobby while she went up to her room to pack her things. It didn't take long, but when she came back down she discovered Mitch had already settled her bill. And that was taking matters too far.

"Mr. Parker, I thought I made it clear to you that I didn't want to accept any charity."

"This is just a loan. I intend to hold the amount out of your first week's pay."

"Even so, you should have discussed this with me first. You can't keep going around making all these decisions on my behalf, no matter how kindly it's meant."

He nodded solemnly. "I'll keep that in mind. Do you have the money to pay Mrs. Pierce?"

Was this how he discussed matters with her? Thankfully she could answer yes to his question, even though paying Mrs. Pierce would take just about all she had left.

He nodded and reached for her bags, but she didn't relinquish them. "Thank you, but I can manage."

"I didn't say you couldn't." He gave her a don't-argue-with-me look as he plucked the saddlebag from her shoulder. "Nevertheless, I insist."

She rolled her eyes at him but surrendered the items. "You are the most stubbornly polite man I ever did meet."

He slung the saddlebag over his shoulder and took firmer hold of the handle of her carpetbag. "Then you either haven't met many men, or they were the wrong kind of men." And with a wave of his hand, he indicated she was to precede him out of the hotel.

When they reached Mrs. Pierce's home, Ivy paused on the front porch. "I can take my bags now."

Mitch stepped up to ring the doorbell. "I've carried them this far—I can take them up the stairs for you."

"But Mrs. Pierce has asked me not to bring guests inside her home."

The door opened just then and Mitch turned to the woman in question. "I'm certain Mrs. Pierce won't mind if I come inside just long enough to deliver these things to your room. Would you, ma'am?"

Mrs. Pierce stepped aside for them to enter. "I suppose that will be acceptable," she said with a decided lack of enthusiasm.

The widow moved to the staircase, then paused. "As I said earlier, I require a week's payment, in advance."

Ivy reddened at this pointed reminder. She should have offered that up immediately. She quickly loosened the strings on her purse and carefully counted out the amount they had agreed on. Looking at her woefully depleted coin purse, she wondered once again if she was making the right choice in staying here.

Mrs. Pierce accepted the money with a regal nod, then started up the stairs. "If you'll follow me, I'll show you to your room."

As Ivy climbed, she noted the elaborately carved banisters and beautiful stained-glass window on the landing. The widow certainly had a beautiful home.

Topping the stairs, Ivy counted seven doors facing the U-shaped landing. Like those on the first floor, they were all closed. Was Mrs. Pierce hiding something? Or just keeping her new tenant out?

Mrs. Pierce led them to the door at the far end of the landing. "This will be your room. I assume it will meet your needs."

Ivy stepped inside and took everything in at a glance. The curtains on the windows were a pretty shade of green. The room was a little smaller than the one at the hotel and the furnishings were obviously odds and ends, but it was nice nevertheless. "I'm sure I'll be quite comfortable here."

Mitch set the luggage down.

Before he straightened fully, Mrs. Pierce gave him a stern look. "I believe your delivery duties are complete."

Mitch sketched a short bow. "Of course." He turned to Ivy. "I'll wait for you outside." Then he unhurriedly made his exit.

The widow turned back to Ivy. "Since you've agreed to do my wash, allow me to show you where the laundry equipment is stored."

Ivy nodded and followed her back downstairs. Laundry was actually her least favorite chore. But it was a task she had to do for herself anyway so doing it for her landlady wouldn't be much extra work.

Later, as she and Mitch walked toward the Barrs' home, Ivy reflected on how fast things were changing. She'd only met Mitch four and a half days ago, but now it felt as if he was a dear friend. She'd planned on being away from Nettles Gap for a week, and now it looked like it would be a month. In just the past few hours, she'd attended a stranger's funeral, confronted a rival for her inheritance, taken a room and a job, found a new plot of ground to cultivate and made several new friends.

"You're quiet. Is something wrong?"

She gave him a reassuring smile. "I was just counting my blessings."

"And what might these blessings be?"

"Well, you, for one."

He frowned, seemingly uncomfortable with her statement, and she felt compelled to explain.

"I could have fallen out there in the woods without help close by. Or I could have arrived in town and had to confront Mr. Mosley on my own. Instead the Good Lord sent someone—you—to help me through both situations."

Mitch shook his head. "You seem to forget, I'm the one who caused your accident in the first place. And it was Adam who did most of the talking with Carter, not me."

She tossed her head. "I stand by what I said." The man obviously didn't know how to accept a compliment. Maybe he just hadn't received enough of them. Well, she could certainly do her part to fix that.

Mitch opened the gate to the Barrs' front walk without responding.

Reggie was in her front yard, cutting blossoms from her rose bushes. After they exchanged greetings, she gave Ivy a sympathetic smile. "Adam told me things didn't go as smoothly as you'd hoped. I'm sorry for the trouble this will cause you, but I'm glad it gives you a reason to stay awhile." Then she tilted her head slightly in question. "You *are* staying, aren't you?"

Ivy nodded and smiled at Mitch. "I am. Thanks to Mr. Parker."

Reggie raised a brow in Mitch's direction. "Oh?"

"Yes, indeed." Ivy enjoyed Mitch's attempt to look bored with her bragging on him. "I was worried about making my money stretch to cover an extended stay. But Mr. Parker introduced me to Mrs. Pierce, who had a room to let, and then he offered me a housekeeping job so I'll have a way to earn some money while I'm here."

Reggie gave Mitch an assessing look. "Well, now, wasn't that nice of Mr. Parker?"

"It was much more than nice—it was providential. I've been thanking the Good Lord for putting him in my path ever since we met." Mitch gave her a stern look, and Ivy decided to relent and stop teasing him. "Which brings me to why we've intruded on your afternoon."

"I assure you it's no intrusion. You're welcome to drop by anytime—with or without Mitch." Reggie started tugging at her gardening gloves. "Is there something I can do to help you get settled in?"

"Maybe. It turns out Mr. Parker doesn't have a garden, which I view as a tragedy. So I've offered to put one in while I'm here. And I'm looking for some cuttings that will work for a late planting."

"Say no more. I can fix you right up." Reggie linked arms with her. "Come on out to my garden—I'm sure we can find what you need." She sent Mitch an airy wave. "You'll find Adam in the parlor."

Mitch was still mulling over what Ivy had said as he went to find Adam. She considered their meeting providential? He'd have thought she would've seen it as the disaster that had kept her from arriving in time to talk to Drum.

"I thought I heard your voice," Adam said, finding him standing in the hallway, lost in thought.

Hiding his embarrassment at having been caught woolgathering, Mitch pulled his thoughts back to the present. He quickly explained why he was there and the two men moved to the back porch.

"So putting in a garden was Miss Feagan's idea?" Adam kept his eyes focused on the two women as they sat.

"It certainly wasn't mine," Mitch said dryly. "Apparently Ivy's not only a skilled gardener, but she loves it, as well." He suppressed a smile. "And because I don't share her belief that every household with a yard should also contain a garden, she thinks me little better than a heathen."

Adam was grinning now. "And she feels it's her duty to convert you?"

Mitch nodded. "With a fervent, missionary zeal." Then he sobered. "So what about Carter? He seemed dead set on fighting her claim. Is there anything she should be worried about?"

Reggie apparently said something amusing because Ivy let out a boisterous laugh, which he found enjoyably distracting. It appeared the two women were becoming fast friends.

Adam rubbed his jaw. "As long as her proof of identity is solid, there's really not anything Carter can do to negate her claim."

Mitch nodded. But he still had a nagging worry that they shouldn't rest easy just yet. Even if Ivy's case was strong, Carter could still make things very unpleasant for her. He intended to be at her side to support her, come what may.

Jack stepped out onto the porch and asked Adam to help him with a tangled string on his yo-yo. Looking at them with their heads bent over the task, Mitch felt a sharp pang of jealousy.

He turned back toward the garden, but this time he didn't see Ivy and Reggie there. He saw Gretchen, smiling as she went about her work, quietly joyful with the knowledge of the new life she carried inside her. A new life that never had a chance to flourish. It took him a long moment to pull himself together, but when Jack wanted to show him a trick with the now untangled yo-yo, he was able to respond with appropriate interest.

Twenty minutes later, Ivy and Reggie strolled back to the porch, still chattering away. Mitch smiled—chattering away seemed to be Ivy's natural state.

When the women drew close, Mitch stood. "Did you two work it all out?"

Ivy nodded. "Reggie has a marvelous garden and she's generously sharing it with us."

Mitch wasn't quite certain how he felt about that familiar use of "us." Especially with those thoughts of Gretchen and his unborn child still lingering in his mind.

"Fiddlesticks," Reggie said. "The garden needed thinning anyway and I was happy to do it. Mitch, you're lucky to have Ivy putting in your garden for you. She really understands plants—gave me a few tips for how to improve my own harvest."

Ivy's cheeks turned pink, and she smiled happily. "You have a fine garden—I just pointed out one or two things that have worked for me." Then she tucked a stray tendril of hair behind her ear. "When will it be most convenient for me to come by and collect the cuttings?"

"Since tomorrow is Sunday," Reggie answered, "how does Monday morning sound?"

"Perfect." Ivy nodded in satisfaction. "I can stop by here on my way to Mi— Mr. Parker's place Monday morning."

Mitch hoped his involuntary wince went unnoticed. Had anyone else caught her stumble over his name?

"Nonsense." Reggie waved away her offer. "Mrs. Peavy and I can harvest the cuttings and shoots Monday morning and load them up in Jack's wagon. Then Jack and Ira can pull the wagon over to Mitch's place." She turned to her son. "Can't you, Jack?"

"Yes, ma'am. My wagon can hold a whole lot."

"Why, thank you, Jack," Ivy said. "I'd be mighty beholden to you."

Then Reggie raised a finger. "That reminds me. You must join our gathering for lunch tomorrow."

Ivy's brow wrinkled. "Gathering?"

Reggie waved the question away. "Mitch can explain, but I won't accept no for an answer." She turned to Mitch. "Don't forget, it's now June so we'll be meeting at Eve and Chance's place."

"I remember."

"Of course you do—you're always so on top of things." She climbed the porch steps. "If you'll excuse me, I need to check on Patricia."

Mitch and Ivy took their leave. They were barely back on the sidewalk when Ivy turned to Mitch. "What is this mysterious gathering that Reggie insisted I should attend?"

"Remember I told you I traveled here from Philadelphia with three other men, and that it was Reggie's grandfather who introduced us to each other before we set out?"

She nodded.

Mitch chose his next words carefully, not wanting to reveal any secrets that weren't his to tell—Reggie's grandfather had sent them to Turnabout with a very specific purpose in mind, one his granddaughter had been furious to learn about.

"When we arrived here, Reggie opened her home to us and we got in the habit of taking our meals together." He suppressed a grin as he remembered what a little tyrant Reggie had been as she insisted they do so to put a good face on a difficult situation.

"Once we all settled into our new lives here," he continued, "it gradually became a once-a-week event—Sunday lunch. It's a tradition that's survived to this day—as members of the group marry and have children, or other relatives come to town, the circle has expanded, but that hasn't stopped us."

"What a lovely tradition. But if it's for the four of you and your families, perhaps I shouldn't—"

He didn't let her finish. "You heard Reggie. She would skin me alive if I showed up without you. And don't worry, the size of the group expands and contracts over time and it seems like every few weeks we seat a different number. Last Sunday we had ten adults, if you count Everett's sister, Abigail, and four children. So one more will scarcely be noticed."

"And so this Eve, who has the unlucky chore of cooking for your large gathering, is she the wife of the fourth member of your group?"

"That's right—Chance Dawson. Eve runs that candy store you eyed when you first got to town. So you'll finally get to sample her wares."

"She must be quite a cook."

"Reggie, Daisy and Eve take turns hosting, swapping up every month. This month is Eve's turn. But they all contribute something to the meal."

"Don't you ever take a turn to host?"

"As a bachelor, I'm exempt. Besides, my dining room isn't big enough." He was tempted to explain further, but held his tongue.

They arrived at Mrs. Pierce's, and Mitch opened the front gate. She stepped forward, but rather than following, he gave her a short bow. "It's best I leave you here."

She cast a quick glance toward the house and nodded. "Mrs. Pierce's rules. Thank you again for all you've done to help me—and not just today."

She looked suddenly small and alone, and he felt as if he were abandoning her. "You're quite welcome. I'll come by in the morning to escort you to church."

She tilted her head in question. "Shouldn't I come by to fix your breakfast?"

"Sunday is your day off," he said firmly. "And I'm perfectly capable of preparing my own meals—just as I've done every day for the past two years."

She grinned. "A man of simple tastes—I remember. Well, then." She paused, as if drawing the moment out. "I suppose I'll see you in the morning."

Mitch waited until she'd stepped inside the house, then

turned and started back toward home. It was getting on toward dusk and Tim would be out lighting the streetlamps in another few minutes.

It had been a very interesting day—several days, he should say. There'd been none of the peaceful solitude he'd planned to enjoy this week. And it looked like that would hold true for the next three weeks, as well.

But strangely, he didn't feel the least bit cheated.

It was undoubtedly the stimulation of having something new and unexpected to focus on.

And Ivy was definitely unexpected.

She was chatty, stubborn and indifferent when it came to propriety. She was also warm, generous and altogether intriguing at the same time. He refused to feel guilty for thinking so—after all, he was merely acknowledging the facts.

When Mitch reached his front gate, Rufus ran to greet him. The dog, no respecter of propriety either, scampered enthusiastically around him, all but tripping him up, until he gave in and stooped down to scratch the animal's neck. "Ivy spoils you. Don't expect to get the same level of attention from me." When Mitch stood, the dog raced off, then returned carrying a stick in his mouth. With a reluctant smile, Mitch accepted the offering and gave the stick a toss that sailed it across the yard.

Rufus quickly returned it to him and they repeated the game three more times until Rufus spied a squirrel and gave chase.

As Mitch entered his house, he thought again about just how much his life had been disrupted. Even when Ivy wasn't here, her dog made sure his time was no longer wholly his own.

What surprised him, though, was how little it bothered him.

* * *

Not wanting to impose on Mrs. Pierce, Ivy had gone to her room almost immediately.

Opening her window to let in some air, she spotted Mrs. Pierce in her very lush vegetable garden, watering the rows.

Her heart went out to the woman. Though she was very serene and elegant on the surface, Ivy sensed a loneliness in her.

Would she welcome an overture of friendship from her tenant?

She began unpacking her few possessions and her thoughts naturally turned to Mitch. She found it strange that he had never taken on his share of the Sunday hosting duties. His comment about the size of his dining room seemed merely an excuse. But if he didn't want to host his friends, she supposed it was none of her business.

But why did he hold himself so aloof from everyone?

His friends were nice people. *Very* nice people. And the fact that they had accepted her so quickly simply because she was his friend spoke volumes for the regard they held him in.

That feeling of being accepted was a gift—one she no longer took for granted.

Lord Jesus, I'm starting to believe You had more blessings in store for me than I ever imagined when You sent Mitch to me out in them woods. I know this won't last forever, but I promise to cherish every minute of it. And when it's time for me to return to Nettles Gap, I will lean on You to give me the strength not to mourn its loss.

But while she was here, she aimed to do what she could to make Mitch see how blessed he was.

Whether he welcomed her attempts or not.

Chapter Thirteen

The next morning, Mitch stopped by Mrs. Pierce's home to escort Ivy to church. The widow walked with them at Ivy's invitation, but when Ivy and Mitch paused to speak to Adam and Reggie, she took her leave and entered the church building alone.

After the greetings were exchanged, Reggie shifted Patricia to her other hip. "Ivy, did Mitch explain about our gathering?"

"He did, and I feel honored to be included, so long as you're certain the hostess is okay with an extra guest."

"Oh, don't worry about that—Eve won't mind." Then she glanced past Ivy. "Oh, look, there they are now."

Reggie waved the new arrivals over and Ivy was quickly introduced to Eve and Chance and their boy, Leo.

Eve Dawson was a petite woman with an infectious smile. "So you're the young lady who rode into town with Mitch and set everyone's tongues to wagging."

"Guilty. And you're the lady who runs the sweet shop."

Eve smiled. "Guilty. You'll have to stop by to sample some of my candies."

Mitch touched Ivy's elbow, as if to lend her added support. "Miss Feagan will be joining us for lunch today."

"Wonderful! It'll give us a chance to get better acquainted." Eve gave Ivy a grin. "Not only that, but it means I won't be the newest arrival at the table any longer."

"You lost that standing six months ago when Daisy's Wyatt was born," Eve's husband said. Chance Dawson was a boyishly handsome man with a charming smile and a teasing tilt to his lips. But it was obvious he only had eyes for his wife.

Eve tapped his arm with a mock pout. "*Must* you be so literal?"

Ivy was enjoying the banter and easy camaraderie the group shared, but her smile faltered when she spotted Carter Mosley from the corner of her eye. The man visibly stiffened when he saw her. Averting his eyes, he walked into the church building without a backward glance.

She had grown used to such snubs at home, but somehow, here, it stung much more.

The church bells pealed and the folks still milling about moved toward the entrance.

Once inside, Ivy spotted Mrs. Pierce sitting by herself. Impulsively, she headed directly for that pew and took the seat next to the widow, and Mitch slid in next to her.

Mrs. Pierce turned, and surprise flashed in her eyes. Then her demeanor closed off again and she gave Ivy a cool nod before facing forward again.

When the service started, Ivy discovered Reverend Harper was quite different from Reverend Tomlin—he was a bit older and lacked some of Reverend Tomlin's stern seriousness. But he seemed equally sincere and concerned for his flock, and she found herself enjoying the service a great deal.

After the service, Mitch introduced her to Reverend Harper as they exited. The man welcomed her with a warm smile and they chatted for a moment about Ivy's plans and how she was enjoying her stay.

Before Ivy could turn back to Mitch, Mrs. Swenson swooped in on him, her three children following like a covey of quail.

"Mr. Parker, how nice to see you on this fine Sunday morning."

Mitch touched the brim of his hat. "Mrs. Swenson."

"Isn't it an absolutely gorgeous day?"

"It is." Mitch glanced back at Ivy, as if wanting her to step forward so they could leave, but Mrs. Swenson wasn't giving way.

"I baked an apple pie this morning," the woman continued. "I wondered if you'd like to join me and my sons for lunch."

"Thank you, but I already have plans." He moved back a step and firmly tucked Ivy's hand on his arm. It was all she could do not to preen.

The imposing woman eyed Ivy frostily. "Miss Feagan, how nice to see you again."

Ivy nodded with a smile. "Mrs. Swenson, what a lovely hat."

The woman eyed the familiar way Mitch held Ivy's arm as she spoke. "Why, thank you, I made it myself. How long did you say you were going to be in town?"

"About three weeks."

Mitch sketched a short bow. "If you'll excuse us, we should be on our way."

Mrs. Swenson dipped her head regally. "Of course. Perhaps you can join us some other time." She turned toward her children. "Come along, boys." Did Mitch have any idea how special he'd made her feel when he took her arm?

More importantly, what would he think if he *did* know?

* * *

Mitch breathed a sigh of relief as the woman walked away. He turned to find Ivy studying him with a speculative gleam in her eye. Ignoring her unspoken question, he asked, "Ready to head to Eve and Chance's place?"

"I need to make a quick stop at Mrs. Pierce's."

"Forget something?"

"I just need to fetch my contribution to the gathering."

"Contribution? Did you cook something?"

"No. I didn't have the proper ingredients to make anything. But I didn't want to go empty-handed, so I gave Mrs. Pierce a few coins this morning for the privilege of plundering her flower garden. I thought flowers might at least brighten the table."

"That's very thoughtful of you." And it was also incredibly generous. He knew she didn't have many coins to spare.

When they reached the Pierce home, the widow was nowhere in sight. Ivy picked up garden shears, gloves and a large basket that had been left at the ready on the front porch. She held the basket out to Mitch. "Mrs. Pierce said I could borrow this to carry the flowers in. Do you mind?"

He accepted the large wicker receptacle and then watched her pull on the gloves while she studied the bounty of flowers with a judicious eye. "I promised I'd only thin the blooms and not strip any one section," she said without taking her gaze from the garden.

With a decisive nod, Ivy stepped forward and went about harvesting select blossoms and greenery. Mitch acted as her assistant, placing the cuttings carefully into the basket. It amused him to listen to her hold a running conversation, talking both to herself and to the flowers. Did she even realize she was doing it?

When she finally stepped back, the basket was full, yet the garden looked nearly as colorful as ever.

"There, I think that will do." She set the shears and gloves back on the porch, then smiled at him as she held out her hand. "I can take that now if you like."

But Mitch shook his head. "I've got it. Are you ready?"

With a nod, she preceded him through the gate.

As they stepped onto the sidewalk, Mitch spotted the Barr household a couple of blocks ahead of them. Both Adam and Ira carried large hampers, undoubtedly food that Reggie and Mrs. Peavy had prepared for their gathering.

"I do hope Eve has something we can put these in," Ivy said. "I didn't feel right asking Mrs. Pierce to borrow her vases."

Mitch detected a hint of nervousness in Ivy's tone. Was she worried about fitting in? He had no doubt she'd be welcomed, but he planned to do his part to make her feel comfortable.

"I'm certain Eve will have something suitable," he said.

Truth be told, he felt a little nervous himself. Hopefully his friends wouldn't read more into his escorting Ivy into their gathering than was there. After all, it was Reggie who had issued the invitation to Ivy. He was merely providing escort.

But he had a feeling the others wouldn't see it in quite that light.

Ivy tried to calm her nerves as they strolled down the street. She saw Reggie and the rest of the Barr household up ahead but had no desire to hail them. She was perfectly content to stroll along with just Mitch for company. She glanced at him from under her lashes and couldn't help but smile. He should have looked ridiculous, this giant of a man carrying her basket of riotously arranged flowers. But instead he looked quite charming.

He shifted the basket to his other hand just then and took her elbow as they reached a street crossing.

She knew those little gestures were no more than what he'd afford any woman lucky enough to be in his company, but it still made her feel special in a way she never had before.

When they arrived at Eve and Chance's place, Ivy braced herself, hoping she wouldn't do anything to make Mitch sorry he'd introduced her to his friends.

The main doors were open wide, with the entrance barred by two swinging half doors, similar to what she'd seen on the saloon in Nettles Gap. But this was no saloon—far from it—and she liked the openness of it.

Ivy stepped inside to see the room was divided in half by a low half wall. On one side was the sweet shop. On the other side was what looked like a toy workshop. Display cases contained all manner of tasty-looking treats, and shelves were filled with wooden and tin toys.

Candy and toys—what a magical place.

Eve came bustling over as soon as she spotted them. "There you are. We were beginning to worry that you'd changed your mind."

"Not a chance," Mitch said, holding out the basket. "Ivy just stopped to pick these for you."

Eve's eyes lit up as she accepted the basket. "Oh, how beautiful!" She turned to Ivy. "And how thoughtful. Come along to the kitchen and we'll find something to put them in."

Ivy felt a strange sense of being set adrift as she left Mitch's side. But he gave her an encouraging smile, almost as if he'd read her feelings.

Braced by that smile, she followed Eve as Mitch was drawn into the circle of menfolk arranging the tables for the upcoming meal.

When Ivy stepped into the kitchen, she found a roomful of women working amicably together. Daisy and Reggie were unpacking hampers of food. Mrs. Peavy was stirring something on the stove. Someone had spread a pallet in the far corner of the room and Abigail sat there with Daisy's baby in her lap, holding up a wooden rattle to amuse Reggie's Patricia.

"Look at the beautiful flowers Ivy brought us," Eve announced.

The women immediately gathered around to admire the contents of the basket. There were oohs and ahhs as Ivy's contribution was examined in detail.

"Wherever did you get such beautiful blooms?" Reggie asked.

"From Mrs. Pierce's garden." Then she quickly clarified. "I had her permission."

"Eileen let you pick her flowers?" Mrs. Peavy remarked. "Well, mercy me, isn't that something? That garden is her pride and joy."

In short order, Eve found a large vase and several jars to place the flowers in. While the others went back to their cooking and babysitting duties, Ivy separated and arranged the flowers.

"You have quite an eye for that," Abigail said.

Ivy shrugged self-consciously. "I like working with plants." Then she smiled at the sixteen-year-old. "And it looks like you are very good with the children."

Abigail grinned with pixielike impishness. "It's not very difficult when you have two sweeties like these."

Ivy nodded, then went back to work on the flowers. It was so nice to be here amongst these women, but rather bittersweet, as well. She wasn't really one of them, no matter how kindly they went about including her. In a few weeks' time, she'd be leaving, after all.

"It's a bit overwhelming, isn't it?"

Ivy glanced up quickly to see Eve watching her with a sympathetic smile.

"Pardon?"

"Being thrown into the midst of such a large group of near-strangers—it can be overwhelming."

Ivy nodded, hoping she hadn't done anything to make her new friends uncomfortable.

"It's only been about seven months since I was the new person here," Eve continued. "And I remember very well how, even though everyone was warm and welcoming, I still felt like an outsider for a while."

So Eve really did understand. "You seem very much a part of the group now. What was your secret?"

Eve laughed. "I suppose marrying Chance helped."

That was no help. Marrying her way in wasn't going to happen for her. No matter how much she'd begun to contemplate the idea.

"But truly, these people accepted me into their midst before Chance ever thought about proposing."

Ivy liked the sound of that.

"There's absolutely no need for you to feel like an intruder," Eve continued. "Those four good men respect each other and are closer than they would have you believe or even admit to themselves. If Mitch thinks you belong here, then that's the only stamp of approval you need with the rest of them."

Ivy suddenly found herself wondering if Mitch had brought other women to this gathering.

Taking herself to task, Ivy reminded herself again that in three weeks she would return home and never see these people again. Even if she did end up with land in Turnabout, Nana Dovie would never leave her home and that was that.

Preferring not to dwell on the thought of leaving, Ivy lifted one of the flower containers. "Where shall I put these?"

Eve put a finger to her cheek. "I think the vase should go on the candy counter. The smaller ones would look nice on the table in a row down the middle. Hopefully our men-folk have it set up by now." She picked up one of the jars. "I'll help. I need to see if the men have finished so I can put cloths on the tables."

The men did indeed have everything set up, so while Eve spread the cloths, Ivy transported the remaining flowers from the kitchen. Almost without conscious thought Ivy glanced Mitch's way and the approving smile on his face warmed her as she worked.

"Now, isn't that a nice touch," Eve's husband said as Ivy placed the last jar of flowers onto the table. "It appears you like prettying up a place as much as Eve does." He grinned and gave a gallant bow. "Which you both do quite well just by your presence."

"Don't mind him," Eve said as she set out the napkins. "He can't help himself—flirting is in his nature."

"Alas, it's true," he said unrepentantly as he placed an arm around Eve's waist. "But who can blame me for flirting with such lovely ladies as yourselves."

Ivy smiled at his outrageous comment and realized she felt a little less like an intruder than she had earlier.

When the food was finally brought out and they were all seated, Mr. Dawson offered up the blessing, giving thanks for the food and the company gathered around the table. Then he stood and cleared his throat. "Before we dig in to this wonderful meal, Eve, Leo and I have an announcement to make." He held out his arm, and Eve stood and stepped into his embrace, then shuffled aside to make room for Leo to stand between them.

Mr. Dawson paused to place a hand on the ten-year-old's shoulder. "As of yesterday, the adoption process is complete. Leo is officially our son."

A chaotic chorus of congratulations erupted as everyone stood to surround the trio. There were slaps on the back for Chance, delighted hugs for Eve and congratulations for the boy.

She was surprised to learn Leo wasn't their natural son. Later she'd ask Mitch to tell her the story of how Leo had come to live with them, but for now she was happy to just share in their joy.

Ivy couldn't tell which member of the newly formed family looked happier. Leo's chest seemed about to burst with pride and the grin on his face could outshine the sun. But Eve's and Chance's faces shone with so much love and joy that it couldn't help but touch the hearts of any who witnessed it.

Once everyone took their places again, Ivy found herself drawn into the conversation, as if she were a long-time friend of these people. Mitch, as usual, didn't say much. But she noticed that when he *did* speak, people paid close attention.

Did he realize how much his friends respected him?

When the meal was over, everyone pitched in to clear the table. Then the men put the room back to order while the women cleaned the dishes and portioned out the leftovers.

Eve placed one of the packets in the basket Ivy had carried the flowers in. "This is for you and Mitch."

Ivy shook her head. "Oh, no, I couldn't. And I'm sure Mitch would agree. The leftovers should go to those who contributed to the meal."

She suddenly realized she'd inadvertently used Mitch's

first name and nervously glanced around. Would anyone notice?

But Eve seemed more focused on the other part of Ivy's statement. "You contributed those beautiful flowers. And Mitch always contributes to the meal, though it doesn't surprise me that you didn't know. That man is more close-mouthed than a stone statue."

Mitch had contributed? How?

Before she could ask, Reggie nodded. "Even though we've each told him it's not necessary, Mitch has placed a standing order with the butcher. Every Saturday, regular as clockwork, either a roast or ham is delivered to whomever is hosting that week's Sunday gathering."

Why hadn't he said something when she questioned him? But she already knew the answer—Mitch wasn't one to boast over his own good deeds.

As the gathering broke up, she studied the family groupings. Only she and Mitch were solo. Would she ever feel the joy of becoming a wife and mother? It was a cherished dream that Lester had tried to steal from her. But being with these people—with Mitch—made her dare to hope she could still have it.

She glanced toward Mitch. She knew why she was still unmarried—Lester had robbed her of her reputation. But it made no sense to her that Mitch was still single. A man such as he—kind, generous, honorable—that kind of man should have no trouble finding a wife. Moreover, a wife who would treat him as he deserved.

The only explanation she could come up with was his grief over the loss of his wife.

He looked her way and gave her a questioning glance. Had he read something of her thoughts in her expression?

She flashed a quick smile, then busied herself with re-tying the string that was wrapped around the food in her basket. Mitch crossed the room to take the basket from her, and she relinquished it with a thank-you, then turned to say something to Abigail before he could question her.

It seemed natural for Mitch and Ivy to leave together—after all, they'd arrived that way. But Ivy was still aware of the eyes of her new friends on them as they did so.

When they stepped out onto the sidewalk, Mitch turned to her. "I suppose you'd like to check on Rufus?"

She nodded and they turned their steps toward his place.

Rufus greeted Ivy with his usual enthusiasm, but his attention quickly turned to Mitch—or more specifically, the basket in Mitch's hand.

"Rufus! No!"

But Mitch accepted the animal's less-than-decorous attention with good humor. "You can't blame him—this food is worth getting excited over. I asked Eve to toss a bone or two in my packet so he'll get his share." He lifted the basket to her eye level. "I'll divide the rest between us. We should each get a nice meal out of it."

"Oh, no, I couldn't accept that."

"Of course you can. The ladies always send me too much—you'd think they were trying to fatten me up for something. Besides, I'm certain sharing this is what Eve intended."

Ivy took advantage of that opening. "Eve and Reggie told me you always furnish the main meat for the meal."

He shrugged. "It seems fair since I don't take a turn hosting."

"But why didn't you say something yesterday?"

"It wasn't important." Then he turned away. "While you and Rufus catch up, I'll put this in the kitchen."

Ivy absently ruffled Rufus's fur, then picked up a stick and tossed it for him, her mind still on Mitch.

The man was such a puzzle. But a puzzle she wanted to solve.

She drifted across the lawn as she played with Rufus and almost before she realized it, she found herself in the backyard. The swing caught her eye and drew her like crumbs drew a mouse.

Mitch must have heard her because a few moments later he stepped out the back door.

He crossed the yard and stopped just out of reach of the moving swing. "Your food is in Mrs. Pierce's basket whenever you get ready to go."

"Mind if I ask you a question?" she asked from her perch on the swing.

His lips curved up in a wry smile. "I find trying to stop you is a waste of energy."

She ignored that bit of teasing. "Why don't you have any of your sketches hanging on your walls or up on your mantel, where folks could see them? They're much too beautiful to keep hidden away."

His expression didn't change, but she saw a slight crease appear on his forehead. She'd come to recognize that as a sign he was about to close himself off again. "Those sketches are purely for my own enjoyment, not for display."

This time she wouldn't drop the subject. And there was only one response to such a stuffy answer. "How selfish."

He blinked, obviously caught off guard by her words. "Hardly that, since I don't ever have visitors."

No visitors? But Mitch had friends here. Good friends, if the gathering today was any indication. Didn't he see that?

"If both of those things you just said are true," she replied, "then you've only proved that the drawings *should* be displayed."

He gave her a puzzled look.

"If they're for your pleasure only, and if no one ever comes here, then it only makes sense for you to display them so that *you* can enjoy them without worry that anyone else will accidentally enjoy them, too." She hoped he caught the irony in that last bit.

"Quite a debater, aren't you." His tone was dry, but she didn't detect any irritation. Still, she wasn't sure if he'd meant the words as a compliment or not. She decided it didn't matter, and forged ahead.

"Have you done any sketching lately? I mean, since we left the cabin."

He nodded.

She stilled the swing and leaned forward eagerly. "May I see it?"

Something flashed in his expression—was it reluctance? Had she overstepped? But then he nodded.

"All right."

She stood, but he held up a hand. "Keep your seat. I'll bring it out here."

Was he merely saving her a few steps? Or was he guarding her reputation again? Or was he forcing her to keep her distance?

When he returned, he didn't hand over his sketchbook immediately. "It's not finished yet. I still have some shading to do."

She stood and smiled, holding out her hand. "I'll keep that in mind."

He finally handed it over and she flipped open the cover. Then she gave a delighted smile. It was a sketch of Rufus. The dog stood on two legs, front paws braced against a tree and barking at something above him. She'd seen him in that very pose dozens of times. "You've captured him perfectly!"

Mitch rubbed the back of his neck. "I thought you might like to have this one."

"You mean it? Oh, Mitch, I'd *love* to have this." Impulsively she threw her arms around him, giving him a big hug. A moment later she realized what she'd done and stepped back, horrified.

The stunned look on his face did nothing to alleviate her embarrassment.

What must he think of her?

Chapter Fourteen

"Oh, my, I mean, oh, Mitch, I'm...I'm so sorry. I don't know what—"

He'd recovered quicker than she had, cutting her stammering apology short by touching her arm lightly. "Please don't apologize. I know it was merely an impulsive gesture of thanks, and I accept it as such."

He was right, of course. That was all it had been. She'd have done the same with anyone, given the circumstances, wouldn't she? And the fact that he'd momentarily slipped an arm around her in response had probably just been reflex, too, on his part.

She tried to cover her confusion with chatter. "It's just that this is the best gift I've ever received."

He gave a self-deprecating smile. "I doubt that, but I'm glad you like it. Now let me have it back so I can finish it."

She gave it up reluctantly and he flipped the cover closed again.

Then she brushed at her skirt, not ready to meet his gaze yet, knowing her cheeks were still a bright pink.

"I should be going." She needed to get away, to take stock of what had just happened without his very distracting presence beside her.

He gave her a long, searching look, and she had the feeling he was reading her thoughts. He finally nodded. "Of course. I'll fetch the basket and then walk you home."

"That's not necessary."

"Perhaps, but it *is* what I'm going to do. Besides, Rufus needs a walk. He's been closed up in this yard for too long."

Her hand went to her mouth. "Oh, my goodness, I should have thought of that myself. I didn't mean to saddle you with all of Rufus's care."

He shrugged. "I enjoy long walks. But, if it'll make you feel better, we can walk him together."

How could she refuse his company when he put it that way? "Of course."

At least that impulsive hug hadn't pushed him away. In fact, as far as she could tell, other than his initial startled reaction, it didn't seem to have affected him at all.

Seeing as how he was her employer, that was a good thing. So why did it leave her with a dissatisfied feeling?

Mitch still felt that impulsive hug, could feel the impact of her throwing herself at him, of her arms wrapping around his chest, of his own arm wrapping around her in return in a gesture that felt all together too right.

It had been highly inappropriate, of course. Holding her, even for so brief a moment, had opened a floodgate of emotions that he'd long held at bay. And opening that particular floodgate was a dangerous thing.

But somehow he couldn't regret that it had happened. He hadn't realized how much he missed that kind of close physical connection.

Of course he couldn't allow it to happen again. It wouldn't be fair to Ivy.

No matter how good it felt.

But if Ivy's demeanor was any indication, he didn't need

to worry about it. She'd appeared to have some very real regrets. And now she was unusually quiet, talking to Rufus in subdued tones and doing her best not to meet his gaze.

He certainly didn't want things to get awkward between them. After all, she'd be working in his home for the next three weeks.

Perhaps it was time *he* made the effort to carry a conversation.

Mitch cleared his throat. "How do you like your new accommodations?"

She glanced his way. "The room is very comfortable. Much cozier than the hotel."

She didn't expand further and there was another silence.

He tried again. "And are you and Mrs. Pierce getting along okay?" Her decision to sit with her landlady during the church service had startled him, but only for a moment. Given that she knew the widow had few friends, he should have guessed she'd show public support.

Ivy nodded. "Of course we haven't spent much time together. I mean, she's a bit standoffish, but that's her right. She doesn't know me very well yet."

Then she gave him a smile that was closer to her usual sunny expression. "We discovered we share a love of gardening, though, so I have a good feeling about how we'll get along in the future."

Gardening was obviously a touchstone for her. "Her flowers *are* nice. I think Eve really appreciated your bringing them to our gathering."

"I'm glad." Her smile widened. "Mrs. Pierce's garden is lovely. There are more flowers out back. There's also one of the largest and most varied herb gardens I've ever seen—I have no idea what some of the plants even are. And she has a luscious vegetable garden, as well."

To his relief, the awkwardness between them had all but disappeared.

Ivy absently tucked a strand of hair behind her ear. "I plan to learn what I can from her while I'm here."

"Are you sure she did it all herself?"

Ivy nodded decisively. "She was out watering it when I returned home yesterday. And this morning I saw her collecting some of the produce. Does that surprise you?"

Mitch found it difficult to picture the elegant Mrs. Pierce working in a garden. He'd thought he hadn't judged the widow, but it seemed he had. "I suppose she didn't strike me as someone who liked getting her hands dirty. You're showing me a side of her I hadn't seen before."

"Nothing wrong with getting your hands dirty. A little dirt under the fingernails can help cleanse the mind of all its worries."

"Another of your Nana Dovie's sayings?"

She grinned. "No, that's one of mine. But that doesn't make it any less true."

"I agree. And I'm glad you've found some common ground with Mrs. Pierce."

"That reminds me, I'll need at least one day off to take care of this laundry business. I can do yours at the same time if you like, as part of my housekeeping duties, I mean."

"That's not necessary." There was no way he would add more to her workload. "I already send my laundry out. And as for a day off, you'll have Sundays off, naturally, and then whichever other day you'd like, though I'd prefer it not be Saturday or Monday."

"That makes sense. I reckon Wednesday would work best, it being the middle of the week."

"Then Wednesday it is."

As they reached Eileen Pierce's gate, Ivy straightened. "I suppose it's time I say farewell to you and Rufus."

He was guiltily gratified to hear a touch of regret in her tone. He hoped they were back to the easy friendship they'd shared before.

Now if he could just keep things that way.

Ivy stooped down to give Rufus one last goodbye hug, and Mitch had to tamp down the memory of that embrace she'd given him. What was wrong with him?

"Be good," she admonished the animal. "I'll see you in the morning." Then she smiled at him. "I'll see you in the morning, too. Thanks for a lovely day."

"You're welcome." He felt an odd reluctance to return to his empty house. "How do you plan to spend the rest of your afternoon?" he asked.

She fingered her collar. "I want to write a letter to Nana Dovie. A lot's happened since I left Nettles Gap and I know she's curious. There's so much more you can say in a letter than a telegram."

And then Ivy closed her eyes and lifted her face as if absorbing the heat of the sun. "It's such a pretty afternoon," she said dreamily.

The unconscious innocence of that gesture, and the beauty of her smile, took his breath away.

Then she dropped her chin and opened her eyes. "I'll probably sit on the front porch to write the letter."

He hoped she hadn't noticed his momentary gaping. But she wasn't looking at him. She brushed at her skirt. "How about you?"

Was she reluctant to part, as well? He shook off the thought.

"I'll probably finish the book I started earlier this week." Strange that he hadn't thought about that book since Ivy had entered his life.

She nodded but didn't turn away immediately. "Oh, I

forgot to ask—what time would you like me to show up tomorrow?"

Mitch considered that a moment. His first thought was to have her arrive at nine o'clock since he liked to have time for quiet reflection when he first got up in the morning. But then he realized that would leave her on her own for breakfast.

"I'd like my morning meal on the table at eight-thirty. Will that be a problem?" He normally ate much earlier, but he supposed he could survive on coffee until she arrived.

"Not at all. What do you like to have for breakfast?"

"Nothing fancy. Biscuits and eggs will do."

She gave him an exasperated look. "Now what kind of breakfast is that? A body needs a hearty meal to start off the day proper—especially a body as large as yours." Her teasing look made it clear she'd meant no offense.

"I'll fix your eggs and biscuits, of course," she continued, "but I'll also add meat and cheese. And some jam for the biscuits. And if I can find potatoes—"

He raised a hand. "Don't go overboard. Adding a bit of meat and some jam will be more than enough."

"All right, you're the boss, I suppose." Her words were delivered with a reluctance that amused him. "I'll shop for supplies first thing and then see you bright and early."

He nodded, waiting for her to turn and go.

But she wasn't finished. "Hopefully I'll arrive before Reggie's cuttings are delivered."

He'd forgotten about her plans for a garden. "If not, I'll see that they're unloaded properly for you."

"Thank you." She gave a little wave. "Well, goodbye."

Was he imagining the wistfulness in her voice? Mitch stayed by the gate until she reached the front porch. Then he turned and headed for his place, Rufus padding along beside him.

It was definitely going to be an interesting three weeks.

* * *

Twenty minutes later, Ivy sat on the front porch, a half-written letter on the table beside her.

She'd been worried that her impulsive gesture earlier would cause some awkwardness between them, causing Mitch to worry that she was much too forward, or that she was throwing herself at him. But it seemed that hadn't been the case. Any surprise he'd felt had been short-lived.

By the end of their walk, it appeared he was prepared to act as if it hadn't happened.

She, on the other hand, couldn't brush it aside quite as easily.

It had only been six days since she'd met Mitch, but she was afraid she might already be developing deeper feelings for him.

Which would never do. Because falling for him would only lead to heartache.

He was kind and generous and honorable—everything a girl could hope for in a husband. But he wasn't romantically inclined toward her. Which was actually a good thing, because if he ever learned all there was to know about him, he would be shocked, and perhaps worse. And she couldn't bear to see that in his eyes.

Besides, he was her employer now, and it would be best to keep things strictly businesslike between them.

No matter how *un*businesslike she felt.

And she would never, ever think about that unfortunate, but very, *very* nice embrace again.

Now if she could just figure out how to make her heart listen to common sense.

Chapter Fifteen

Ivy gave Rufus a quick pat when she arrived the next morning, but then moved briskly toward Mitch's back door. She was determined to be businesslike today. She would focus on doing a good job and earning her pay—nothing more.

She smelled the coffee as soon as she opened the door.

"Good morning," Mitch said, sitting at the table with a cup, giving her that smile that she was quickly getting addicted to despite herself. He stood and crossed the room to take the basket from her. Those gentlemanly gestures were quite addictive, as well.

"Good morning," she said briskly. "That coffee smells good."

"Help yourself. The stove is already stoked and ready for you."

She grinned. "Hungry?"

He shrugged. "I wouldn't turn down a good meal."

She'd have to make sure she got here a little earlier tomorrow. Those were chores she should be doing herself if she was going to be earning her pay.

Ivy hung her bonnet on a peg by the door, then paused.

There, on one of the other pegs, was a nicely starched apron. When in the world had he gotten it?

She lifted it from the peg and put it on, then spun around to face him. "Very nice. Thanks."

He gave a casual wave. "You can thank Daisy—it's one of her extras," he said casually, though she thought she detected a note of pleasure.

"But you're the one who got it for me, so again, thank you."

"You're welcome." Then he gave her a stern look. "You're planning to have breakfast with me, right?"

It was time to establish limits. "I don't think that's appropriate. It's important that we maintain a businesslike relationship." She was fast coming to hate that word.

He leaned back in his chair. "Now who's being overly concerned with propriety?"

She was determined to stand her ground. "I want to make certain we do this right. Remember—no special treatment."

He raised a brow at that. "You remember that first night when we ate at Reggie and Adam's home?"

She nodded, wondering where he was going.

"Didn't Mrs. Peavy, Reggie's housekeeper, sit down to eat with the family? Are you saying that was inappropriate?"

"Well, no, but—"

"No buts. If it's appropriate for the Barr household, it's appropriate for this one."

Now she was confused. She couldn't find a hole in his argument, but she was sure there was one somewhere.

When she didn't answer right away, he smiled. "I'll take that as agreement, so the matter is settled." He moved to the hall door. "I'll be in the study if you need me for anything."

Unable to come up with a response, Ivy clamped her mouth shut and went to work preparing the meal.

He sure wasn't making it easy for her to maintain her distance.

Then again, if she insisted on maintaining a strict working relationship with him, it would make it harder for her to fulfill her goal of helping him learn to let down his guard a bit and take joy in what life had to offer.

Somehow she'd have to figure out how to strike a proper balance.

And protect her own all-too-vulnerable heart in the process.

Mitch felt quite pleased with himself as he sat in his study, listening to the sounds of Ivy in his kitchen, preparing his breakfast. She'd liked the apron and he'd convinced her to share his meals. Two victories in her first ten minutes officially on the job. Perhaps he'd be able to maintain control of the situation after all.

When she called him in to eat, he tried to ignore the fact that it wasn't just hunger that hurried his steps toward the kitchen.

As with the other meals she'd prepared for him, it was simple but hearty fare. They passed the time in easy conversation, with him allowing her to do most of the talking. He found the personal glimpses of her life and character that slipped into her conversation absolutely fascinating. Her ability to laugh at herself, and to find blessings in the darkest of situations was both admirable and charming.

But there was one thing missing from her stories, something that he thought might give him a further insight as to what her life at home was like. During a rare pause, he decided to touch on it.

"It sounds like you and Miss Jacobs lead an interesting life on that farm of yours."

She nodded. "I wouldn't trade it for anything else in the world."

He ignored the little twinge he felt at that and moved on. "I assume you don't spend all your time there, though. What's life like in Nettles Gap itself?"

She shifted in her seat, as if suddenly uncomfortable. "Nettles Gap is a lot like Turnabout, only smaller. We have a church, a school, a livery and so on. The railroad bypassed us, but the stage still comes through every Tuesday, and Mr. O'Hara runs a freight wagon from the train station at Bluehawk a couple of times a month."

Was she deliberately avoiding his question? "I wasn't asking about the town's commerce, I was asking what sort of social life you have there. What do you do for fun?"

She'd forked up the last bit of egg from her plate, and now she slowly chewed her food. He had the feeling there was something here she really didn't want to talk about. Should he change the subject?

Before he could decide, a knock sounded at the front door.

Ivy quickly stood, something like relief on her face. "I thought you said you never have visitors."

"I usually don't." He stood and moved toward the hall, but Ivy stopped him with a raised hand.

"Hold on. I'm the housekeeper, remember? I should be answering the door."

He frowned, letting his exasperation show. "Nonsense. Whoever is at the door is no doubt here to see me, not you."

She fisted her hands on her hips. "That's neither here nor there. You hired me to be your housekeeper, and I intend to do my job."

He tried another tack. "You wouldn't be trying to put off doing the dishes, would you?"

His teasing had the desired effect. She relaxed and grinned. "Maybe." Then she waved a hand in surrender. "All right, you answer the door and I'll get started on the dishes."

As Mitch headed down the hall, his thoughts returned to the strange way she'd reacted to his question. What was she hiding?

He opened the door to see Ira Peavy standing there. Behind him, at the foot of the porch steps, was Jack with a wagon crammed full of plants.

"Reggie said you'd be expecting these," Ira said with a grin. "Where do you want them?"

"By the back door, if you don't mind. I'll let Miss Feagan know you're here." He glanced down at Jack. "I think there may be a few extra buttermilk biscuits and some honey if anyone is hungry."

Jack's eyes lit up. "Yes, sir!"

When Mitch returned to the kitchen, he found Ivy energetically scrubbing a plate.

"I was wrong," he said when she looked up. "It *was* for you. Jack and Ira are here with your cuttings. They're bringing them around back."

A dazzling smile lit her face. "Oh, I'd almost forgotten! If you'll have them unload everything next to the porch I'll tend to the planting as soon as I'm done cleaning up in here."

With a nod, Mitch stepped outside, hiding a grin at the way Ivy seemed to suddenly be moving at double speed. She was obviously eager to finish her chores so she could tend to the plants. He'd tell her to let the dishes wait, but he knew she wouldn't welcome anything that hinted at special treatment.

Besides, he needed a few more moments to figure out how he was going to get her talking about her life in Nettles Gap again.

Ivy flew through her chores, listening to Mitch, Mr. Peavy and Jack chat as they unloaded the wagon. Of course it was mostly Mr. Peavy and Jack doing the talking. Good to know Mitch wasn't quiet just with her.

Then again, she sure wished he'd been less chatty when he started asking about her life in Nettles Gap. She wasn't going to lie to him, but she'd rather not be too forthcoming about certain aspects of her life there.

Better to focus on something more positive. Like the wagonload of cuttings. She was already picturing where she'd place each plant, and she couldn't wait to get started.

As soon as she'd put away the last plate, she stepped outside. The wagon had already been unloaded. Mr. Peavy and Mitch stood nearby talking and Jack was across the yard, playing with Rufus.

Ivy looked over the plants and frowned. "There must be some mistake. There's more here than Reggie and I agreed on."

"No mistake," Mr. Peavy said. "Reggie loaded this wagon herself."

Her new friend had been more than generous. There were the peppers, peas, snaps and cucumbers they'd discussed. And sage, rosemary and lavender. But there was also squash, okra, parsley, thyme, mint and a few other things she'd have to take a closer look at to identify.

"Make sure you tell her how much I appreciate this. And, if you don't mind, also let her know I plan to stop by and thank her in person as soon as I can."

"By the way," Mitch said, "I told Jack there might be some biscuits and honey left from breakfast."

"Of course." She refrained from casting a longing look at the plants and waved for the boy to follow her. "Come on inside and I'll fix you right up."

Fifteen minutes later, Ira clapped Jack on the shoulder and said it was time to go, and the two took their leave.

With a happy sigh, Ivy turned to her garden-in-the-making. She knelt, ignoring Mitch's amused expression, to look through the bounty Ira and Jack had delivered.

"Oh, look," she exclaimed. "There's even cuttings from her rosebush. We'll have to plant these near your front porch."

"If you like." There was a decided lack of enthusiasm in his voice.

She glanced up curiously. "Don't you like roses?"

"I don't *dislike* them."

Was he not certain how to care for them? "They're not really hard to nurture and they'll definitely brighten up your front yard."

Again that disinterested shrug. "I've managed just fine with a not-so-bright front yard."

Was he being deliberately contrary? She refused to let it deter her. "Wait and see. You're going to like the difference it makes."

He straightened. "I'll get the garden tools while you finish sorting the plants."

He was offering to help her again. "Please don't feel you need to join me if you've got something else to tend to. After all, this *is* part of my job now." She grinned. "The fun part."

"There's nothing else requiring my attention at the moment." He gave her a searching look. "Unless you'd rather do this alone."

Was it her imagination or was there a hint of vulnerability behind his polite question? She smiled. "Not at all.

I'll be glad of the company. I just didn't want to keep you from anything important."

"You're not." He rolled up his sleeves and went to get their tools. And for the next few hours, Ivy was blissfully happy playing in the dirt. She started with the herb garden, arranging and planting the sprigs of sage, rosemary, lavender, mint, basil, parsley and thyme. Mitch worked beside her but, to her surprise, deferred to her direction on how she wanted things done.

When at last she had the final herb planted, she leaned back and admired their work. "We did a good job if I do say so myself."

"It looks like more than what I'll ever use." He gave her a dry smile. "I don't bother with herbs when I do my own cooking."

"That's because you didn't have a handy source before. You just wait—once you get used to flavoring your foods with fresh-picked herbs, you'll never want to go back to bland food again."

He shot her a skeptical look that made her laugh. "I'll get scrap timbers from the lumber mill to edge the garden with," he said.

"That'll look nice. And it's good to see you taking pride in the garden."

He raised a brow. "You made it clear you expected me to take ownership."

She grinned. "Good to know you were paying attention."

He glanced toward Rufus, who was sniffing around the edges of their plot. "What's to keep your mutt from digging all this up as soon as we go inside?"

"Rufus knows better than to dig in any garden of mine. Don't worry. He'll let it be." Then she grimaced. "Unless a squirrel scampers through it. Then it's a whole nother story."

She stood and stretched the kinks out of her back. "Time to tackle the vegetable garden."

"Are you sure you don't want to take a short break first?" he asked.

She glanced skyward, shading her eyes with her hand. The sun had climbed higher and the day had heated up accordingly. She was a bit stiff, but not ready to quit just yet.

"The sooner those cuttings get planted, the better." She gave him a challenging look. "But if you're tired, by all means take a break. I can finish this up."

He shook his head as he reached for a carefully wrapped tomato cutting. "You, Miss Feagan, are an unrelenting taskmaster. Lead on."

Ivy loved the way he treated her as if her opinions mattered. He deferred to her judgment in this particular task, but when she asked for his opinion he didn't hesitate to give it, and his thoughts were sound. It was as though he thought of them as equals.

And he seemed to be a bit of a mind reader, as well. He brought the water bucket and dipper around periodically without being asked, as if he could sense when she was ready for a refresher, sometimes even before she'd realized she needed it herself.

A girl could get spoiled being around a man who showed that kind of consideration.

Mitch once again fetched the bucket and ladle. Looking at Ivy's flushed face, he decided she needed more than a quick water break. "Time to get out of the sun for a few minutes."

She swiped her forehead with the back of her hand, then took the dipper from him. After gulping down a nice long drink, she stood. "All right. I could stand to enjoy a patch of shade for a few minutes."

Instead of going to the house as he'd expected, Ivy headed for the oak tree and sat down on the swing, but didn't set it in motion.

He followed and leaned back against the trunk of the tree.

"I wonder what Nana Dovie is doing right now," she said dreamily.

"She's probably wondering the same about you."

"Probably." She absently scratched Rufus's ear. "She's having to take care of all the chores herself while I'm gone."

He could hear the worry in her voice and he wanted to comfort her. But he dare not risk a repeat of what had happened yesterday.

"If things work out with this inheritance," she mused, "I'll be able to do some things to make our life easier. Rebuild the barn and purchase a wagon. Get a new milk cow. Maybe even get a newfangled washing machine."

"Those are all good investments. But isn't there something you want for yourself? Maybe buy some nice clothes or take a trip?"

She looked affronted. "Are you saying my dresses aren't nice?"

Had he insulted her? "No, no, not at all," he said hastily. "I only meant—"

She laughed. "I was just teasing, I know what you meant. My clothes are just fine for the life I live. And I wouldn't want to go off traveling without Nana Dovie, and she's not one for leaving the farm."

"You mentioned that once before." He left it at that, not wanting to press.

"It's the strangest thing. She's always been something

of a homebody. But when I was younger she also enjoyed her weekly trips to the mercantile and going to church. And she was always the first one to visit a family who was in need of comfort. But lately…"

Her voice trailed off and she set the swing in a lazy, dragging motion before she continued.

"Lately she hasn't been able to leave our place. She's tried—even went so far as to climb up in the wagon once or twice. It's not that she doesn't want to leave, it's that she can't seem to make herself leave. She's even stopped going to church."

So that meant Ivy was tethered to the farm, as well. As anxious as she was about returning, perhaps this time away was good for her.

The soft vulnerability of her demeanor had him once more longing to comfort her. This time it was harder to push away thoughts of yesterday's embrace. But a heartbeat later her mood had shifted as she suddenly popped up off the swing, startling Rufus into a surprised yelp.

Mitch straightened immediately. The stricken look on her face had him taking a half step in her direction.

"Oh, my goodness. I forgot to get lunch started."

Mitch relaxed. "Is that all?"

"Is that all?" She waved a hand in dismay. "It's the job you hired me for, isn't it?"

"There's nothing that says you have to cook something to prepare a meal. Many's the day I've had a cold lunch. Some cheese and fruit will be adequate. I told you, I'm a man of simple tastes."

She sniffed disdainfully. "It may be too late to cook a proper lunch, but I think I can do better than *that*."

"Be that as it may, what I'm paying you for is to do some work around here. And you've definitely earned your wages this morning," he assured her.

She nodded, then halted. "That reminds me of something I wanted to do."

He watched as she turned and headed toward the back of his lot, Rufus trotting at her heels. What was she up to?

She walked all the way to the fence where the weeds had taken over. To his surprise, she started picking wildflowers. When she had an armful, she headed back. "Aren't these beautiful?"

He looked over her bounty of posies dubiously. It was a mismatched lot that seemed composed mostly of weeds. But she had such a pleased look on her face that he found himself nodding. "What do you plan to do with them?"

"Why, brighten up your house, of course." She hefted her burden of blooms. "I suppose it's too much to hope you have a vase or two?"

When he shook his head she merely smiled. "That's okay. I can use a glass or jar. Won't it be nice to have such a happy splash of color in the house?

"Very nice indeed." But the splashes of color he was thinking about were the sparkling green of her eyes, the pink in her freckled cheeks and the soft auburn of her hair.

Being trapped on that farm was a hardship for her, that much had been obvious in her demeanor when she spoke of it. Surely there was something he could do to free her?

The fact that by doing so it might free her to live here in Turnabout was merely an incidental benefit.

By the next morning, Mitch was certain he was better prepared to keep an appropriate distance between himself and Ivy. She arrived right on schedule and went about preparing breakfast while he sat at the table with his newspaper, and the conversation was appropriately inconsequential.

He escaped to his study right after breakfast, channeling his edgy feelings into his sketching for a few hours. He was still there when he heard a knock at the front door.

"I'll get it," he called back to Ivy.

Who in the world could that be? Had Reggie decided to send additional cuttings? He'd had no visitors except deliverymen in the two years he'd been here, and now two visitors in two days? It seemed his life was changing in more ways than he'd imagined as a result of letting Ivy into it.

His smile faded as soon as he opened the door.

Hilda Swenson stood on his front porch, along with her three boys.

What in the world was she doing here?

Chapter Sixteen

"May I come in?"

Mitch opened the screen door wider, though in fact that was the last thing he wanted to do. "Of course."

His visitor turned to her sons. "Peter, keep an eye on your brothers. I won't be long."

"Yes, Momma."

As she stepped inside, she sighed dramatically. "They're good boys, but it is *so* hard on them not having a father in their lives."

Mitch ignored her very obvious hint and ushered her into his parlor. "What can I do for you, Mrs. Swenson?"

"Oh please, how many times must I ask you to call me Hilda?" Her gaze scanned the room, seeming to miss nothing. "I hope you don't think it forward of me to come calling, but now that you have a *housekeeper*," she said, with a note of false enthusiasm in her voice, "I decided there could be no hint of impropriety. And it was something that could not wait."

"And what might that be?"

"My oldest son, Peter, will move up to your class next year. And I'm afraid his mathematical skills are not at the level they should be. Miss Whitman suggested I have him work with a tutor this summer."

Janell Whitman was Turnabout's other schoolteacher. She worked with the younger students and Mitch with the older ones. He considered her a good teacher—by the time students moved from her classroom to his they were well prepared.

"If Miss Whitman suggested it, then I'm confident that is what you should do. Would you like me to provide the names of some of my students who would make good tutors? There are several excellent candidates."

"Actually, I was hoping you would take the job."

Mitch stilled. Was she using her children to get to him?

But Mrs. Swenson seemed not to have noted his reaction. "Peter will respond much better to an adult than to a young person. I would help him myself, but I'm afraid I have no head for numbers," she said as if it were something to be proud of. "My talents are much more feminine and domestic."

Mitch tried to maintain an impassive demeanor. "Surely there is someone else in town—"

She didn't let him finish. "My boy deserves to have the very best. And who better than a schoolmaster? Since Miss Whitman will be out of town most of the summer, that leaves you."

She sat without invitation, obviously planning to stay awhile. "Besides," she added coyly, "this will give the two of you an opportunity to get to know each other before school starts. You'll find Peter is a very attentive student, eager to learn."

So why had he fallen behind? But Mitch refrained from asking that aloud. "This is what I'll do. I'll give Peter a set of problems to work on at home. I'll look over his work when he's done and assess what kind of help he needs."

She flashed a bright smile. "That sounds more than fair. Peter will benefit from the extra attention, I'm sure of it."

Mitch stood. "If you'll excuse me, I'll write down the problems for him."

"Of course. Take your time—I don't mind waiting."

Trying to ignore the victory in her voice, Mitch headed to his study. As he pulled out a piece of paper, he heard voices coming from the yard. Glancing out the window, he spotted Ivy and Rufus entertaining the three boys. He watched, enjoying the uninhibited abandon with which she joined in their play.

It was several minutes before he remembered what he'd stepped into his study to do. Turning back to his desk, he carefully wrote out the arithmetic problems. As he worked, the sound of laughter and horseplay drifted in through the window. He'd heard that same sound many a time from his classroom.

But he'd never before been as tempted to join the participants as he was today.

Mitch finally leaned back and studied the list of problems. Satisfied that it was complete, he returned to the parlor only to find his guest examining his things. Strange—when Ivy had done that, it hadn't really bothered him. But the widow's actions struck him as intrusive.

When she looked up and spotted him, she smiled as if there was nothing to be embarrassed about. "Your home could certainly use a woman's touch."

"I like to keep things simple."

She laughed and it was a very soft, feminine sound. Nothing like the boisterous joy of Ivy's laugh.

"Isn't that just like a man?" she said archly. "But if a woman ever puts her mark in here—softer curtains, flowers, a few delicate bits of bric-a-brac—you'd wonder why you ever resisted."

What would she think of the wildflowers Ivy had added to his kitchen and study?

He handed her the papers he'd brought with him. "Ask Peter to work on these and bring them back to me tomorrow." Then he remembered tomorrow was Ivy's day off. And he'd rather not be alone when the woman returned. "Make that the day after. And I would caution you not to help him."

She placed a hand over her heart. "I wouldn't dream of it." Then she fluttered her lashes. "Besides, as I said, I have no head for numbers."

Did she honestly think that made her more attractive to him? "Then I'll see you on Thursday."

Her nose wrinkled. "What's that smell?" Then her eyes widened in alarm. "My goodness, is something burning?"

Mitch sniffed the air, then turned abruptly and raced for the kitchen. He knew what had happened even before he pushed open the door. Ivy must have been distracted by the children and left something on the stove for too long.

Sure enough, when he entered the kitchen, smoke billowed from the stove grates. Grabbing a cloth, he opened the oven door and pulled out the now blackened lump of what had undoubtedly been a loaf of bread. Wanting to get the still-smoking mess out of the house, he headed for the back door, pushing it open with his hip.

Ivy glanced up as soon as he stepped outside. The expression on her face would have been comical if she hadn't looked so stricken.

He tossed the blackened mass from the pan toward the fence. Rufus rushed over to check it out, but after one good sniff, he gave a violent sneeze and bounded away again.

Ivy approached the porch like a student caught passing notes. "I am *so* sorry—I lost track of time."

"Nothing to get distressed over. I've eaten meals without bread before—it won't hurt me to do so again."

She clapped a hand over her mouth "Oh, my goodness, the stew!" She gathered her skirts and rushed to the back door. "I hope I haven't ruined that, as well."

Mitch barely managed to get the door open for her before she raced inside. Then she halted abruptly.

Following close behind, he caught sight of what had stopped her in her tracks.

Hilda stood at the stove, stirring the contents of the pot, looking for all the world as if she were the lady of the house.

"Hello, dear." Both her tone and smile were condescending. "I hope you don't mind. I added some water to the pot to keep it from burning." She tapped the spoon on the rim of the pot before setting it on the spoon rest. "I think I got to it just in time. And I hope you don't mind but I also added a pinch of salt and rosemary to it. It was rather bland, and a worldly man like Mr. Parker surely likes flavor in his food."

"Thank you," Ivy said evenly, "but I'll take over now."

"Of course. I was just trying to help." Her smile took on a feline quality. "You seem to have been otherwise occupied."

Mitch sensed Ivy's stiffening and quickly stepped forward. "I'll see you and Peter on Thursday, then."

Mrs. Swenson turned to Ivy. "I'm sorry if my boys distracted you, my dear. When you're a mother yourself someday, you'll learn how to manage both a home and children."

Mitch took the woman's elbow and ushered her from the room before Ivy could respond. "Allow me to escort you to the door. I'm certain your sons are eager to reclaim your attention."

By the time Mitch returned, Ivy stood at the sink, scrubbing the blackened bread pan with great determination. She paused a moment to glance his way. "I'm truly sorry."

"You don't have to keep apologizing. As I said, it's really nothing to concern yourself over. I've burned more than one meal myself." He tried to shift the focus to something more positive. "You seemed to enjoy entertaining those boys."

Her expression softened. "I did. They came to the kitchen door and asked if it was okay to play with Rufus. I told them yes, but then Davey, the youngest, seemed a little afraid, so I went out to put them at ease. I'd only meant to be a minute, but then Davey asked me to push him on the swing.

"They're good boys," she continued as she returned to her scrubbing. "A little too quiet for young'uns, but they relaxed after a bit. Andy, the middle boy, really took to Rufus. They don't have a dog of their own, but it sure sounded as if they'd like to have one."

She'd make a good mother someday, he decided. A sudden image of her with a babe in her arms and a toddler at her feet flashed through his mind with the clarity of one of his sketches. The sweet tenderness of it nearly took his breath away.

"I'm not off to a very good start, am I?"

It took him a minute to focus on her meaning. "I wouldn't say that."

"You're kind, but yesterday I fed you a cold lunch and today I burned the bread to a charred lump."

He didn't like the defeat in her eyes. "Look at it this way—it hasn't been boring." He'd meant that as a bit of levity, but he realized it was true. His life had been turned upside down since she entered it, but he hadn't felt so alive in a very long time.

"I hope my negligence didn't spoil your visit with Mrs. Swenson."

There was a note in her voice he couldn't quite read. "It wasn't a social call. Her oldest son needs some tutoring."

"Peter? He seems to be a very serious youngster. Maybe a mite *too* serious."

"You could tell that from a few minutes of play?"

She shrugged. "I could see how dutifully he watched over his brothers, and how he didn't let himself relax and just have fun."

"That's typical of the oldest child in a family. I see it in my students."

She eyed him thoughtfully. "You said you're the oldest."

Was she trying to draw comparisons? "Yes. And I did keep an eye on my sisters. But Peter has the added burden of being the man of the house now that his father is gone."

"How long ago did his father pass?"

"About a year and a half ago."

She dried her hands on her apron and moved to the stove. "Those poor boys. It must be hard on them not having a father in their lives."

"They'll manage, as others have. And there are good men in this community to serve as role models for the boys until she marries again."

She smiled. "Good men, like a certain schoolteacher I happen to know."

Mitch paused, unsure how to respond as feelings he couldn't quite identify washed over him.

She considered him a *good man?*

Ivy had been doing her best not to dwell on the poor showing she'd made in front of Mrs. Swenson.

She did have her pride, after all. But more than that, she couldn't bear the idea of letting Mitch down. And right now he looked slightly dazed. What was he thinking? She wished he would say something. But he just continued to stare at her in that unnerving way.

Trying to cover the silence, she said the first thing that came to mind, "Do you plan to help him? Peter, I mean."

He finally relaxed his gaze and rubbed his chin. "I'll help, yes, but I haven't yet decided quite how. I gave his mother a test for him that will let me know the extent of his need. Once I look over the results, I'll decide."

Relieved that their discussion was back on safer ground, Ivy nodded. "I suppose that means she'll be returning here. Do you know when?" She was eager to snatch at this chance for domestic redemption. "I want to be prepared with refreshments next time."

"That's not nec—"

"It's *absolutely* necessary. When you have visitors in this home, it's my job to help you be prepared to welcome them properly."

And that woman would not find her lacking again. She refrained from examining too closely why Mrs. Swenson in particular could get her back up this way.

"Then yes, I expect her to return on Thursday, but we didn't discuss a time."

Ivy waved that minor obstacle aside. "No matter. I'll just prepare something that keeps well."

"If it's important to you, then by all means do so."

Ivy hesitated a moment, then decided to say what was on her mind. "Mrs. Swenson seems quite smitten with you."

Mitch frowned uncomfortably. "I believe *smitten* is too strong a word."

Ivy didn't agree. But perhaps he was still mourning his late wife too much to see anyone else in that light. "You must have loved her very much."

His surprised look brought heat to her cheeks. She hadn't intended to say that aloud. "Your wife, I mean," she added hastily. "Not Mrs. Swenson."

"Gretchen was a sweet, gentle woman who deserved better than me."

"I doubt she thought so."

"Nevertheless," he said, his tone relentlessly firm, "that was it for me. I don't plan to ever marry again."

Ivy felt as if she'd been slapped. She'd always known, of course, that any kind of permanent relationship with Mitch was out of the question, that after her case with Carter was settled she'd likely never see him again.

But just because her head knew that didn't mean her heart had accepted it.

"You shouldn't slam the door on the possibility. I mean, you never know wh—"

"That may be true for others, but my situation is different. I stand by my statement, and now I'd prefer we move on to another topic."

Ivy went back to work preparing a meal from scratch. He must have loved his wife deeply to refuse to marry another.

Surely she wasn't jealous of a dead woman?

Trying to move past her own reaction, Ivy realized she'd obviously touched a very raw nerve with Mitch, but it had been illuminating. He was even more stubbornly closed off than she'd imagined. And that was no way for a person to live.

She was more determined than ever to open his eyes. Now if she could just figure out how...

Mitch had seen the hurt look Ivy tried to mask before she turned away and felt a pang of regret for putting it there. But he knew he'd done the right thing. Now there would be no misunderstanding. If she had in fact formed any sort of affection for him, she was now aware that it could lead no further than friendship.

And if that thought left a sour feeling in his gut, well, it was just what he deserved.

She was quieter than usual as she worked at the stove. He wouldn't have been surprised if she refused to sit down to the meal with him, but to his relief that wasn't the case. But all through the meal he couldn't shake the feeling that she was studying him, but to what end he couldn't imagine.

He also found himself missing her cheerful chatter. Even the leading questions that normally started her talking failed to elicit more than direct responses.

When had her babble become so dear to him?

And what was he going to do when she returned to Nettles Gap for good?

Chapter Seventeen

Ivy rose early Wednesday morning. She wanted to get started on her laundry duties before the hottest part of the day.

Doing the laundry for herself and Mrs. Pierce wasn't much more work than doing it for herself and Nana Dovie. Mrs. Pierce's clothing was of a finer quality, but surprisingly worn. Perhaps she wanted to cling to her mourning clothes as long as possible.

As Ivy worked, her mind kept replaying yesterday's conversation with Mitch. She couldn't believe such a man could feel truly fulfilled leading a solitary life. Surely, in time, he'd find a woman who could bring him joy again.

But it obviously wouldn't be her. Still, she couldn't let that stop her from her self-appointed mission to help him. It was the right thing to do.

No matter how much it hurt.

When she'd hung the final load on the line, it was nearly noon.

It would be a while before the laundry was dry enough for her to take down. Perhaps she'd head over to Mitch's place. Just to see if he needed anything. And to check on Rufus, of course. She went to the back porch, then hesitated. She could see Mitch through the screen door. He was seated at the table, sketch pad spread out. Would he welcome her presence or was he savoring his solitude?

He looked up then, taking the decision from her hands.

She was gratified to see his smile of greeting. "Well, hello. Come on in."

"Actually, I'm just taking a break while I wait for the wash to dry. I thought I'd see if the garden needed watering and maybe give Rufus a walk."

Why did she suddenly feel so shy?

To cover her nervousness, she sat on the porch steps to greet an exuberant Rufus. A moment later, Mitch joined her outside, leaning against the nearby porch support. "I watered the garden earlier. And you should be enjoying your day off, not looking for additional chores to do."

She leaned back to avoid more of Rufus's slobbery kisses. "I don't really consider gardening and taking a stroll with Rufus doing chores."

"Have you eaten lunch yet?"

"I'll get something a little later." She was certain she could find something edible on her walk with Rufus. And she was still hoarding a bit of the hardtack he'd given her a few days ago.

"I was about to head over to The Blue Bottle to speak with Chance. Why don't you join me? I'm sure Eve would be glad to see you."

"That's really not necessary. I'll need to get back to check on the laundry in a little bit." She took a deep breath. "Actually, I had another reason for coming."

"Oh?"

"I wanted to apologize for yesterday. I overstepped with my comments about Mrs. Swenson and about your wife."

His expression closed off and he was silent for a long

moment. Then he straightened. "I insist you accompany me for lunch. We need to discuss your duties."

Ivy was confused. That was it? He wasn't going to acknowledge her apology? Then his words registered. Was he unhappy with her work? Or had her prying questions yesterday brought on his dissatisfaction? Or was it a combination of both? "Of course."

As they strolled toward The Blue Bottle, Ivy kept waiting for Mitch to speak up on whatever he wanted to discuss with her, but instead he seemed more interested in learning how her morning had gone.

By the time they reached their destination she realized she'd done most of the talking.

Mitch held the door as she stepped inside. She was very careful not to brush against him as she passed, but even so his closeness was highly distracting. It was getting harder and harder to deny her feelings.

Eve was transferring chocolate treats from a tray to a display stand on the counter. Chance sat at a workbench across the room, painting a wooden train.

"Mitch, Ivy—welcome!" Eve set the tray down and wiped her hands in the folds of her apron. "Can I interest you in something sweet?"

Mitch nodded a greeting. "Everything smells so good. Why don't you fix us a cup of whatever tea you have today, along with some of those fancy sandwiches you make."

Eve's brows lifted in surprise, but she recovered quickly. "Of course."

Then she turned to Ivy. "Just have a seat and I'll bring that right out."

Based on Eve's reaction to Mitch's request, Ivy gathered he didn't normally order tea and sandwiches. Was he doing all this for her benefit? And when was he going to let her know what he wanted to discuss with her?

As Ivy took her seat, she noticed Mitch and Chance deep in discussion. She couldn't hear what they were saying, but from the hand gestures Mitch was making, it appeared he was describing something he wanted Chance to build.

As she watched, she couldn't help but compare the two men. Chance was boyishly handsome with a ready smile and deep blue eyes. He always seemed relaxed and ready to enjoy whatever life tossed his way.

On the other hand, there was nothing boyish about Mitch. He was mature, impressive, solid. He exuded responsibility and dependability. There was something so admirable, so attractive in the quiet strength that was a natural part of him, and the control and grace with which he wielded that strength.

And while there might be some who preferred Chance's sunny good looks, she personally was partial to a man whose face reflected character and control, and whose manner suggested authority without being overbearing.

As soon as Eve stepped out of the kitchen, Mitch and Chance wrapped up their business.

Eve placed a cup of tea in front of Ivy, and a plate of daintily cut sandwiches on the table. "Today I have a peach tea. And two kinds of sandwiches—cheese and apple, and a chopped egg and vegetable mix."

It all sounded quite exotic to Ivy.

"Perfect," Mitch said as he joined them and took his seat.

Eve returned to the counter to finish unloading her tray of bonbons, leaving Mitch and Ivy to their tea and sandwiches.

Mitch picked up one of the tiny sandwiches, then moved the plate closer to her. "Help yourself."

She obediently took one and nibbled on it, watching

Mitch surreptitiously. He should have looked silly with that dainty cup and tiny sandwich in his huge hands. But he seemed completely at ease and entirely unselfconscious.

"Is something wrong with your sandwich?"

His question brought the heat to her cheeks as she realized she'd been staring rather than eating. "No, it's quite good." She took a large bite to prove her point and followed it with a sip of the delicious tea.

She turned to Eve. "You'll have to teach me how you make this tea. I'd like to fix some for my Nana Dovie when I go back to Nettles Gap."

Eve smiled. "Of course. Stop by whenever you have a few minutes and we'll brew a pot together."

Still very aware of the man sitting at her elbow, Ivy kept her gaze on Eve. "Where's Leo?"

"Ira took Leo and Jack fishing this morning. They're not back yet so either the fish are biting well and they don't want to quit, or they're not biting and they don't want to give up."

The talk of fishing put her in mind of the fishing she and Mitch had done back at the cabin, and she couldn't resist a quick look his way.

Sure enough, he was watching her with a smile.

"Ivy enjoys fishing, too," he said. "Even digs her own worms and baits her own hook. Or so she tells me."

"Is that so?" Chance said. "Maybe when Eve teaches her to make that tea, she can teach Eve to fish."

Eve shook her head firmly. "I'll cook 'em, but I'll leave the catching to those who enjoy it."

Chance gave an exaggerated sigh, then smiled "I suppose I'm still getting the better end of that bargain."

Eve blushed prettily under his smile, but gave a sassy toss of her head. "That you are."

A pang stabbed Ivy as she watched the affectionate exchange between them. She was very happy for them, of course, but it was hard to realize she would likely never experience that same closeness and intimacy with anyone. No one in Nettles Gap would look twice at her, and moving away from there was not an option.

This time, she resisted the impulse to look at Mitch. Instead, she focused on her food.

When they finally took their leave, Ivy decided she'd waited long enough. "You said you wanted to talk about my duties?"

"So I did. Do you know how to sew?"

That wasn't at all what she'd expected. "Depends what you mean by sewing. I can mend and patch just about anything. And I can make up a new piece of clothing if I have a pattern to work from. But I'm not very good at fancy work."

"How about curtains?"

Her spirits rose immediately. Was he ready to add some color to his place? "Of course. As long as you want something simple without ruffles and such."

He gave her a dry smile. "Definitely no on the ruffles."

"Are you planning to replace all the curtains or just some?"

"Neither. I want to add curtains to the kitchen window."

Ah, well, that was a start. "Do you already have the fabric?"

"No, but I'm sure we can find something at the mercantile."

He'd said *we*. If he really was willing to let her help select it, maybe she could talk him into something colorful. "I did notice they have a nice selection." She was already imagining a print of some sort with a bright blue as the prominent color.

"Shall we go take a look?" he asked.

"I probably should be getting back—"

"It won't take long, and there's no time like the present."

She was surprised by his insistence. "All right, I suppose the laundry *could* probably use a few extra minutes to dry."

When they arrived at the mercantile, Mitch placed a hand lightly at the small of her back and guided her down one of the aisles. Ivy was certain it was a reflexive gesture, totally impersonal and meant to be polite rather than affectionate.

But her reaction to it was anything but impersonal.

The table where the bolts of fabric were stacked was at the far end of the store and she remained acutely aware of the protective warmth of his touch the entire way. The walk seemed to take forever and end too quickly at the same time.

As soon as they reached the fabric table, Mitch stepped away from her and reached for a bolt near the top of the stack. "What do you think of this one?"

She tried to focus on the fabric. It was a tan-and-brown plaid with a thin maroon stripe providing the only hint of color.

She stifled a grimace. There was nothing inherently wrong with it, but she'd had something a little brighter in mind. "Perhaps something with a little more color."

To her relief, he didn't seem insulted. "Which one would you recommend?" Then he gave her a stern look. "No flowers."

She laughed, and the smile he gave her warmed her right down to her toes.

However was she going to make it through the rest of her time in Turnabout with her heart unscathed?

* * *

Mitch watched as Ivy studied the bolts of fabric. He hadn't been able to resist the urge to touch her, even if it was just to put a protective hand at her back.

He'd have to watch that in the future. Ivy was the last person he wanted to mislead.

She studied the bolts intently, as if it were a decision of utmost importance. He decided he liked the way her nose crinkled and her lips quirked up on one side when she was mentally working through a problem.

She fingered a yellow print covered with white flowers and then another that had white-and-yellow polka dots on a green background.

To his relief, she dismissed both of those and continued looking. With a triumphant grin she pulled out a bolt of blue gingham. Grabbing a corner of the fabric, she turned to him with a smile. "How's this?"

He pretended to study it critically. "It's not neutral, but I think I can live with it."

Mitch had turned to signal Doug Blakely, the owner of the mercantile, that they needed help when another customer walked in. To his chagrin, it was Hilda Swenson and her boys.

The widow caught sight of him at the same time, and her expression brightened. She immediately headed his way. "Mr. Parker, how nice to see you. Are you doing your shopping, too?"

When she spied Ivy, her expression slipped for just a moment, but she recovered quickly. "Miss Feagan. I thought you were off on Wednesdays."

Now, how had she learned Ivy's schedule?

"I am. I'm just helping Mr. Parker pick out some fabric for kitchen curtains."

"How very nice." The widow glanced at the fabric Ivy

had picked out. "Oh, my dear, surely you're not thinking of going with that gingham."

Mitch started to protest, but Ivy spoke up first.

"I know it's not the most colorful of prints, but I'm trying to keep in mind that this is for a bachelor's home."

So she'd picked up on his more conservative tastes, had she?

Mrs. Swenson nodded. "Of course. But just because men don't appreciate florals doesn't mean we must choose something dull." She stepped past Ivy and dug through the bolts stacked on the table. She finally pulled out one from the bottom of the pile. It had alternating stripes of red and blue separated by narrower strips of white.

"This one is much brighter and still has a masculine look to it, don't you agree?"

Ivy nodded. "You're right, this is a much better choice. I don't know how I missed it."

The woman preened. "I'm just more familiar with the offerings here." She glanced Mitch's way. "I confess I'm always on the lookout for ways to make my home cozier and more welcoming. Mr. Blakely lets me know when he has something that might interest me."

Mitch cleared his throat. "I think the fabric Miss Feagan selected is fine."

Ivy, however, disagreed. "But this one Mrs. Swenson found will work out much better than the gingham."

Before Mitch could respond, Mrs. Swenson spoke up again. "If your duties keep you too busy to sew, I'll be happy to make these curtains for Mr. Parker. Mr. Swenson used to say I was quite the seamstress. He took pride in showing off my domestic talents." She lifted her chin proudly. "And of course I make most of the clothes for myself and the boys." She fanned out one side of her skirt, inviting them to admire it.

"That's quite kind of you," Ivy responded, "but I consider this part of my job and wouldn't feel right letting someone else take care of it."

"But I—"

Mitch had had enough. "That's indeed a generous offer, but as I'm in no hurry, I'm certain Miss Feagan can work it into her schedule."

With a disappointed smile, the widow nodded. "Of course. But the offer stands if that changes." Then she tightened the strings on her purse. "Now, I'll leave you to finish making your purchase. And I'll see you tomorrow to discuss Peter's tutoring needs."

Later, when they stepped outside, Mitch offered Ivy an apologetic grimace. "I'm sorry if Mrs. Swenson's interference upset you. She can be overbearing at times."

"Not at all. She means well and she was right about the fabric." She hefted the parcel in her hands. "This piece is much better than the one I selected." She gave him a curious look. "I would think you'd be flattered by the attention. She's a handsome woman with a number of nice qualities that would make her a fine wife for some lucky man."

"She'd be better served to turn her attention elsewhere. I've tried to make my disinterest as clear as I can without being outright rude."

They stopped in front of Mitch's house and he opened the gate. Ivy handed him the fabric as Rufus raced to greet her.

She finally straightened. "Thank you for the tea and the company, but it's time I headed back. In this heat, I'm sure at least part of the laundry has dried."

"Of course. I'll see you in the morning."

Ivy started to turn away, then paused. "By the way, would you mind if I spoke to Mrs. Pierce about purchasing produce from her garden? She's harvesting more than she can use, and I like the idea of picking it fresh myself."

"Not at all. Tell her to keep tabs on the amount and I'll pay her once a week when I pay you."

Mitch watched Ivy walk away, surprised once again at her thoughtfulness. First her tactful handling of Hilda's interference and now this scheme to help Mrs. Pierce out.

He slowly headed for his backyard. He'd actually enjoyed their little shopping expedition today. Strange how even the most mundane tasks took on a sense of adventure when he was able to view them through her eyes.

He was going to miss that when she was gone.

That and much more than he cared to admit, even to himself.

Chapter Eighteen

Mitch was working on a sketch of Ivy seated on the swing when a knock at the door sounded the next morning, and he reluctantly put down his pencil. This time, he had no doubt as to who it was.

He wasn't happy at the interruption. It had been a long time since he'd had any interest in sketching a person, but he could see already that this sketch was going to be his finest work to date. If he could just capture her smile…

But before he could get up, Ivy appeared in the hallway and gave him a very firm look. "I'll get it."

With a smile, he settled back in his chair. She'd shown up at his kitchen door this morning with a determined look in her eye. She'd made quick work of breakfast and then shooed him away, saying she had baking to do and didn't want to be distracted.

He'd heard her humming and talking to herself for the past few hours and it had influenced his sketching, infusing the figure coming to life beneath his pencil with a joyous abandon.

"Mrs. Swenson, good day to you." Ivy's words carried clearly to him, and he smiled at her formal tone. "I believe

Mr. Parker is expecting you. If you and your boys will have a seat in the parlor, I'll let him know you're here."

Mitch put away his sketchbook as he waited for her to appear in the doorway, which she did almost immediately.

"Mrs. Swenson has arrived."

"So I heard."

She gave him another stern look. "I'll have refreshments ready in a few moments."

He knew it would be useless to tell her not to bother, so he merely nodded. He would let her have her moment, even if it might give Hilda Swenson the impression she was welcome here.

He straightened the papers on his desk, then headed to the parlor.

As soon as he stepped into the room the widow gave him a beaming smile. She sat on the sofa and her three boys occupied the other seating in the room.

He decided to remain standing for the moment.

"Peter, hand Mr. Parker your papers, please," she instructed.

The boy solemnly complied.

Mitch smiled down as he accepted the papers, trying to put the youngster at ease. "Thank you, Peter." He didn't like the idea of discussing the boy's work in front of his siblings. "Perhaps Peter and I should step into my office to review this."

"Oh, there's no need for that. I'm sure his brothers can learn from whatever you have to tell Peter."

Before Mitch could insist, Ivy returned carrying a tray loaded down with two teacups and a platter of sandwiches similar to what they'd had at Eve's place yesterday.

"I thought you might enjoy a bit of refreshment while you have your discussion." She set the tray down on a small table next to the sofa, then turned to the two younger boys.

"If you'd care to join me in the kitchen, I just took a tray of cookies out of the oven and need someone to taste them." Then she turned to Mrs. Swenson. "If it's okay with your mother, that is."

Mrs. Swenson graciously gave her permission and the two younger boys hopped up, eager to follow Ivy.

Before they exited, Ivy turned to Peter. "Don't worry. There'll be cookies left when you're done with your business here." Then she turned and ushered Peter's brothers out the door.

Had she overheard his request for more privacy with Peter? Or was she just intuitive when it came to the feelings of others?

Mrs. Swenson recaptured his attention as she reached for a teacup. "It was very charitable of you to hire Miss Feagan as your housekeeper," she said complacently.

Charity had had nothing to do with it, but he didn't feel the need to explain himself. "She's earning her wage."

"I'm certain she is. And she's providing a nice woman's touch to your place." She glanced at the wildflowers Ivy had placed on the mantel this morning. "In fact, I predict that you'll miss all these little niceties once she leaves."

Mrs. Swenson met Mitch's gaze head-on, as if she was intentionally reminding him that Ivy would be leaving soon. Mitch made a noncommittal sound, then turned to Peter. "Before I review your papers, why don't you tell me which parts of this test gave you the most trouble?"

Twenty minutes later, Mitch had finished his assessment. Peter seemed to have grasped all but a few of the basic principles. And the boy had meticulously detailed his computations, so it was easy to see where he'd gotten off track.

Mitch put a hand on Peter's shoulder and turned to the boy's mother. "There's no need to be concerned. Peter has a good understanding of the basics, and I think just a few sessions will set him on the right path."

Mrs. Swenson nodded. "And you'll work with him?"

He glanced down at the boy. "I'll be happy to."

"Then we should discuss payment."

Mitch frowned. "That won't be necessary. As I said, it won't take more than a couple of sessions, and I consider this part of my role as his teacher."

"Then at least let me bake something for you."

"That won't be—"

"Nonsense. I must repay you somehow. And I do so love to bake. Mr. Swenson used to say I was quite the dessert maker."

Apparently the late Mr. Swenson had seen no wrong in his wife. "I'm certain you are. But I have a cook so—"

Again she interrupted his protest. "I won't take no for an answer. Now, which days would be best for you to work with Peter?"

Mitch decided the sooner this was over, the better. "Let's plan on tomorrow and Saturday."

"Perfect."

"And it would be better if I saw Peter alone."

Her expression fell.

"It will allow him to focus solely on his work," he said smoothly. "I'm sure a good mother such as yourself can understand how important that would be."

The bit of praise from him seemed to restore her good humor. "Of course."

Mitch stood. "I won't keep you." He smiled down at the boy. "And don't worry, Peter. We'll have you tackling these math problems with confidence in no time."

Mrs. Swenson stood, as well. "I'm certain Peter will be grateful for your attention. I'll just fetch my other two boys and we'll be on our way."

Mitch wasn't at all sure Ivy would welcome Mrs. Swenson into her kitchen again. "Why don't I fetch them for you?"

She ignored his offer and moved toward the doorway. "No need. I know the way. Besides, I'm sure Peter is eager for the treat your housekeeper promised him."

He found her insistence on referring to Ivy by role rather than name irritating. When they reached the kitchen, Mrs. Swenson paused on the threshold so abruptly Mitch almost bumped into her.

"What is going on in here?" The widow's voice vibrated with outrage.

Mitch stepped past her and had to hide a grin.

Both boys stood on upside down crates around the table. They wore aprons made of large dish towels and were stirring the contents of a large bowl. Flour was everywhere, including the boys' faces and clothing. Ivy stood beside them, a damp cloth in her hand, and it appeared she'd been laughing just prior to their arrival. As for the boys, they were watching their mother with identical guilty expressions.

Ivy, still looking amused, spoke up first. "Don't worry. It's only flour." She gave the boys approving smiles. "Andy and Davey volunteered to help me make up a fresh batch of cookies. Unfortunately, the flour canister tipped over and a breeze from the window did the rest. My fault entirely." She began wiping the younger boy's face. "I'll have them cleaned up in no time."

Mrs. Swenson marched over, took the cloth from Ivy and began vigorously wiping her son's face. "And just what were my sons doing wearing aprons and mixing cookie dough?"

Ivy frowned uncertainly, as if unsure why the widow was angry. "I apologize if you disapprove. I assure you I wouldn't have let them do anything that—"

Mrs. Swenson cut her off. "Baking is not a skill my boys should be taught, nor do they need to be clothed in an apron. Baking is women's work."

"Quite the contrary," Mitch said, his voice deliberately cold. "Where I come from, some of the finest and most respected pastry chefs are men."

Mrs. Swenson's expression of righteous indignation faltered for a moment, but she recovered and rounded on Ivy again. "Be that as it may, I will thank you to refrain from assigning my sons work of any sort."

It took everything Mitch had not to cross the room and stand between Ivy and Mrs. Swenson's misguided tirade. His desire to protect her—and everything about her that was joyous and charming and thoughtful—was nearly overwhelming.

Ivy held her tongue with difficulty.

Yes, the woman was only being protective of her children, but her response seemed out of proportion to the offense.

She'd appreciated Mitch's ready defense and while a part of her felt the woman deserved a bit of a set down, she did understand that the woman was only being protective of her children. And it wasn't right to argue with her in front of her sons.

Ivy took a deep breath, reminding herself that she was an employee in this house, and needed to act accordingly. "Please accept my apologies, Mrs. Swenson. Of course I should have asked your permission before allowing your sons to help me. But you can be proud of what polite, helpful boys you're raising here."

The widow seemed to collect herself and gave a short nod. "Thank you. And I'm certain you meant well. I'm sorry if I was abrupt."

With the truce now having been called, quick work was made of getting the children cleaned up. Ivy handed Peter his promised treat and the Swensons finally made their exit.

Ivy went to work scrubbing down the table. To her surprise, however, Mitch returned to the kitchen after he saw his guests out.

She paused long enough to meet his gaze. "Was she still angry?"

"I think she'll get over it."

Was that a glint of amusement in his eyes?

She tried to remain contrite. "I should have thought it through before I invited the boys to help."

"Perhaps. But based on the condition of the kitchen, I'd guess they were enjoying themselves."

Her grin broke through. "That they were."

"And I daresay, Mrs. Swenson may think twice before she brings them here to suffer under your influence again." He gave her a mock frown. "Which is such a shame."

This time she laughed out loud. "You, sir, are not fooling anyone."

He grabbed the broom and helped her finish cleaning up the mess, whistling as he went.

Ivy thought she'd never heard a finer bit of music.

As they exited the church together on the following Sunday, Everett called Mitch over to discuss something about a story he was working on. Ivy waved him on, secretly pleased that he'd glanced her way before leaving her side.

She was looking forward to again having Sunday lunch with Mitch's friends, people she was beginning to think of as her friends, too. She'd once again made arrangements to purchase flowers from her landlady's garden, and was trying to decide whether she should go on and take care of that or wait for Mitch when Mrs. Ortolon approached her.

"How are you this fine Sunday morning?" she asked Ivy.

"I'm doing quite well, thank you. And you?"

"My rheumatism is acting up, but I can't complain," she said with a long-suffering sigh. Then she gave Ivy a sympathetic smile. "But what about you? I understand that you'd fallen and injured yourself when Mr. Parker found you. I hope you've fully recovered."

"Yes, ma'am." Ivy glanced toward Mitch, thinking what a fine hero he made.

"Well, it's unfortunate that you were hurt all the same. But I must say, that aside, it sounds like a very romantic way to meet."

Ivy nodded, smiling at the memory of those two days at the cabin. "He *was* quite heroic. Bandaged my head, then just lifted me up and plopped me onto that great big horse of his like I didn't weigh more than a pup." She smiled at the memory. "He made me ride while he walked all the way to the cabin. He even cooked me a broth and tended to my mule."

The woman's sharp intake of breath brought Ivy's gaze quickly back around.

"The cabin?" The woman's eyes had narrowed. "I thought Mr. Parker found you on the trail back to town."

The warmth rose in Ivy's cheeks as she realized her slip. Mrs. Ortolon watched her like a child eyeing a new toy.

What had she done?

This was exactly what Mitch had warned her about.

Ivy scrambled for a way to divert the woman's suspicions. "Actually, I was on my way here, but when Mr. Parker found me I wasn't far from the cabin so he took me there first to tend to my cut and let me rest for a bit. Then we came on to town."

Strictly speaking, that sequence of events *was* correct. So why did she feel as if she'd just told a fib?

"Of course."

From the look on her face, Ivy could tell the woman wasn't going to let the matter drop.

Mrs. Ortolon watched her closely. "I believe that wagon you two rode into town on came from the Morrisons' place just outside of town."

"Yes, ma'am. They generously loaned it to us when Mr. Parker told them of our situation."

"Isn't Reggie's cabin quite some distance from the Morrisons' place?"

Ivy didn't like the speculative gleam in the woman's eye. She wished Mitch were here to extricate her from this mess.

As if he'd heard her unvoiced plea, Mitch appeared at her side. "Mrs. Ortolon, how nice to see you."

"Thank you. Miss Feagan and I were just having an interesting conversation on the circumstances of your meeting."

Mitch's expression didn't change and his demeanor remained unruffled, but Ivy could sense tension in him.

"Yes, it was quite fortuitous. But if you'll excuse us, Miss Feagan and I are meeting friends for lunch."

As they moved away, Ivy cast a guilty glance his way. "I'm sorry. I'm afraid I may have let more slip than I intended to."

"What exactly did you tell her?"

Ivy quickly related the conversation. When she was done, Mitch grimaced.

"I'm so sorry."

"You aren't the first to let a secret slip to that woman.

She can sniff out gossip like a buzzard scents carrion." He let out a heavy breath. "What's done is done. The question now is, what do we do about it?"

Ivy worried at her lip. "Do you really think it's that bad? I mean, she doesn't know anything for certain."

"That won't matter. She'll relay what she knows and follow it up with 'surely you don't think they…' or 'far be it from me to surmise, but…' And before long the damage will have been done."

Ivy didn't like the set, tight-jawed look on Mitch's face. She liked even less that she'd put it there. If he was right, then this development didn't just affect her—there would be repercussions for him, as well. And it was all her fault. She'd done to him what Lester had done to her, though in her case it hadn't been deliberate.

How could she have been so careless?

Chapter Nineteen

Mitch remained silent as he escorted Ivy to Mrs. Pierce's home. But his mind was churning furiously, trying to process what Ivy's slip of the tongue meant for the two of them. There was a small chance, of course, that nothing would come of it. But he needed to be prepared for the worst. He needed to prepare *Ivy* for the worst.

And come what may, he would make sure she didn't suffer for this. Even if it meant he had to go back on his vow to never remarry. Surprisingly that prospect didn't bother him as much as it would have a mere week ago.

He placed his hand on the gate to Mrs. Pierce's front walk, but didn't open it. He waited for Ivy to meet his gaze, but she didn't seem inclined to do that anytime soon.

"Ivy," he said gently, "we need to talk about this."

She finally looked up, and the regret in her eyes was almost his undoing. "I'm so sorry," she said. "You warned me, but I didn't take it seriously enough."

He touched her arm. It was supposed to be a gesture of comfort, but he felt something more pass between them. "It's not the end of the world. If the worst happens, I promise to step up and give you the protection of my name."

She withdrew her arm from his hold. "I wouldn't dream of asking you to make such a sacrifice."

By the tone of her voice and the injured pride in her expression he realized he'd flubbed his offer. "I truly wouldn't mind."

She opened the gate, her posture stiff. "I know you mean well, but there's no need. Now, let me take care of the flowers so we can be on our way." And with that, she marched toward the porch.

Mitch rubbed the back of his neck. What now? How could he make this right?

"Ivy, I'm sorry if—"

"You've nothing to apologize for. It was an honorable gesture. But we both know how you feel about getting married again, so you'll be relieved to know I release you from all responsibility."

Was she wielding the garden shears with just a little more vigor than necessary? "Will you please just put that down and talk to me face-to-face for a moment?"

She ignored his request. "There's nothing further to say. And we don't want to keep your friends waiting."

And no matter how much he tried, she refused to budge from her position.

It was a quiet walk to The Blue Bottle.

As soon as they stepped inside, it was obvious from the sympathetic looks that everyone had already heard the rumors.

Ivy excused herself and scuttled off to the kitchen as if she couldn't get away from him fast enough.

Mitch watched the kitchen door close behind her, his frustration curling his hands into fists at his sides. Surely there was something he could do to fix this.

He turned to find all three of his friends regarding him with sympathy. He grimaced. "How bad is it?"

Adam answered first. "Reggie was approached by two different people who heard second- and thirdhand that you and Ivy spent time together at our cabin."

"Mrs. Ortolon was flitting around the churchyard like a bee in a flower garden," Chance added.

"It was entirely innocent," Mitch explained through his clenched jaw. "She was injured and her mule had come up lame. We had no choice."

"We never thought otherwise," Adam assured him.

The other two men nodded agreement, and Mitch felt some of his stiffness ease. He thanked them with a nod and rubbed his jaw. "I plan to do the right thing, of course," he said. "I'm just having trouble convincing Ivy that marrying me *is* the right thing."

Everett clapped him on the back, and Mitch remembered that the newspaperman had once been in a similar situation when Eunice Ortolon had discovered an unlocked door that connected his apartment to Daisy's.

"She hasn't had time to think it through," his friend said in that clipped British accent of his. "Give her time. She'll come around."

Mitch certainly hoped Everett was right.

Ivy stepped into the kitchen, tightly clutching the basket of flowers. What sort of reception would these women give her? If they turned cold or distant, she wasn't sure she could bear it. In fact, it might be best for everyone if she just found an excuse to leave now, before things got awkward or uncomfortable. If she said she felt ill, that wouldn't be a lie—her stomach was tied in knots so tight she'd never be able to eat a bite anyway.

But the women were so unbelievably supportive she almost broke down and cried right there.

Immediately she was engulfed by her friends. Mrs. Peavy

took the basket of flowers, Reggie led her to the table and Eve placed a warm cup of tea in her hands.

What should she say? Explanations tumbled around in her mind, chaotic thoughts out of sequence and incomplete. What came out was "It wasn't Mitch's fault."

"Of course it wasn't." Eve patted her hand. "And I'm sure it wasn't yours, either."

"Nothing happened."

"You don't have to explain yourself to us." Reggie took the chair beside her. "We know Mitch is honorable, and we can see what high regard he has for you."

Mitch held her in high regard?

She looked at Reggie. "I stayed two nights at your cabin and borrowed some of your things—I'm sorry I didn't tell you sooner."

Reggie waved a hand dismissively. "Don't give that another thought. I'm just glad it was there when you needed it."

Why were these women being so nice? Would they feel the same if they knew her whole story?

Daisy placed a hand on her shoulder. "You look like you could use a bit of fresh air. Why don't we step out back for a moment?"

Ivy frowned, not certain why Daisy had issued the unexpected invitation, but she saw something in the woman's eyes that convinced her to accept the offer.

They walked in silence for a moment, and then Daisy spoke up. "I understand how you're feeling, because something very similar happened to me."

Ivy shot her a disbelieving look. "What do you mean?"

"I mean Everett and I were the subject of some rather unpleasant gossip, and were more or less backed into a corner where we had to announce our engagement."

"How awful. But, I mean, it seems obvious you two love each other."

Daisy's smile softened. "Very much. Only it wasn't so obvious then, and I didn't much cotton to the idea of marrying someone who didn't really want to be married."

So Daisy *did* understand. But then again, Daisy wasn't dragging a sullied past into the marriage with her. "Thank you for sharing that with me."

"I told you because I don't want you to lose heart. I've seen the way Mitch looks at you, and you at him. The two of you are good with and for each other."

Ivy wished that were true. "Thank you, but this is more complicated than it appears. We're friends and that's as far as it *can* go. I'll be returning to Nettles Gap in a couple of weeks and then Mitch can get on with his life."

"I don't believe that will be as easy for him as you think."

Ivy's heart fluttered at that. But much as she wanted to believe it, she was sure Daisy was mistaken. Besides, what was the use? There were too many obstacles in their way. And now this.

She mustered a smile. "We ought to be getting back. It'll be time to set the table by now."

Daisy touched her arm lightly. "Please think about what I said. And no matter what you decide, remember that you have friends here."

There was no further mention of the gossip, and the meal proceeded as it had the previous Sunday. But this time Ivy studiously avoided looking Mitch's way.

She couldn't keep him from her thoughts, though. She remained acutely aware of his every movement, his every word. And try as she might, she couldn't forget what Daisy had told her.

Later, as they left The Blue Bottle together, Ivy nervously waited for Mitch to say something. Would he press her to marry him again, or had he accepted her refusal as the out he needed?

When they reached the crossroad where they would normally turn to go to his home, Ivy halted. "Perhaps I should leave you here."

He frowned down at her. "We need to talk. The sooner we settle this matter, the better."

"I consider it already settled."

His frown deepened. "Do you really want to have this discussion here on this street corner?"

She glared at him. She was not going to let him bully her into giving in. "I certainly don't think it advisable for us to have it inside your house right now."

His jaw worked for a moment, and then he nodded. "Agreed. We can have our discussion as we walk Rufus." He arched a brow. "Assuming that's acceptable?"

She supposed she couldn't put him off forever. She gave what she hoped was a regal nod. "It is."

No sooner were they following an exuberant Rufus out the front gate than Mitch said, "We must announce our engagement immediately."

Well, at least he wasn't beating around the bush. "We'll do no such thing."

"I understand that this isn't the ideal arrangement for either of us, but there's no other solution. You may think you don't care about your reputation, but believe me, when everyone starts whispering and staring, you'll change your mind."

"I won't." She took a deep breath. It was time to be totally honest. "And I'm not guessing. I've already been through that, and I know exactly how it feels."

He stopped in his tracks. "What do you mean?"

She turned to face him, her gaze locked to his with

all the intensity she could muster. "My reputation was already shredded five years ago."

Mitch saw the pain behind her brave facade. Who had hurt her? He suddenly wanted to find whoever was responsible for that haunted look in her eyes and make him pay.

They were passing the deserted school yard, and he led her to one of the swings. He leaned against a tree and waited for her to explain.

She finally met his gaze. "Aren't you going to ask me what happened?"

"Only if you want to tell me. But I know whatever happened, you were wronged."

He saw her eyes fill with tears then, but she didn't allow them to fall. Instead, she nodded and pushed the swing into a lazy rocking motion. "I'd like to tell you about it."

"Then I'm honored to listen."

"When I was sixteen, a young man decided to court me. To this day, I'm not really certain why. He was quite prominent in our community—the son of the mercantile owner—and several girls had made it clear they would welcome his advances. The thing was, I didn't share his feelings and tried to tell him so. But he apparently thought I was just being coy."

Mitch thought of his situation with Mrs. Swenson. But how much worse must it have been for her?

She wrapped her arms around the ropes holding up the swing. "Finally, at one of the town dances, when he was being particularly insistent, I made my feelings very clear, telling him in no uncertain terms just how I felt. Unfortunately, the encounter was not as private as I'd thought and Lester felt humiliated."

So this cad's name was Lester.

"Lester couldn't accept what I'd done—not when I'd so

inadvertently but thoroughly stomped on his pride. So he figured out a way to get even."

Mitch hadn't even heard what the cad had done and already he was ready to throttle him. It was probably just as well the oaf wasn't in striking distance.

"We had a goat that liked to wander off. He never went far, but one day I had trouble finding him and ended up going farther into the woods than I'd realized. Then I found the animal tied to a tree. Before I could do more than wonder what was going on, someone placed a bag over my head and tied my hands behind my back. Then, without saying a word, he forced me to walk what seemed a long ways. The more I struggled, the tighter his grip on my shoulder."

She rubbed her shoulder, as if reliving the experience. Mitch's hands fisted helplessly at his sides, but, sensing she needed to keep going, he didn't say anything.

"He finally stopped and then pushed me to the ground. I struggled to get back on my feet, more afraid than I'd ever been in my whole life, wondering what would happen next. But nothing did. I couldn't hear anyone, and because the sack was over my head, I couldn't see anything, either. I finally realized he'd just abandoned me there. I stumbled around for a bit, then somehow managed to get that sack off."

That was his girl, resourceful even when scared out of her wits.

"Whoever had tied me up was long gone. But I had no idea where I was. I didn't have any choice but to start walking. After about twenty minutes, a stranger found me. At first I thought it was the person who'd tied me up and I started running from him. But he caught up with me and was very kind. Said he'd been out hunting when he spotted me. He untied me and helped me find my way back to town."

She stopped, but he had a feeling there was more to the story, so he bided his time without responding. But it was very hard not to pull her into his arms then and there.

"We came out of the woods in a spot near the Lowells' farm. They were having a barn raising and most of the town was there. It was late evening and folks were gathering up their things. I was so relieved to see familiar faces I almost sobbed."

She paused for a long moment. "And just as we cleared the woods, the man who'd rescued me pulled me into a tight embrace and gave me a kiss, right on the lips. I could hear the gasps even from a distance."

He wanted to gather her into his arms and give her what comfort he could. But not here in the open. He'd be doing her no favors if he did that.

"He finally stepped back," she continued, "gave my cheek a pat, then turned and marched back into the woods, leaving me to face everyone alone. I knew I looked a sight—my dress was dirty and torn, my hair in wild disarray." Her expression turned grimmer still. "And then I saw Lester, smirking at me, enjoying my disgrace. And I knew—deep in my heart, I *knew*—that he had planned the whole thing."

She pushed the swing in motion again. "After that, my reputation was in shreds. Everyone believed the worst. I was shunned by most everyone in town." She looked up at him. "So you see, there's no need to worry about my 'good name,' because I haven't had one in a very long time."

Everything inside Mitch was wound tight enough to explode. He could barely breathe right now the need to avenge her was so strong. If the cowardly little weasel had been in Turnabout, there was no telling what he would have done. But right now he had Ivy's feelings to consider. And he was more determined than ever to give her the protection of his name. "Perhaps that's true in Nettles Gap, but not here."

She smiled sadly. "I think the events of today paint a different story."

"Not if you marry me. Even if it's an in-name-only arrangement, if you move here you'll have a fresh start and friends who will welcome you into their midst."

She firmly shook her head. "That's a very generous offer, especially given your feelings about getting married again."

Was that what was holding her back? He should never have told her how he felt, even if he'd thought at the time he was protecting her.

Or maybe he'd just been trying to protect himself.

"Besides, once this case is resolved I'll be headed back to Nettles Gap."

"But you don't have to—head back to Nettles Gap, I mean. Once the judge settles this case you'll own land here. Why not move here where you can get a fresh start? Turnabout is a really good place for that."

"I told you, Nana Dovie won't leave home, and I won't leave Nana Dovie."

It seemed they were at an impasse. "Then at least marry me before you go. You can return to Nettles Gap as my wife. That should change your standing in the community."

For a moment he thought she would agree, but then she shook her head. "Thank you, but I can't."

"Can't? Or won't? You need to take emotions out of this and be reasonable."

"I *am* being reasonable. When I marry, it's going to be for love. Otherwise, everything I've gone through the past five years has been for nothing."

Mitch had no response to that. The fact that her words indicated she didn't love him was irrelevant.

So why did he feel this stab of disappointment?

Brushing that thought aside, he tried again. "If you can't do it for yourself, then do it for me."

"What do you mean?"

"I don't want to be known as a man who won't take responsibility for his mistakes."

She winced, then straightened. "I think your reputation is strong enough to survive this, especially once I'm gone." She lifted her chin. "But if you're really worried, I can make it obvious that you asked and I refused."

"Will you do it to save me from the advances of women like Mrs. Swenson?"

At least that won him a grin. "Coward. I'm afraid you'll have to find another way to deal with the women who are attracted to you." She stood and brushed at her skirt. "Now, I think Rufus has chased enough squirrels for the afternoon."

"We're not through with this discussion."

"I am. At least for today." She whistled for Rufus and began to walk away.

Mitch shook his head and followed the frustrating woman.

Ivy held herself together by sheer willpower. She was doing the right thing, so why did it hurt so much? For all his support and kindness, Mitch had never once mentioned love.

She didn't know why she'd thought he might—perhaps it was Daisy's comments that had planted that idea in her mind. But it was now crystal clear that he was proposing marriage out of a sense of obligation and nothing more. He wanted to protect her and that was admirable, but it wasn't the same as love.

The problem was, she now realized, *she* loved *him*.

There it was, plain as the sun in the sky and every bit as big. She loved him, and because she did, she couldn't allow him to sacrifice himself for her.

No matter how sweet the thought of a life with him sounded.

Mitch walked her to Mrs. Pierce's house and left her at the front gate. She could tell he was unhappy with her decision, but there was no help for it. And after she'd returned to Nettles Gap, he'd realize she'd been right.

The first thing Ivy did when she stepped inside the house was seek out her landlady, whom she found doing some stitchwork in the parlor.

"I suppose you heard the whispers," she said without preamble.

Mrs. Pierce looked up from her stitchery. "I don't indulge in idle chitchat much these days." There seemed to be a wealth of meaning in her words.

Ivy took a deep breath, drew her shoulders back and met the woman's mildly curious gaze. "They're saying that Mr. Parker and I spent time together at the cabin before coming into town."

The widow set the cloth and needle on the sofa, and then folded her hands in her lap. "And did you?"

Ivy tilted her chin up. "I was injured and Mr. Parker didn't have a way to get me into town right away."

"So that means yes."

Ivy gave a short nod. It was hard to tell what the woman was thinking. "If you want me to move out, just say the word."

"What you did or did not do is none of my concern so long as you continue to pay the rent and follow my rules."

Some of the rigidness left Ivy's spine. "Of course."

"Will you be continuing to work for Mr. Parker?"

"For now. We want to go on as before."

"I see." Mrs. Pierce picked up her sewing again. "If, by some happenstance, you find yourself no longer able to work for Mr. Parker, I may have some work for you myself."

Ivy was both surprised and touched by the out-of-the-blue offer. "What kind of work?"

"I hear you are making curtains for Mr. Parker's kitchen, so I assume you can sew."

Ivy nodded.

"I have decided it's time to add a bit of color to my wardrobe again. But none of my older gowns fit as they should. I need someone to take them in for me."

"I would be more than happy to help you with that task in the evenings."

"Then we will come up with a price per garment that we can agree on and adjust your weekly rent payment accordingly."

"Mrs. Pierce, I meant I would be glad to help you as a *friend*."

The woman paused midstitch for just a heartbeat. Then she nodded. "Thank you."

"If you like, you could select several pieces now and we could take a look at what needs to be done."

The woman rose gracefully from the sofa. "I suppose that would be acceptable." She moved to the doorway, then paused and glanced back at Ivy, her demeanor cool. "And afterward, perhaps you would care to join me for supper." Her expression softened. "And please, call me Eileen."

"I'd be honored."

Ivy watched Eileen leave the room. This had definitely been a day of emotional highs and lows. She'd let slip the secret that brought her and Mitch under judgmental scrutiny. But then God had used the opportunity to show her what good friends she had in the women who were part of the Sunday lunch gathering.

Mitch had tried to convince her to marry him and in doing so had made it clear that he didn't love her. But she had discovered that she loved him, and though it was a bittersweet realization, it was one she still treasured.

And now she had this new opportunity to crack through the wall Eileen Pierce had built around herself and forge a friendship.

Dear Lord, I'd hoped this little vacation from everyone looking down their nose at me would last while I was here. But I did this to myself so I don't have any call to be complaining. Thank You for giving me a passel of blessings to help offset the trials. Please help me to focus on those blessings, and to make my peace with the trials.

And chief among those blessings was Mitch. No matter the outcome, she would never be sorry for this time she'd had with him.

And she still had to find a way to help him. On top of everything else, she had to make sure this gossip didn't hurt him.

But how?

The next morning, Ivy did her best to hold her head up and smile as she walked through town. She hoped for the best but braced herself for snubs.

The first few people she encountered seemed more uncertain than affronted. She received tentative smiles and nods in return for her greetings. She saw a couple of women on the other side of the street whispering behind their hands, and she tried to convince herself they were talking about something besides her.

Then, as she passed Daisy's restaurant, Abigail stepped out onto the sidewalk. She linked her arm through Ivy's with a smile. "Mind if I walk to the mercantile with you? I need to pick up some flour for Daisy."

"Of course." Had this been Abigail's idea or had Daisy put her up to it? Regardless, Ivy was grateful for the show of support. Especially when they arrived at the mercantile to find Mrs. Ortolon there talking to two other ladies.

The conversation came to an abrupt stop when they entered. Abigail ignored it all, and keeping her arm firmly locked with Ivy's, she approached the counter and greeted the proprietor as well as Mrs. Ortolon and her friends.

Ivy almost felt sorry for them. Abigail was relentless in her cheerful chatter, giving them no choice but to respond or seem churlish. When they parted company, Abigail gave her a very tight, very public hug. "Don't forget you have friends here," the girl whispered. And then she was gone.

Buoyed by that encounter, Ivy had no trouble keeping a smile on her face as she walked the rest of the way to Mitch's.

She arrived to find him standing outside talking to two young men.

He immediately waved her over. "I'd like to introduce you to Calvin and James Hendricks. I've hired them to paint my house and shutters."

Both youths tipped their hats respectfully in response to her greeting, then turned back to their work.

Ivy frowned. Mitch's house didn't really need painting. Maybe she'd had some influence on him and he'd decided to add some color. She leaned forward, eager to check out the paint cans, then dropped back on her heels in disappointment. It was stark white, the same color as his existing walls.

She shook her head. "While you're going to all of this trouble, might I suggest you at least think about painting your shutters red to match your door."

Mitch studied his house for a moment, then nodded. "Good idea." He turned to the older of the young men. "Calvin, we may need another can of the red paint."

Calvin saluted with his paintbrush. "Yes, sir, I'll take care of it."

As Ivy watched this exchange, it suddenly hit her—Mitch had hired the Hendricks brothers not because he had a pressing need to paint his home, but to serve as very visible chaperones for the next few days.

She didn't know whether to be grateful or irritated. Then she decided she was a little of both.

As she climbed the back porch steps, she mentally reviewed her basket of groceries and what she could remember of the pantry contents and decided it would stretch to feed two additional people who would likely have hearty appetites after working out in this heat all morning. She'd decided last night that one way to try to help him was to get him to talk about his wife. It was an understandably touchy subject for him, but she needed to understand, and she also felt it would be good for him to share his hurt, as well.

She just had to find the right time....

Mitch watched as Ivy dusted the bookshelves. She seemed unusually pensive this afternoon. Was the gossip taking its toll on her? Perhaps it was time to renew his efforts. "So, have you been thinking about what we discussed yesterday?"

She didn't turn around. "It would be hard not to."

Her dry tone gave nothing away. "And are you ready to see reason and admit marriage is the best course of action? I assure you, I *will* let you go your own way afterward if that's what you want."

She was silent for a long moment, and he wished she would turn around so he could see her face. Finally, she did.

"I told you, when I marry, it will be for love."

There was a finality in her tone that seemed to slam the door on the subject. But it was the words themselves that struck him hard. She was saying she wouldn't marry him because she didn't love him.

Not that he was looking for love from her. It was just, well, didn't she feel even the least bit of affection?

"Do you mind if I ask you something personal?"

There was something in her tone that told him he wouldn't like the question. Still, he couldn't bring himself to deny her, so he gave a short nod.

"What was your wife like?"

Mitch kept his expression carefully neutral, but it took some effort. "The first word that comes to mind when thinking of Gretchen is *gentle.* She was a very sweet, very delicate woman."

Ivy nodded. "You must have loved her very much."

Mitch straightened a few papers on his desk, not meeting her gaze. He had cared for Gretchen, very much. But—

He realized Ivy was still waiting for his answer. "Everyone who knew Gretchen loved her." He moved a stack of papers on his desk by a half inch. "And she loved me, right up until the day she died, though I never did quite figure out why."

"I know why." Her soft words caught him by surprise and he glanced up quickly.

She reddened and turned back to her dusting. "That's why you're so set against getting married again, isn't it? You're still in mourning and don't want to go through the pain of losing someone again." She shot him a look over her shoulder. "But that's the wrong way to look at it. If you don't let yourself love again, it's true you might never again hurt as deeply, but you'll never find joy, either. And that would be very sad."

"I've asked you to marry me, haven't I?"

"Because you feel like you must, not because you want to."

"Why does that matter?"

She shrugged. "Because it does."

He hesitated a moment. She'd bared her soul to him yesterday. Now it was his turn. "You're wrong."

That earned him a startled look.

"About the reason behind my decision to not marry again," he explained. "It's not because I mourn Gretchen so deeply. It's because I killed her."

Chapter Twenty

Ivy wasn't certain she'd heard right. "By accident, you mean."

His lips compressed in a hard line. "It was a deliberate action on my part that led to her death."

Just as she'd thought. "Then you didn't kill her. You just feel responsible for whatever happened." She crossed the room to stand in front of his desk. "Tell me what happened."

He raked a hand through his hair. "Gretchen didn't believe in violence, not for any reason, not even in self-defense. She believed one should always turn the other cheek, no matter what. And I tried to live that way, for her sake."

"Tried?"

"Pacifism doesn't come easily to me. But I was successful, for a time. Then one of our neighbors, a fellow named Early, started a feud over land boundaries. And no matter how much Gretchen pleaded with me to just give in, I wouldn't do it. I'd worked that land with my own two hands and I intended it to be a legacy to my children someday."

"It was your right to stand up for what was yours."

Mitch continued as if she hadn't spoken. "The dispute

escalated. I took Early to court and won my case. I was quite proud of myself. I'd managed to hold on to my land without resorting to violence."

He made a sound that was full of self-derision. "But the man's son decided to ignore the judge's orders and began tearing down fences. Before I could do anything about it, he broke his neck when his horse threw him. Unfortunately, it happened on my property. When I carried his body back to his father, he didn't believe it was an accident."

How awful that must have been—for all parties.

"No matter how I tried to explain, Early blamed me. That night he came riding onto my place all drunk and wild-eyed and ready for blood. Gretchen begged me to stay inside, but I stepped out with my rifle. There was a gunfight and a stray bullet found its way into the house and killed Gretchen."

His gaze finally met hers again and she was shocked at the bleakness she saw there. "She was carrying our baby at the time," he said dully.

Jagged shards of horror pierced Ivy's heart at the thought of what he'd gone through. She came around to his side of the desk and took both of his hands. "Oh, Mitch, I'm so sorry. That must have been terrible for you." She squeezed his hands. "But her death was *not* your fault."

"Wasn't it? If I had done what Gretchen wanted, if I had turned the other cheek and not taken him to court, Gretchen and the baby would still be alive."

"You can't know that for sure."

"Their chances would certainly have been better."

"But what would have happened to you?"

"Me? I would have been poorer, but I imagine I would have survived, as well."

"Physically. But if you had done as your wife wished

and let that neighbor run roughshod over you, it would have eaten away at the part of you that needs to take care of your family and build a home that is safe and secure. It would have made you feel less of a man and more than likely affected the way you viewed your relationship with your wife."

He gave her a self-mocking smile. "Don't you believe in turning the other cheek, in reserving vengeance for the Lord, the way it says in the Bible?"

"There is a time and place for that. But there is also a time to stand up and defend yourself and your loved ones. And yes, that's biblical."

He didn't seem entirely convinced.

"Mitch, have you prayed about this?"

"I haven't come to terms with God on this matter yet." He said this almost defiantly, as if trying to shock her. "I went a little crazy for a while. Nearly killed Early and did some property damage." His lips twisted in a grimace. "It should have been me who died that night, not Gretchen."

"Don't you dare say that. Don't even think it. God left you here for a reason—don't try to second-guess Him. It's hard when we lose our loved ones, but we've got to trust that God is in control and that He loves us." She saw a flicker of doubt in his eyes. "He *does* love you," she said firmly. "There's nothing you can do that He won't forgive, if you just ask Him to."

Mitch pulled his hands from hers and stood. "If you'll excuse me, I think I'll go see how the Hendricks boys are doing." And with that, he strode from the room.

Ivy stood there for a long time after he'd gone, her heart breaking for him. The story he'd related had been truly heartrending—to have lost not only his wife but his unborn child in such a manner—how had he borne up under such pain? That was a terrible burden to carry all on his own. No wonder he was afraid to give his heart again.

But his thinking was flawed. Somehow she had to make him see that.

It had become her new goal.

Later that afternoon Ivy answered a knock at Mitch's door to find Carter Mosley standing there, hat in hand.

"Miss Feagan, could I speak to you for a few minutes?"

She opened the door. "Of course. Come in."

Mitch stepped out into the hall. "Who is it?" Then he saw Carter and his eyes narrowed. "Is there something I can do for you?"

"Actually, I came to speak to Miss Feagan."

"Perhaps you should wait to do your talking when the judge arrives."

Ivy held up a hand. "No, it's all right. I'd like to hear what he has to say."

Mitch crossed his arms. "Then I hope the two of you won't mind if I sit in."

"Not at all." Carter fingered the brim of his hat. "Look, I know I wasn't very civil last time we spoke, and you have every right to be angry, but I'm sorry for that and I hope you'll hear me out now."

Mitch waved an arm toward the parlor. "Let's talk in here."

As soon as they took their seats, Carter began. "I won't lie. I didn't believe your story. And I'm afraid I acted badly." He gave her a penitent look. "For that, you have my apologies."

Ivy relaxed. "Of course. You were grieving your uncle's death and it was unfair of us to spring that on you so quickly."

He nodded acceptance of her forgiveness. "I didn't

leave it there. I sent one of the hands, a man I respect, to Nettles Gap to check things out and learn what he could about you."

Ivy tensed again. Surely he had heard about her ruined reputation. Would he spread the stories here to enforce the current gossip?

"Sonny talked to a number of people there," Carter continued. "And he learned that you are exactly who you say you are, Robert Feagan's daughter."

"And?" At least the story about what Lester had done to her wouldn't come as a surprise to Mitch.

"*And,* after reading the papers my uncle left me, including a journal, I'm withdrawing my objections to your claim. I'd like us to settle this matter without going to court."

Ivy blinked. It was impossible to believe his man hadn't heard the gossip from Nettles Gap. Why hadn't he brought it up? But Carter was watching her with something very akin to neighborly sympathy. Was silence on the matter his way of strengthening his apology?

"I'd like that, too," she said with a more genuine smile.

Mitch leaned forward. "What sort of settlement did you have in mind?"

"Something that will be fair to all parties, that will honor Uncle Drum's wishes. We can work through the details when we get down to drawing up the paperwork." He stood. "I need to get back to the ranch, but with your permission, I'll set up an appointment with Mr. Barr for later in the week. Hopefully we'll be able to work things out to everyone's satisfaction in very short order."

Ivy accepted his outstretched hand and shook it. "That's my hope, as well."

"Once we determine what portion of the estate you're

entitled to," Carter said diffidently, "I hope you'll consider letting me buy you out."

Ivy smiled. "Of course. And I want you to know that I don't intend to take advantage. My pa didn't put all the hard work into the place that you and your uncle did, so I'm not looking for an even split."

Ivy was thrilled that they wouldn't be going to court. And the thought that she would have money to bring back to Nana Dovie...

But her joy was short-lived. Because she was just now realizing that the sooner she and Carter settled, the sooner she'd be on her way back to Nettles Gap. And away from Mitch.

Mitch listened to the rest of the exchange without comment. It appeared things were going to work out to Ivy's satisfaction. And while he was happy to see she wouldn't be going through a contentious legal battle, he wasn't as happy about what that meant. Once they met with Adam this week, there'd be nothing left to hold her here. She'd be free to return to Nettles Gap and her Nana Dovie... without marrying him.

He couldn't let her do that. He had a responsibility here, and a reputation of his own to protect. After all, what parent would want their child's teacher to have a questionable reputation?

He had to convince her to marry him. He simply had to. He was just being practical, after all.

But from somewhere deep inside, a voice whispered, *Coward,* over and over.

The next morning, instead of Abigail accompanying Ivy to the mercantile, Reggie "happened" to be going in the same direction. They met Jack and Ira outside the newspaper office and Ivy picked up Mitch's newspaper. And once again, Ivy felt deep gratitude for the new friends she'd made in Turnabout.

Once she arrived at Mitch's place, she greeted the Hendricks brothers and invited them to share in her planned lunch of pan-fried chicken and gravy with garden vegetables, then headed inside to fix breakfast for Mitch.

She handed him his newspaper, glad he would have that to occupy him while she cooked breakfast. Perhaps it would keep him from renewing his arguments for why she should marry him before she left.

Ever since she'd realized yesterday that she only had a few days left in Turnabout, the time seemed to be speeding by much too quickly. By the end of the week she'd be headed back to Nettles Gap. For just a moment she'd had a wild urge to send word to Carter to delay their meeting with Adam.

But this little interlude had to end sometime, and perhaps it was better that it happen quickly. Now that the story of their time at the cabin had come to light, it would be less awkward for Mitch if she were no longer around as a reminder.

He could go back to his normal routine. She prayed, however, that he wouldn't isolate himself so much in the future and that, someday, someone would come along whom he could love enough to share himself with.

Someone sweet, gentle, delicate.

Someone, obviously, unlike her.

Just before lunch, there was a knock at the door. As Ivy bustled to answer it, she grinned. For a man who "never had visitors," he certainly had received his share of callers lately. Perhaps things were changing for him.

She opened the door and her smile, along with everything inside her, froze.

"Hello, Ivy."

Lester Stokes, the man who'd ruined her life, stood there, smiling like a fox facing a cornered rabbit.

Chapter Twenty-One

For a moment Ivy couldn't speak. What in the world was Lester Stokes doing in Turnabout?

"Well," he said in that cocky drawl she hated, "aren't you going to invite me in?"

Ivy made no move to step aside. "What are you doing here?"

She saw a flash of irritation in his eyes, but his smile never faltered. He stepped closer. "I really think it would be best—"

He halted abruptly, and Ivy realized Mitch now stood behind her.

He must be an intimidating sight to a bully like Lester Stokes.

"Care to introduce me to your friend?" Mitch's tone was mild, but Ivy suddenly felt as if nothing bad could touch her.

"Of course. This is Lester Stokes." She felt Mitch's subtle stiffening.

"Lester, this is Mr. Mitch Parker, my employer."

Mitch stepped forward and offered his hand to Lester. "Are you an acquaintance from Nettles Gap?"

Lester quickly withdrew his hand. "That's right. Ivy and I grew up together."

Lester gave Ivy a meaningful glance. "If you have a few minutes, I need to talk to you." He cut a quick glance Mitch's way. "On a personal matter."

Mitch leaned against the doorjamb with folded arms, apparently oblivious to Lester's hints.

Lester frowned in annoyance, then turned back to Ivy. "I'm afraid I have bad news about Miss Jacobs."

Ivy's heart stuttered painfully, her mind dishing up all sorts of awful possibilities. "Is she all right?"

"She fell and hurt herself. Doc says she shouldn't be alone until she heals. My ma is with her, but I thought you should know as soon as possible."

"Yes, of course." She turned to Mitch, her thoughts racing. "I'm sorry. I need to go to her."

"Tell me what I can do to help."

Lester spoke up before Ivy could. "Everything is taken care of. I've already booked a return passage on tomorrow's train. And my sister, Dory, is with me—she's at the hotel right now—so Ivy shouldn't feel any discomfort with our traveling together."

Ivy's mind was awhirl with disjointed thoughts of things she needed to take care of before she left and images of a hurting Nana Dovie needing her. She should never have stayed away so long. "My meeting with Carter and Adam—"

"I'll let them know to reschedule."

"Tomorrow is laundry day—"

"I'm certain Mrs. Pierce will understand."

"Rufus and Jubal—"

"Ivy." Mitch took her hands, forcing her to focus on his words. "Don't worry. I'll watch over your animals until you return. And I'll see that those who need to know, do.

As for your housekeeping duties—" he gave her a crooked smile "—I'll manage to cook my own meals and care for my own house just fine."

She took a deep breath, drawing strength from his supportive presence. "Thank you."

She turned to Lester and was surprised by the furious look in his eyes. Was he so bothered by the fact that she'd found a friend and champion in Mitch?

"Thank you for bringing me the news. I'll be ready to leave when the train pulls in tomorrow."

Mitch eyed Lester critically. "I wonder why you didn't send a telegram. Miss Feagan could have already made it to Nettles Gap by now."

Ivy frowned. In her concern over Nana Dovie, she hadn't thought things through. Mitch was right—why *had* he come? And why Lester, of all people? He'd be the last person who'd want to do her any favors.

"I thought it best Ivy receive such upsetting news from a friend rather than a telegram," Lester said. "And I didn't want her to have to make the trip alone."

Since when did Lester consider himself her friend? Then Ivy took herself to task. Carter was proof people could change. Perhaps this was Lester's way of making up for past wrongs.

"I know this has come as a shock," Lester continued. "Why don't I escort you to your lodgings so you can rest?"

"Thank you, but if I do that I'll just go crazy worrying. It's best I keep busy." She started to untie her apron. "And I should send Nana Dovie a telegram to assure her I'll be there tomorrow."

"I'll take care of that for you," Lester said quickly. "And I'll come by when you're done here and take you to supper. I'm certain Dory will appreciate your company."

"You don't need—"

"I insist." Lester gave Mitch a terse nod, then turned and left before Ivy could protest further.

Mitch didn't like this—something about Lester Stokes's story seemed off.

Once Ivy closed the door, he crossed his arms. "Is this the same Lester you mentioned once before?"

Ivy nodded.

Mitch's hands fisted at his sides. Just the thought of what that snake had put Ivy through was enough to make him throw his vows of nonviolence to the winds. "Then I don't want you traveling with him tomorrow. I'll escort you to Nettles Gap myself."

She placed a hand on his arm. "Thank you. But that won't be necessary. Lester is obviously trying to make amends, and with Dory tagging along, I'm sure he'll be on his best behavior."

"I'm not so sure his motives are as benevolent as you appear to believe."

She waved away his concerns. "I'll be fine. I'm not a naive sixteen-year-old any longer. If Lester does resort to some of his old tricks—which I highly doubt—I can take care of myself."

"Be that as it may—"

"Please. There's enough gossip circulating about us as it is. How do you think it will look if you follow me back to Nettles Gap?"

"How it will look is not my primary concern."

She gave him a teasing smile. "I never thought I'd hear those words from Mr. Propriety himself." Then she moved past him toward the kitchen. "Now, lunch should be just about ready. Would you ask Calvin and James to get washed up and join us?"

Mitch watched her head down the hall, frustration almost smothering him. No matter how much he reasoned or cajoled, she still refused to marry him. And now she was leaving in the morning. She'd return, of course, once Miss Jacobs was better. But only to complete the negotiation with Carter. After today, he wouldn't have her to himself, or even in his life again. Order and peace would be restored.

And he couldn't garner even a speck of enthusiasm for that prospect.

The next morning, Ivy settled into her seat on the train and stared out the window. Mitch stood on the platform, Rufus at his side, watching as the train pulled away. Perhaps it was best this way, for them to have this clean break now, before the gossip could do any more damage.

But there was no denying how much she was going to miss Turnabout.

And Mitch.

When the train turned a curve and the town finally disappeared from sight, Ivy sat back and smiled at Dory beside her. "Thank you again for coming here with your brother."

The girl glanced nervously toward Lester, then gave Ivy a shy smile. "You're welcome. It was a chance for me to see someplace other than Nettles Gap."

Lester, who sat across the aisle from them, stood. "Dory, change seats with me. Ivy and I need to talk."

Something about Lester's tone raised Ivy's hackles. "What about?"

Lester didn't answer her until he was comfortably settled beside her. "First, I wanted to put your mind at ease. Miss Jacobs is not injured—in fact, as far as I know, she's as healthy as the day you left her."

Ivy stiffened, her relief quickly followed by anger. Lester Stokes had fooled her *again*. But before she could say anything, he pressed on.

"I just needed a good excuse to get you back to Nettles Gap with minimum resistance and fuss."

Icy spider legs scuttled up her spine. "Why?"

"Because of your inheritance, of course."

How did he even *know* about that? Surely Reverend Tomlin hadn't said anything.

"Someone came to town last week looking for information on you and your pa. I convinced him to tell me what was going on. Imagine my surprise when I found out that you're going to be a prominent landowner soon."

"So?"

"So, you're going to marry me, and as your husband, I'm going to gain control of that land."

Marry him? Ivy was so astonished she hardly knew what to say next. "What makes you think for even a minute that I'd consent to such a thing?"

"Because I'm not going to give you much choice. I can call in your precious Nana Dovie's loan if you don't."

Ivy blanched, then recovered. It was Lester's father who held the note on their place. And he was a much fairer man than Lester had ever been. Besides, that would soon be a moot point. "If my claim holds, it won't matter. I'll be able to pay the loan without any trouble."

"But not before we've already repossessed the farm. There are ways to delay the judge's arrival. And there are also ways to throw doubt on your claim to be who you say you are. Oh, you'll win your case eventually, but think of the damage that can be done by the time you do."

She stared at him defiantly. "I don't need to wait for the judge. Carter Mosley and I have discussed settling this between us."

Some of his confidence seemed to slip. "You haven't signed any papers yet, have you?"

"No, but I gave my word—"

"Then it's not too late to back out. From what I can tell, you have a claim to half of the whole estate."

"But that's not what I agreed to. And with this offer from Carter, I should be able to get matters settled quickly, so there's nothing for you to hold over me." Surely he couldn't force her hand.

His expression turned ugly. "You think not? Do you really believe you can get matters settled and have money in hand before I evict Miss Jacobs?"

She hesitated and he grinned triumphantly. "I've heard how she can't leave her place. I hear she gets agitated and downright hysterical if she tries. I wonder how it will affect her if the sheriff comes by to toss her out?"

"You might be that cruel, Lester Stokes, but I don't think your father is. Especially if I tell him about the money I'll have shortly."

"My parents are on a business trip. He left me in charge until he returns, which may be as much as a month from now."

Ivy felt trapped, but struggled not to show it. "How can you do this? You already have so much."

His face twisted. "I have nothing—it's all my father's. Gaining control of that land means I won't have to live under his thumb anymore."

The dark determination in his expression scared her. "What if I just sign over a part of my inheritance to you?"

He seemed to think about that for a minute, then shook his head. "I know you've gotten cozy with that boss of yours. No doubt he'd help you find some way to wiggle out of the deal. No, the only way to be certain is for us to get hitched."

Ivy frantically tried to come up with a way out. How could she marry Lester after she'd spurned Mitch, saying she'd hold out for a love match?

But if she didn't, Nana Dovie would lose her home, and worse. She couldn't bear to think what it would do to that dear lady if she were forced to leave.

Nana Dovie had made many, many sacrifices to raise her, and now it was time for Ivy to return the favor, no matter how distasteful the task before her might be.

"Nana Dovie must never, under any circumstances, learn why I'm doing this."

His face contorted into a triumphant smirk. "Agreed."

Chapter Twenty-Two

Mitch knelt in the garden, pulling weeds. Rufus lay nearby with his head forlornly resting on his front paws. It had been two days since the train had carried Ivy away, but it felt more like two months.

Mitch could barely stand to be inside the house. It seemed too quiet, too empty.

He felt empty.

He sat back on his haunches and stared at Rufus. "What's happening to me? I never considered myself melodramatic before."

The dog gave a halfhearted bark.

"Don't worry, she hasn't abandoned you. She'll be back in a few days to meet with Carter and Adam. Which means I'll have one more shot at getting her to see reason."

Rufus set his head back down on his paws, watching Mitch with doubtful eyes.

"I don't understand why she's so resistant to the idea of marrying me. I know she's been hurt, but given our situation, compromises must be made."

He stabbed at the ground with the trowel. "If I can put my feelings aside and enter into marriage again after vowing I never would, then surely she can do the same."

He pointed the trowel Rufus's way. "And as for this matter of holding out for a love match—" Mitch slowly lowered his arm. "Perhaps, if she married me, love would come with time."

This time Rufus's bark was more enthusiastic.

Mitch gave him a wry grin. "One thing you do have going for you is that you're a good listener."

Suddenly the dog lifted his head, an alert look on his face. A moment later he was up and racing to the front yard.

Did they have company? Had Ivy returned already?

Mitch followed the dog in long strides. He rounded the corner to see not Ivy but Zeke Tarn from the train depot. Swallowing his disappointment, Mitch slowed his step.

Zeke descended the porch steps. "Oh, hi, Mr. Parker." He held out a telegram. "This just came for you."

Mitch's pulse kicked up a notch. He pulled a coin from his pocket to give Zeke, then stepped inside before he allowed himself to open the telegram.

It was from Dovie Jacobs.

And it contained a single line:

IVY NEEDS YOU.

Mitch pulled the buggy to a stop and studied the place. According to the farmer he'd passed on the road about a mile back, this was Dovie Jacobs's farm.

He smiled at the profusion of flowers bordering the fence and porch. Ivy lived here, all right.

Rufus jumped down and ran to the house, barking with tail-wagging enthusiasm.

Mitch followed, his pace nearly as hurried. That cryptic telegram had proven what Mitch already knew in his heart:

he should never have let Ivy go with that snake—the man was nasty business. If he'd done anything to hurt Ivy—

The door opened before Mitch reached it, and he found himself facing a petite gray-haired woman with sparkling green eyes and gnarled hands resting on top of a walking stick.

He removed his hat. "You must be Ivy's Nana Dovie."

She'd been studying him with a piercing gaze. Then she smiled. "And you must be her Mitch."

He gave a short bow, liking the sound of "her Mitch." "Yes, ma'am, and I'm very glad to meet you. I came as soon as I received your telegram." He tried to look past her into the house. "Where's Ivy?"

"In town." She frowned at him. "You're almost too late."

His disappointment in not seeing Ivy gave way to concern. "Too late for what?"

"To stop the wedding."

Mitch felt as if the breath had been knocked out of him. "Ivy's getting married?"

"She is. To that weasel Lester Stokes."

"She loves him?" He refused to believe such a thing.

The woman snorted. "Ivy has more sense than that. But that's what she tried to have me believe."

He studied her, noting her firm stance. "So his report that you were injured was just a ruse."

"I'm healthy as a horse." Then her eyes narrowed. "Is that how he got her to come home with him?"

Mitch nodded. "It's why I let her go." He should have listened to his gut.

"That was a mistake."

"Yes, ma'am, it was." He tried to rein in his impatience. "Do you know the real reason she's agreed to marry him?"

"I have a good idea."

He waved a hand toward the two rockers on the porch. "Then let's talk."

* * *

Ivy shifted in the saddle. The horse she rode belonged to Lester's family. She didn't like the idea of being beholden to him, but he'd insisted, saying her borrowing it would go a long way toward making the community believe they were serious about their marriage.

The two of them had spent the morning with Reverend Tomlin making arrangements for the ceremony, which was to be held at Ivy's home tomorrow morning. The preacher had wanted them to wait until Lester's folks returned, but Lester had brushed that concern aside. He'd used Ivy and Nana Dovie's financial situation as an excuse, and assured the clergyman that they would schedule a second ceremony when his parents were available.

Reverend Tomlin had shot her several concerned looks throughout the discussion, but she'd done her best just to smile and let Lester do the talking.

And all the time her mind was desperately trying to find a way out of this mess, as it had been ever since Lester had made his twisted proposal.

A part of her wished she'd accepted Mitch's offer of marriage—he might not love her either, but at least he respected her. For one heartbeat of time, she thought about sending for him—her white knight who always seemed set on rescuing her.

But she discarded the thought almost immediately. Not only would it not be fair to *him*, but the thought of his coming to resent her later was unbearable.

If only Nana Dovie weren't so tied to this place, she'd let Lester have the farm and take her someplace where they could both make a fresh start.

Like Turnabout.

But, as Nana Dovie liked to say, if wishes were fishes…

As their small farm came into sight, Ivy frowned. Whose carriage was that?

She nudged the horse into a faster gait. It wasn't the reverend; she'd just left him. And no one else, other than an occasional peddler, ever came out here. Was Nana Dovie okay?

Then a familiar figure came bounding out the front gate. Rufus!

Her pulse kicked up a notch. There was only one explanation—Mitch was here.

But why? Could it be that he'd missed her as much as she'd missed him?

As soon as she arrived at the house, Ivy slid from the horse's back and smoothed her skirt. Then she paused to make certain her bonnet was on straight.

Taking a deep breath, she headed inside. She found Mitch sitting at the kitchen table with Nana Dovie, sipping a cup of coffee.

He stood as soon as she entered, and the sight of the warm smile on his face was almost enough to make her fling herself into his arms. Instead, she merely smiled.

"What are you doing here?"

"Ivy Kathleen, what kind of question is that?" Nana Dovie gave her a stern look. "And he's here because I sent for him."

"Nana!"

"You didn't think I would let you marry that bully Lester Stokes without doing something about it, did you?"

Ivy cast a quick, embarrassed glance Mitch's way. She couldn't believe Nana Dovie was involving him in all of this. She turned back to her. "It's all settled. Reverend Tomlin will perform the ceremony here tomorrow morning. It'll just be us, you and Dory."

Please don't let Mitch still be here. She couldn't bear the idea of him watching her marry Lester.

"There's not going to be a wedding."

She blinked at the absolute certainty in Mitch's voice. "Listen, Mr. high-and-mighty Mitch Parker, you can't just walk in here and give me orders."

"You told me once that you would only marry for love. Do you love Lester Stokes?"

"Who I love or don't love is none of your business."

"So you don't love him. That means you're being coerced. Perhaps the fact that his father owns the note on this place has something to do with that."

"Don't you *dare* offer to pay that note. I won't be taking charity from you or anyone else."

"Ivy Kathleen!" Nana Dovie looked truly shocked. "Didn't I teach you what a terrible sin pride is? And that ingratitude is nearly as bad?"

"Yes, ma'am."

"Besides, last time I looked it was my name on the deed to this place. Don't you think it should be my decision as to whether or not to accept an offer of help?"

"But—"

Nana Dovie patted her hand. "I know, dear, you're just trying to help and be very brave in the process. But I can't let you do that for me. And no, I'm not taking Mr. Parker's money."

"Then what—"

"I'm taking you both away from here." Mitch's tone brooked no argument.

"But—" Ivy turned and took the older woman's hands. "Nana, I can't let you do this."

"I've held you back for too long. That stops now." She smiled in satisfaction. "The way you described Turnabout,

I think it's going to be a mighty nice place to set down new roots."

Ivy was afraid to let the hope building inside her unfurl. She looked from Mitch to Nana Dovie and back to Mitch, trying to make sense of it all.

Mitch gave her a reassuring smile. "Miss Jacobs and I discussed several things we think will make this trip smoother for everyone."

"Such as?"

This time Nana Dovie spoke up. "There's a medicine I know how to mix up that helps a person relax, relax so deeply they sometimes fall into a deep sleep. I'll take this medicine tomorrow just before we leave, and with any luck I won't even notice I've left home until I wake up in Turnabout."

Ivy wasn't convinced. "You've told me yourself that medicines can be tricky—different people react differently. How do you know it'll work?"

"Because I've tested it on myself. Don't look so shocked. I've wanted to take you away from here ever since Lester spread those lies about you five years ago. I just didn't have anywhere to take you before now."

Ivy stepped up and gave her a fierce hug. "Oh, Nana Dovie, I love you so much."

The woman waved her away. "Now, you two have important roles to play if we're going to make this work. First, I'm not certain I'll be able to get around very well, if at all."

"Don't worry, ma'am, I'll see that you get where you need to go, with nary a hair out of place."

Ivy smiled up at him, remembering the ease with which he'd carried her.

"And I'll also need a place to stay when I get there," Nana Dovie continued. "A nice, quiet room where I can be alone whenever I want to."

"I'm sure Eileen Pierce will rent us another room at her place. And if not we can share mine until we can make other arrangements." Then Ivy looked around. "But this house, all your things..."

"They're just things, child. What's important are the people and the memories—and those we bring with us. We'll find new things when we settle in this new place."

She stood. "I'll hear no more arguments. Now, you two go to Arnold Hemp's place. He'll be willing to take on the animals we've got here along with the tools and equipment for a fair price. Tell him he can also have whatever produce from the garden he can cart off, but he has to get it all before noon tomorrow."

She walked them to the door. "Don't spend a lot of time dickering with him, but make sure you get enough to stake us for the next couple of weeks." She gave Ivy a look that, on a younger woman, would have been called sassy. "After that, I expect you to use that inheritance of yours to take care of my needs." Then she made shooing motions. "Now off with you. There are preparations to be made."

Mitch helped Ivy into the wagon, savoring the luxury of having her beside him again.

Once she'd given him directions to Mr. Hemp's farm, he set the wagon in motion, trying to figure out how to say all he was feeling. He didn't want to mess it up this time.

"I'm sorry Nana Dovie asked you to come all the way here." She stared straight ahead.

"I'm not."

She turned to study him.

He tried for a light tone. "Rufus missed you."

She nodded, then faced forward again.

He cleared his throat. "We both did."

This time, when she turned to face him, there was a curious mix of hope and doubt in her expression. But she finally gave him a soft smile. "I missed both of you, too." She shifted slightly. "I'm sorry for being so rude earlier."

"You've been carrying a lot on your shoulders the past few days."

"Still, I owed you better than that. Thank you for riding to my rescue yet again."

"It was my pleasure." Did she have any idea how deeply he meant those words?

"I can see Nana Dovie likes you."

"The sentiment is returned. She's quite a lady."

"I hope she knows what she's doing."

Mitch placed a hand over hers. "Have faith."

Her gaze flew to his. Was it a reaction to the touch or his words? He was pleased when she didn't pull her hand away. Instead, she repositioned it so that their palms touched and their fingers intertwined.

At that moment, she could have asked him to carry the world on his shoulders and he would have gladly attempted to do it for her.

Chapter Twenty-Three

It was difficult to convince Mitch to leave Nettle's Gap without confronting Lester. But Ivy had finally gotten through to him. She thought, more than anything else, it had been his memory of the consequences of ignoring another woman's entreaty that finally did the trick.

To her great relief, the trip to Turnabout went surprisingly well. Nana Dovie slept through most of it.

There *was* a bit of trouble at the train station when they tried to board. The conductor suspected the elderly woman was ill and at first refused to allow her on the train. But after a long discussion, and a bit of money changing hands, the man relented and Mitch was allowed to carry the slumbering woman aboard.

When they arrived in Turnabout, Mitch marched all the way from the train station to Eileen Pierce's home carrying Nana Dovie. With Ivy and Rufus flanking him on either side, they attracted every bit as much attention as they had when Ivy had first arrived in town beside him on that borrowed buckboard.

Mrs. Pierce, unruffled by their unannounced appearance on her doorstep, seemed pleased to be able to earn income from a second boarder. Within minutes of their arrival, a slowly awakening Nana Dovie was comfortably ensconced in the room next to Ivy's.

Afterward, Ivy walked Mitch as far as Eileen's front door.

He took her hand. "I'll see that your things are delivered from the depot. And I'll send word to Carter that you're back and ready to settle your business with him as soon as possible."

"Thank you." She didn't withdraw her hand, and neither did he.

"And don't worry about Rufus, he's welcome to stay with me again."

She grinned. "I'd better watch it or he'll start thinking he's your dog."

He gave her hand a slight squeeze. "I know this isn't the right time for a long discussion on the matter, but I hope you'll reconsider my offer of marriage. Especially now that you're moving into the community permanently."

"Thank you, Mitch. You'll never know how much it means to me that you care so much." She gently tugged her hand free. "But as I said before, barring blackmail, I intend to hold out for a love match."

Her little attempt at humor didn't elicit so much as a smile.

"Aren't friendship and respect strong enough emotions to base a marriage on?" he asked.

Was that what he felt for her? "Not for me. Because I know what love feels like. And I want someone to feel that for me."

He went very still. "There's someone you love?"

She nodded. Why was it so hard to say the words? "With all my heart. But he doesn't feel the same for me." She touched his cheek. "So while I will always cherish his friendship and respect, marrying him would eventually break my heart, knowing he doesn't return my feelings."

And with a quick kiss to his cheek, she turned and raced back up the stairs, feeling a bittersweet triumph.

She'd just told Mitch Parker that she loved him.

Mitch stood on Eileen Pierce's front porch, too stunned to move. His heart pounded so hard he could hear it thrumming in his ears. She loved him? For one shining moment, his whole being thrummed with exultation.

Then he sobered. This changed everything. A businesslike arrangement was one thing. It was safe and practical and had purpose—namely her protection.

But love—that was messy, complicated. If she loved him then he could disappoint her, fail her. Even if he loved her in return.

Who was he kidding? There was no *if* about it—he loved her, had loved her long before he'd allowed himself to admit it.

But knowing it didn't give him the right to act on it. Not with his history.

Perhaps she was right to refuse him.

Over the next few days, Ivy and Carter reached an agreement on how to split the ranch, and in the end, Ivy found herself the recipient of more money than she'd ever thought to see in her lifetime. While it wasn't a fortune by some standards, and Carter would be paying it off to her over a course of several years, she was confident it was enough to find a place for her and Nana Dovie to start their new lives.

Word reached them that Lester had not taken their leaving well. He had, in fact, set a torch to their house—his house, she supposed—in a fit of anger.

Nana Dovie took the news in stride, surprising Ivy with the prediction that he'd probably regret his actions once his pa returned home.

And despite Mitch's fears, mainly due to the support of his circle of friends, Ivy was not ostracized. While there were some who would always give in to the urge to whisper and gossip, for the most part Ivy was made welcome throughout the town.

But there was one welcoming smile she missed. She'd barely seen Mitch since she'd told him of her feelings four days earlier.

Had she made a mistake?

"Where is Ivy?" Mitch stood, hat in hand, on Eileen Pierce's front porch.

Nana Dovie, who was shelling a bowl of peas, eyed him as if she could read his secrets. "Out back in the garden," she finally said.

Of course. Where else would she be? "Thank you."

Before he could step away, she spoke up again. "There's something different about you today. You're carrying yourself with a sense of purpose. Does this mean you've finally come to your senses?"

He didn't pretend to misunderstand. "Yes, ma'am. I only hope I'm not too late."

She waved him away. "Well, what are you waiting for? Go tell her how you feel."

He nodded and jammed his hat back on his head. "Yes, ma'am."

Mitch marched around the house, trying to figure out just what he'd say. He still hadn't settled on the right words when he caught sight of her.

She spotted him at the same time, and the welcome smile on her face gave him hope.

"Mitch, hello. Come see the size of these tomatoes."

"Very nice. But it's you I'm here to see."

Something flashed in her eyes and he prayed it was love. "Is there something I can do for you?"

"Yes. You can marry me."

She frowned, and this time it was sadness in her eyes. He winced, knowing he was the one who'd put that there.

She turned away, tugging another tomato from the plant. "Please, I've told you how I feel. Let's not go through it again."

"No, we haven't been through *this* before. I *want* to marry you. Not because I feel I have to. Not because I feel responsible for you. But because I *love* you."

She shook her head vehemently, not turning around. "Stop. I know you think this is the right thing to do, but I can't bear it." She turned to face him and he was almost undone by the pain glistening in her eyes. "You're a good man, but you have to accept that you can't fix every problem—the gossip has all but died down, the inheritance is settled, Nana Dovie and I are happier than we've been in a long time. And much of this is thanks to you."

She took a deep breath. "As for what I said the other day, I probably shouldn't have said anything. I'm happy to have you as a dear friend. So please, don't throw yourself on your sword over this."

"You're not listening." He took hold of her arms. "I. Love. You."

Her eyes searched his face and he hoped she could see what he truly felt.

"But I thought you never wanted to marry again."

"So did I. Then you came into my life, and everything changed. I've fought it for as long as I can. I may not deserve you but I've finally realized I can't go on without you."

* * *

Ivy was afraid to believe what she was hearing, though she very much wanted to. This had to be just another way he'd found to *help* her, whether she wanted that help or not.

"But I'm not the kind of woman you're drawn to—I'm not gentle or delicate."

"True. In fact, you're the most stubborn, down-to-earth, speak-your-mind female I've ever met. And you're also strong, generous, spirited, courageous and sensitive to the hurts of others. You'd willingly sacrifice yourself in marriage to a wretchedly cruel and selfish man to save your dear friend's refuge. And you are quick to extend grace and forgiveness to those who have wronged you."

The look in his eyes as he uttered those beautiful words chipped away at her resistance. Could he really mean what he was saying?

His hands slid down her arms, his fingers twining with hers. "What you are is the woman I love. And you're absolutely right. This community has accepted you so there's no reason that you have to marry me. Except that I'll be totally and completely lost without you."

He gave a crooked smile. "Marry me so you can bring color and life to my home, which seems so unbearably empty without you. Marry me so you can enjoy that swing in my backyard that seems so forlorn now. Marry me to tend to my garden and decorate my yard with riots of flowers. But most of all, marry me because I love you with all that I am."

He traced the line of her jaw with a finger as tears slid down her cheeks.

"I love you, Ivy Kathleen Feagan. I've been every kind of fool and I'm so sorry it took me this long to realize it. But I promise to say those words to you every day for the rest of my life, if you'll let me."

This time there was no doubting the truth. It was there in his words, in the slight tremble of his fingers, in the ragged emotion shining from his eyes.

She lifted a hand to his cheek. "Oh, Mitch, I love you so much. It would make me very, very happy to spend the rest of my days as your wife."

With that, he pulled her into a hug and twirled her around. Then he set her on the ground again and very gently bent down to give her a kiss. A kiss that promised he would love, protect and cherish her, now and forever.

He was her hero, the man who would fearlessly slay all of her dragons and quietly make all of her dreams come true.

Epilogue

Mitch studied his new bride across the expanse of Eileen Pierce's backyard, not caring if his expression reflected how hopelessly smitten he was. He still couldn't quite believe Ivy was well and truly his at last.

The wedding service, which had been held at Mrs. Pierce's place so Nana Dovie could comfortably attend, had ended nearly an hour ago and it seemed as if he'd barely been able to say two words to Ivy since. He tried to tell himself to be patient—after all, he had the rest of his life to spend with her—but he decided he'd been patient long enough. Excusing himself from the discussion with Dr. Pratt and Sheriff Gleason, he circulated through the crowd with purpose, closing in on his bride.

After a half dozen stops to accept congratulatory slaps on the back, Mitch finally made it to her side. The warm smile with which she greeted him set his pulse racing. He leaned forward and kissed her cheek, then whispered in her ear, "What do you think, Mrs. Parker—is it too early for us to make our exit?"

Her low, throaty laugh had him wanting to tug her to him for a proper kiss.

But before she could give him an answer, Reggie approached. "There you are. I'm ready to take photographs of the happy couple if you'll spare me a few minutes."

Ivy shot him an apologetic look and squeezed his hand before turning to Reggie. "Of course. Just tell us what to do."

"I'm set up right over there." Reggie led the way to the flower-bedecked arch where they'd recited their vows earlier. Along the way, Ivy squeezed his arm and nodded off to her left. "I do believe Mrs. Swenson has found a new object for her affection."

Mitch glanced in the direction she'd indicated and smiled. Mrs. Swenson was engaged in conversation with Carter Mosley of all people, and the two seemed to have more than a passing enjoyment of each other's company.

A few moments later, Reggie was fussily posing Mitch and Ivy while some of the guests drifted over to watch. At last, Reggie was satisfied and she took two photographs— one with just the two of them, and one with Nana Dovie between them.

"I wish your sisters could have come," Ivy said. "Then we could have a true family photograph."

"They're eager to meet you, as well." Mitch dropped a kiss on the top of her head. "We'll plan some trips soon." He knew his sisters were going to love Ivy, and she them. But he hadn't wanted to wait a moment longer than he had to for the wedding.

His plans to lead his bride away were foiled yet again when Reggie stopped him. "If you don't mind, there's one more photograph I'd like to take. And this one's for me."

Mitch raised a brow. "You want a picture of me and Ivy?"

"Not exactly." She turned and glanced to the folks gathered behind her. "Adam, Everett, Chance—you three come over here and stand next to Mitch."

Adam raised a brow. "What are you up to?"

Reggie took Adam's hand, then looked at the four men. "I remember when you all first arrived here two years ago—and I know we didn't see eye to eye back then. But this town is the better for all of you being here, and I am, too." She pitched her voice so only they could hear. "I'd like to have a picture of my three would-be grooms, and my one true love, to hang on my wall."

As Mitch stood shoulder to shoulder with his friends, he thought again how they'd all set out to find fresh starts here in Turnabout.

What they'd found was so much more than any of them had ever expected—a community that welcomed them in with open arms. And more importantly, good women to cherish and be cherished by, and to build their lives and futures with.

He met Ivy's warm gaze and thanked God again for not giving up on him when he'd given up on himself, for leading him here to Turnabout and for bringing Ivy into his life to show him how to love and laugh again.

The flash of Reggie's camera released him from his pose and he marched toward his wife and captured her hand in his. "Time to go," he said.

She laughed. "Is everything ready?"

"The hamper and bags are already in the carriage."

"What about the fishing poles?"

"They're there, as well."

"And you're sure Reggie doesn't mind us borrowing her cabin."

"She insisted. After all, I never did get in that week I'd planned on."

"I hope you're not looking for peace and quiet this time out."

"No, ma'am. This time I'm looking for excitement and

adventure." He grinned. "I even have the materials to construct one fine tree swing. Ready?"

She nodded, and hand in hand, they slipped away, together, the way Mitch intended them to be forever.

* * * * *

Dear Reader,

I've had a wonderful time writing the Texas Grooms series and I hope you've enjoyed the stories, as well. I have to admit, though, that Mitch's story was by far the most difficult of the four to write. He was such an enigmatic character to me throughout the series. I knew he had some serious hurts in his past and that he carried a lot of guilt around, but the particulars stayed hidden for a long time.

When I finally discovered the source of his wound, I then had to find the right heroine for him, one who could bring light back into his life, who could help him recapture his belief in himself and his faith in God. And I think I found her in Ivy Feagan—a woman who is an interesting mix of empathy, courage and levelheadedness. From the moment she stepped up and introduced herself to me I knew this was the lady for Mitch.

This is not the last of my visits to Turnabout. I'm currently working on books that will follow the lives of some of the townsfolk who will be familiar to those who have been following these books. For more information, please visit my website at www.winniegriggs.com or follow me on facebook at www.facebook.com/WinnieGriggs.Author.

And as always, I'd love to hear from readers. Feel free to contact me at winnie@winniegriggs.com with your thoughts on this or any other of my books.

Wishing you a life abounding with love and blessings.

Winnie Griggs

Questions for Discussion

1. Ivy first appears on the scene dressed in male clothing, traveling alone through the woods on a trip to a
   place she's never been. What sort of opinions or con-
   clusions did you draw about her based on this opening?

2. Mitch traveled to the cabin for some solitude, yet he
   seemed to adjust well to Ivy's intrusion. Why do you
   think that was?

3. While at the cabin, Ivy seemed to think Mitch was
   going overboard with his insistence on a strict adher-
   ence to the proprieties. Do you agree with her? Why
   or why not?

4. Why do you think Drum Mosley never told his
   nephew, Carter, about the change to his will? Do you
   think he was right to withhold the information?

5. Why do you think Ivy was so insistent about putting
   in a garden for Mitch?

6. What did you think of Mitch's interaction with Ivy's
   dog, Rufus? Do you think it said anything about his
   character, and if so, what?

7. Was Ivy's almost instant trust of Mitch believable
   given the situation? Why or why not?

8. What was your first impression of Eileen Pierce? How
   did this change over time?

9. Did Carter's eventual change of heart regarding Ivy's sharing the inheritance ring true to you?

10. Do you think Ivy was foolish to leave town with Lester and his sister given their history? Why or why not?

11. Though they didn't have a name for it during this time period, Nana Dovie was obviously suffering from agoraphobia. Have you ever encountered anyone with this condition before? Did the way they finally got Nana Dovie to leave her home and travel to Turnabout seem believable to you?

12. Why do you think it took Mitch so long to admit he loved Ivy?

SPECIAL EXCERPT FROM

Love Inspired

*Join the ranching town of Jasper Gulch, Montana,
as they celebrate 100 years!*

Here's a sneak peek at
HER MONTANA COWBOY
by Valerie Hansen, the first of six books in the
BIG SKY CENTENNIAL *miniseries.*

For the first time in longer than Ryan Travers could recall, he was having trouble keeping his mind on his work. He couldn't have cared less about Jasper Gulch's missing time capsule; it was pretty Julie Shaw who occupied his thoughts.

"That's not good," he muttered as he stood on a metal rung of the narrow bucking chute. This rangy pinto mare wasn't called Widow-maker for nothing. He could not only picture Julie Shaw as if she were standing right there next to the chute gates, he could imagine her light, uplifting laughter.

Actually, he realized with a start, that *was* what he was hearing. He started to glance over his shoulder, intending to scan the nearby crowd and, hopefully, locate her.

"Clock's ticking, Travers," the chute boss grumbled. "You gonna ride that horse or just look at her?"

Rather than answer with words, Ryan stepped across the top of the chute, raised his free hand over his head and leaned way back. Then he nodded to the gateman.

The latch clicked.

The mare leaped.

Ryan didn't attempt to do anything but ride until he heard the horn blast announcing his success. Then he straightened as best he could and worked his fingers loose with his free hand while pickup men maneuvered close enough to help him dismount.

To Ryan's delight, Julie Shaw and a few others he recognized from before were watching. They had parked a flatbed farm truck near the fence beside the grandstand and were watching from secure perches in its bed.

Julie had both arms raised and was still cheering so wildly she almost knocked her hat off. "Woo-hoo! Good ride, cowboy!"

Ryan's "Thanks" was swallowed up in the overall din from the rodeo fans. Clearly, Julie wasn't the only spectator who had been favorably impressed.

He knew he should immediately report to the area behind the strip chutes and pick up his rigging. And he would. In a few minutes. As soon as he'd spoken to his newest fan.

Don't miss the romance between Julie and rodeo hero Ryan in HER MONTANA COWBOY by Valerie Hansen, available July 2014 from Love Inspired®.

LIEXP0614R

SPECIAL EXCERPT FROM

Love Inspired
SUSPENSE

When a widow is stalked and taunted by memories from her tragic past, can the man who rescued her years ago come to her aid again?

*Read on for a preview of PROTECTIVE INSTINCTS by Shirlee McCoy, the first book in her brand-new **MISSION: RESCUE** series.*

"Who would want to hurt you, Raina?" Jackson asked her.

"No one," she replied, her mind working frantically, going through faces and names and situations.

"And yet, someone chased you through the woods. That same person nearly ran me down. Doesn't sound like someone who feels all warm and fuzzy when he thinks of you."

"Maybe he was a vagrant, and I scared him."

"Maybe." He didn't sound like he believed it, and she wasn't sure she did, either.

She'd heard something that had woken her from the nightmare.

A child crying? Her neighbor Larry wandering around? An intruder trying to get into the house?

The last thought made her shudder, and she pulled her coat a little closer. "I think I'd know it if someone had a bone to pick with me."

"That's usually the case, but not always. Could be you upset a coworker, said no to a guy who wanted you to say yes—"

She snorted at that, and Jackson frowned. "You've been a widow for four years. It's not that far-fetched an idea."

"If you got a good look at my social life you wouldn't be saying that."

Samuel yawned loudly and slid down on the pew, his arms crossed over his chest, his eyelids drooping. The ten-year-old looked cold and tired, and she wanted to get him home and tuck him into bed.

"I'll go talk to Officer Wallace," Jackson responded. "See if he's ready to let us leave."

"He's going to have to be. Samuel—"

A door slammed, the sound so startling Raina jumped.

She grabbed Samuel's shoulder, pulled him into the shelter of her arms.

"Is someone else in the church?" Jackson demanded, his gaze on the door that led from the sanctuary into the office wing.

"There shouldn't be."

"Stay put. I'm going to check things out."

He strode away, and she wanted to call out and tell him to be careful.

She pressed her lips together, held in the words she knew she didn't need to say. She'd seen him in action, knew just how smart and careful he was.

Jackson could take care of himself.

Will Jackson discover the stalker and help
Raina find a second chance at love?

Pick up PROTECTIVE INSTINCTS to find out.
Available July 2014 wherever
Love Inspired® Suspense books are sold.

A Hero in the Making

by

LAURIE KINGERY

Nate Bohannan won't let anything stand in the way of his grand plans in California. Even if it means traveling there with unreliable huckster Robert Salali. But after a destructive bender in Simpson Creek, Texas, the unscrupulous Salali runs out, leaving Nate to carry the blame—and the debt. He can fix broken furniture…but can anything fix the despair in café owner Ella Justiss's eyes?

When her café was destroyed, Ella felt sure she'd lost her dreams along with it. Yet somehow Nate's cheerful care and optimism fill her with hope again. Painful secrets from her childhood make Ella wary of men. When danger threatens, will Nate be the hero Ella can finally trust—and love?

Brides
OF SIMPSON
CREEK

Small-town Texas spinsters find love with mail-order grooms!

Available July 2014
wherever Love Inspired books and ebooks are sold.

Find us on Facebook at
www.Facebook.com/LoveInspiredBooks

LIH28270

Love Inspired

THE BACHELOR NEXT DOOR

by
Kathryn Springer

Dedicating all his time to the family business isn't easy for
Brendan Kane. But he owes his foster parents big-time for
taking him and his brothers in. And if he has to give up the
possibility of a relationship—so be it. So when Brendan's
mother hires Lily Michaels to redecorate the family home, it
doesn't matter to Brendan that Lily is beautiful. And funny.
And smart. He has no time for distractions. Can Lily show him
there's more to life…and that it includes a future together?

Castle Falls

Three rugged brothers meet their matches.

*Available July 2014 wherever
Love Inspired books and ebooks are sold.*

Find us on Facebook at
www.Facebook.com/LoveInspiredBooks

LI87896